THE KISS LEFT THEM

D1385907

TYLER

COURTHOUSE STEPS

GINGER CHAMBERS

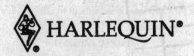

HARLEQUIN®

TORONTO • NEW YORK • LONDON
AMSTERDAM • PARIS • SYDNEY • HAMBURG
STOCKHOLM • ATHENS • TOKYO • MILAN • MADRID
PRAGUE • WARSAW • BUDAPEST • AUCKLAND

For Steve, Beverly and Chris...
who always believed

First published in Great Britain 1999
by Harlequin Mills & Boon Limited,
Eton House, 18-24 Paradise Road, Richmond, Surrey TW9 1SR

Special thanks and acknowledgement to Joanna Kosloff for her
contribution to the concept for the Tyler series.

© Harlequin Enterprises II B.V. 1993

Special thanks and acknowledgement to Ginger Chambers for her
contribution to the Tyler series.

ISBN 0 373 82511 0

110-9911

Printed and bound in Spain
by Litografia Rosés S.A., Barcelona

TYLER

American women have always used the art quilt as a means of expressing their views on life and as a commentary on events in the world around them. And in Tyler, quilting has always been a popular communal activity.

COURTHOUSE STEPS

Courthouse Steps is a variation of the Log Cabin pattern. Light and dark colours are evenly paired at opposite sides of a central block to form a giant step. Perhaps the first Courthouse Steps quilt was made as a wedding present, and the giant step was the one that led to the altar!

Dear Reader,

Welcome to Harlequin's Tyler, a small Wisconsin town whose citizens we hope you'll soon come to know and love.

Tyler faces many challenges typical of small towns, but the fabric of this fictional community has been torn by the revelation of a long-ago murder, the details of which will evolve right through the series. In *Courthouse Steps*, this intriguing mystery culminates in an emotional trial that profoundly affects the lives of everyone scarred by Margaret Lindstrom Ingalls's life of careless desperation.

Phil Wocheck has already testified to the police and the grand jury about what really happened that fateful night, but he's not about to share that information with anyone—not even his own son. What's going to become of them? Edward and Alyssa, Jeff and Cece, Liza and Cliff and little Margaret Alyssa, Amanda and Judson? Their world seems to be hanging from a single thread, which could snap at any moment.

So join us in Tyler for a slice of small-town life that's not as innocent or as quiet as you might expect, and for a sense of community that will capture your mind and your heart.

The Editors.

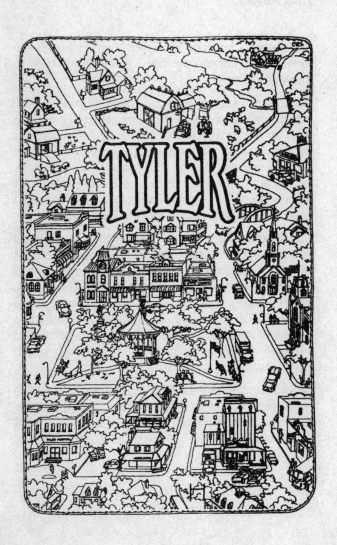

CHAPTER ONE

AMANDA SAW him across the lobby. He was standing in a cluster of people, but he was easily the most likely to draw the eye. Tall, dark-haired, in command—the set of his handsome features reflected a quick mind and a steely determination. The group he was with seemed to hang on his every word. Several individuals nodded; one left to do his bidding. He turned to a shorter man at his side, murmured something for his ear alone, then broke away from the small group himself. His walk was assured as he started across the room.

Amanda's heart rate jumped when she saw that he was coming toward her. She looked around for somewhere to hide. She didn't want to meet him like this! She wasn't ready! When she'd come to the courthouse in Sugar Creek, it was to tie up the last threads in a case that had nothing to do with her grandfather. She hadn't expected to run into Ethan Trask!

She sidled quickly toward a high rectangular table where other people were filling out forms. Picking up a form herself, she pretended to study it, but in reality she continued to watch the man…her adversary. His reputation had preceded him. He was the state attorney general's ''Avenging Angel.'' When he was assigned to a case, he almost always won it. Brilliant, she'd heard him described. Merciless, as well.

She held her breath as he paused near her. Had someone told him that she was here? She spared a glance toward where he'd been standing and saw that the group had dispersed. No one was waiting to see what would happen next. Her blue gaze whipped back to the man and moved quickly over his angular face and strong, straight nose. She braced herself for his sharp word of greeting and the reactive flash of confident recognition that she would be no match for him.

Instead, his gaze lingered only briefly on her face before moving on. She was just another woman among many who had business in the courthouse. She might have been there to arrange bail for a boyfriend or to act as witness at a trial. He had no business with her, as far as he knew. No reason for recognition. Amanda remained frozen near the table. It was only when she saw him walk safely through the double doors of the building's main exit that she allowed herself the freedom to breathe again. Her heart rate took longer to settle.

She had known he was coming. *Everyone* knew he was coming; his picture had been in the *Tyler Citizen* on and off for a week. It was only a matter of when. Now he was here. In person. No longer a face in newsprint or a terrifying reputation to be feared. She had seen him, looked straight into his eyes, and she had discovered that this time reality was every bit equal to the gossip.

"Amanda…hello," someone called from a short distance away, drawing her out of her panicky thoughts.

Amanda looked up to see a fellow attorney struggling to contain an armload of notebooks and files. She forced a smile. "Sharon! Hello to you, too! I thought you were still visiting your parents in Florida.''

Her friend grimaced. ''I'm supposed to be, but I got called back. A custody hearing was moved up, so here I am. Have you heard? Ethan Trask is scheduled to set up his office in the courthouse today. Have you met him yet? Walk with me—I'm already behind schedule.''

Amanda checked over her shoulder to make sure that Ethan Trask hadn't changed his mind and reentered the building. ''No,'' she said, settling in at her friend's side. ''I haven't met him yet, and I wish I never had to.''

Sharon Martin glanced at her with compassion. ''I don't envy you one bit. Neither does anyone else, with the possible exception of our usual showboater. He'd love to take on Ethan Trask. Winning or losing wouldn't matter, as long as he got plenty of media attention.'' Sharon hesitated. ''Have you given any more thought to finding a co-counsel? I'd offer to help, but I'd be next to useless. You need someone who really knows their way around a criminal court.''

''I could always ask Larry,'' Amanda murmured dryly. Larry Richardson was the ''showboater'' Sharon had referred to. Not only did the man have an ego the size of Wisconsin concerning his abilities as a criminal defense lawyer, he also thought he was God's gift to women.

''Yeah, sure.'' Sharon's tone held just the right amount of sarcasm. ''First he'd insist on being lead counsel. You'd have to do everything *his* way. Second, he'd inflate his fee. Third, you'd do all the work and he'd take all the glory. Fourth, you'd have to fight for your virtue every time you stepped into an empty room with him. And fifth…he wouldn't care nearly as much as you do about proving your grandfather innocent. Don't ask Larry!''

''I'll take your advice under consideration, Counselor.''

Sharon, who looked tanned and rested from her week in Miami, ignored Amanda's teasing words. ''The strain is starting to show, Amanda. Seriously, get some help. Have you thought of asking Professor Williams?''

Sharon and Amanda had attended the same law school in Illinois, and Professor Williams had been their favorite instructor. Several years ago he had retired and moved back to his family's longtime home on nearby Lake Geneva.

''I've thought of him,'' Amanda admitted.

They paused at the base of the wide, curving stairway that was the centerpiece of the graceful old building. Sharon glanced toward the upper floors. ''I've got to go. Give him a call, Amanda. If our positions were reversed, I would.''

Amanda waved her friend away and continued down a long hall that branched off the lobby. She had contemplated placing a call to Professor Williams on more than one occasion, but had hesitated each time because he'd been reported to be in ill health. And with all the upset about her grandfather's upcoming trial, she hadn't taken the time she once would have to pay him a friendly visit. She had been too busy trying to catch up loose ends so that she could devote herself completely to her grandfather's case.

As she neared the county clerk's office, a man who'd been slouching against the wall looked up and jerked forward. ''Miss Baron! Could I have a word with you, please?'' He pressed closer. ''Would you give me a quick statement about Ethan Trask? How does your grandfather feel about his assignment to the case? Does he think he'll get a fair trial? Have you had second thoughts about representing your grandfather? Have you seen Ethan Trask yet? Have you talked with him?'' He readied a notepad and a stubby pencil.

The barrage of questions set Amanda on edge. She still wasn't accustomed to such attention. Strictly a small-town lawyer, she handled small-town problems. The most notorious case she'd ever been involved with concerned a male dog of very mixed breeding that had fallen under the spell of a certain champion female show dog next door. Spike had displayed surprising versatility and enterprise in getting out of his backyard in order to pay his calls, and the show dog's owner had been furious about the little Spikes that had frequently turned up in his litters. He had sued the neighbor, whom Amanda represented, and the story had passed from local color to newspapers across the state. She had given a few quick interviews and been done with it. She and Rob Friedman, the owner and publisher of the *Tyler Citizen,* had had a few good laughs out of it. But ever since her grandfather's indictment, Amanda found little to laugh about.

She took a quick breath and said, ''There's been no change in my grandfather's representation. He has every faith in my ability and in the state to give him a fair trial. As to Mr. Trask…he doesn't frighten either one of us. We're each still getting a good night's sleep.''

''But considering Ethan Trask's reputation—''

Amanda flashed a naturally sweet smile. "I'll leave it at that. Now, if you don't mind, I have business to attend to."

The reporter held back as she stepped into the clerk's office. She might look cool and confident, which was the impression she very much wanted to give, but she felt far from that inside. If truth be told, her sleep patterns were awful. She kept having the same dream, that a monster was out to get her and, no matter where she took cover, always found her. From the drawn look of her grandfather, she suspected he was having much the same experience.

Amanda took care of her business as quickly as possible and made her way out of the courthouse. She had only one close call. As she was about to leave through a side door, she came face-to-face with the small, slender man who had been with Ethan Trask. She recognized him instantly. He had jet-black hair, warm brown eyes and just the slightest trace of a Latin accent when he excused himself and stood aside for her to pass. He was not a handsome man. His nose was too large for his face, his mouth was too wide. But he held himself with such confident élan and had such quick charm to his smile that Amanda found herself smiling, too. Yet if he was in any way connected with Ethan Trask, he had to be dangerous.

Reacting instinctively, Amanda ducked her head and hurried away.

THE HALF HOUR it took for Amanda to drive from Sugar Creek to her office in Tyler included a quick stop at Marge's Diner, where she picked up lunch. Holding out the bag of food to her secretary, she teased, "Amanda to the rescue! Are you starving?

That took longer than I thought. I fully expected to find you expired on top of your desk."

"Don't be silly," Tessie Finklebaum grumbled.

Tessie had been a legal secretary for longer than Amanda had been in the world. She'd seen everything, done almost everything, and was surprised by nothing. She had to be getting close to seventy, but she kept the date of her birth a deep, dark secret. It was as secret as the true color of her platinum-tinted hair. Each morning Tessie went for a two-mile "hike," as she termed it, and two evenings a week she attended an aerobics class. It was not in a person's better interests to call her "old."

Amanda pulled up a chair to her secretary's desk. The set of offices they shared was rather small, comprising her own office in the rear and the secretarial space in front. But she'd tried to decorate the place with a little taste, bringing a chair or two from home and cheerfully accepting Tessie's array of houseplants.

Amanda dug into the paper bag and divided its contents. She placed two tuna sandwiches, two bags of chips and two cans of soda on the napkins her secretary had spread on the desk. "I saw Ethan Trask today," she remarked easily.

Tessie fixed her with a piercing look. "You did? What did he say?"

Amanda grinned. "I didn't say I talked with him, I just saw him. Then I ran away like a craven coward. Tucked my little yellow tail between my legs and took off. What do you think of that?"

"I'd say you probably did the right thing. What was he like?"

Amanda leaned back. "Oh…tall, dark, handsome and terrifyingly competent. Nothing special."

Her secretary shook her head. "You better get yourself some help, young lady."

"That's what Sharon Martin said."

"You should listen to her. Ethan Trask will eat you alive."

"Thanks for your vote of confidence. I told a reporter I was perfectly assured of my ability."

"Are you?"

"I'm scared to death."

Tessie picked up her sandwich and started to munch. For a time they ate in silence. Finally, Amanda pushed away from the desk, her meal half-eaten.

"I'm going to make a couple of calls," she said. "If anyone needs me, ask them to wait."

"Sure thing, boss."

Amanda shook her head as she entered her sanctuary. For Tessie to call her "boss" was something of a joke. They both knew who was boss in the outer office, and it certainly wasn't Amanda. Tessie must think her in extreme need of a pick-me-up…which she was. Because joke all she wanted, she was truly terrified.

She had tried to tell everyone from the start that her grandfather should hire a lawyer more experienced with trial procedure, an expert in criminal defense. But no one had listened. They all told her she would do a great job. No one understood that criminal defense was an art form, just as was criminal prosecution. An ordinary, run-of-the-mill lawyer couldn't just walk in off the street, prepare a case of this magnitude and expect to win. She certainly couldn't. And if her grandfather ended up spending the rest of his life in jail because of her inability…

Amanda reached for her telephone index and punched in a number with the Lake Geneva area code. Ten minutes later, she had gained an appointment with the professor. After that, she punched in the number of the Ingalls mansion. Clara Myers, her grandfather's longtime housekeeper, answered the phone.

"Clara, hello, this is Amanda. I'm not going to be home for dinner this evening. Actually, I just had lunch…. Yes, I know how late it is. Would you please tell my mother that I'll speak to her when I get in, and tell Granddad…tell Granddad I might have some interesting news for him. No—" she quickly changed her mind "—don't say that last part. Just tell him I love him, and that I'll talk to him later, too."

She stared at the phone once she'd hung up. Then her gaze drifted to her rows of law books, which looked almost as pristine now as they had when she first received them, a gift from her mother and grandfather upon graduation from law school five years before.

Law, the body of rules that kept the fabric of society from coming apart… She had fallen in love with it when she was fifteen and one of her high school classes had gone on a field trip to the courthouse in Sugar Creek. She had watched the lawyers maneuver back and forth, watched as the defense team tried to use the cold and impersonal rules to the advantage of their client, watched as the state's representative held fast to the ideal of those rules. And from that day she had forgotten her earlier plan to become a veterinarian. She had haunted the library in Tyler, reading every book she could get her hands on that gave a view of the legal process.

She liked to think that, since becoming a lawyer herself, she had helped people. She hadn't won every case these past five years, but she had certainly attempted to. Most of her work involved technical expertise: what paper to file and where. Few cases actually went all the way to a trial. She tried very hard to mediate between people, to help them settle their differences before they resorted to further legal action.

Amanda sighed, her pretty face, normally so ready with the high-voltage Baron smile, unusually serious. The law *was* cold and impersonal, which meant that emotion held no place in judicial decisions. Just because a jury didn't like the way a defendant looked or behaved didn't mean they could take out their disapproval on that person by finding him guilty. Their decision had to be based solely on the evidence presented.

But in this instance, it was her grandfather she would soon be defending, and she wanted him to have every advantage that the system could offer—every bit of warmth she could stir in the jurors' hearts.

Her gaze moved to the newspaper clipping she had pinned to the wall earlier in the week—a picture of Ethan Trask. On it she had drawn the concentric circles of a target, with the bull's eye the tip of his nose. At that moment, the tip had a dart sticking out of it. Not that she had made such a superb hit, though she'd tried for a quarter of an hour. She had ended up by marching over to slam the dart in at point-blank range.

Ethan Trask. The man she had seen so confidently

issuing orders in the courthouse such a short time ago. The attorney general's "Avenging Angel."

"Oh, Granddad," Amanda groaned softly, beneath her breath, "if only it were anyone else!"

CHAPTER TWO

THE COTTAGE beside the wide lake nestled comfortably in the trees. Its look was ageless. It might have stood there for two years or two hundred. Amanda waited at the front door for Professor Williams to answer her knock. She shifted restlessly from foot to foot.

When at last the door swung open, a slightly older version of her favorite and most valued instructor greeted her. Like the man who had been with Ethan Trask, he, too, was her par in height. Only instead of being slender, Professor Williams was more than adequately insulated against any sudden disruption in the world's food supply. His cheeks were round, his midsection rotund, and he had just enough unruly white hair left on top of his head to remind Amanda of an elf. His eyes contradicted the image. Instead of being benign and merry, they were probing and sharp. After his first sweeping glance, Amanda knew the Professor had guessed the reason for her visit.

"You're wasting your time," he said. Still, he motioned her indoors. "The only sport I'm interested in right now is fishing—bass, walleye, bluegill."

The interior of the cabin was just as comfortable as the exterior. Neatly kept, with an overstuffed couch and chairs, it was perfect for a retired bachelor.

Amanda decided not to equivocate. "You're the only person I can ask, Professor."

"Why's that?" he shot back. "Are you trying to tell me I'm the only person with a half a brain left in this state?"

"No."

"Good, because I wouldn't believe you." His eyes narrowed. "You always did tell the truth, even when it wasn't in your best interests."

"Isn't truth what the law is all about?" Amanda countered. "I seem to remember you had a special lecture you liked to give—"

"I did," he interrupted her. "But I gave it so many times I don't care to hear it again." Finally he smiled. "It's good to see you, Amanda Baron. Even under these trying circumstances. You're a feast for the eye as well as the spirit."

Amanda inclined her head, managing a small smile. The professor looked her over more carefully. "I've kept up with what's been happening via the newspapers. I read about your grandfather's arrest and his indictment. Events of that sort are good fodder, especially when they happen in a nearby town. How is your family holding up?"

"Not very well, I'm afraid. They're all trying to act as if everything will turn out all right, but they're scared silly that it won't."

"And you?"

"Me most of all."

The professor showed her to the couch and invited her to sit down while he went to make coffee. Soon he was back with two large mugs. "Do you take cream or sugar?" he asked.

"No, I like it straight." She accepted a cup and

took a small sip of the steaming liquid. It did little to warm her.

Professor Williams sat back, his cup untouched. "So, what is it you're afraid of?" he asked.

"What am I *not* afraid of is a better question! I don't know what I'm doing, Professor! I've never handled a criminal case before...at least, nothing more serious than some crazy local kid assaulting someone, or somebody else robbing a store. This is *murder* we're talking about here! Life imprisonment. And my grandfather is the person charged! Everyone believes I can handle it—my mother, my brother, my sister...my grandfather. They all think that just because I have a law degree, I should be able to waltz into court and get Granddad off. I've tried to explain that it's not that easy, but they won't listen." She set down her cup, afraid to hold it any longer in case it spilled.

"I believe you can do it," the professor said quietly. "You have a very quick mind, Amanda."

"But if I lose, if I do something wrong...if I overlook something, if I pick the wrong jurors...Ethan Trask will—"

"You have a very tough adversary."

"The battle won't be fair!"

"Which is why you came to me."

Amanda sat forward, her chestnut hair lightly brushing her shoulders. "I thought possibly if you would be my co-counsel..."

He was already shaking his head. "It's been three years since I left teaching and ten since I set foot in a courtroom. When I retired, I took leave of all that."

"It's not something a person forgets," she maintained. "Not someone as capable as you. I've read your memoirs. I've read all the cases."

"I didn't say I've forgotten anything," he corrected her sharply. "I said I took *leave* of that life. I swore to myself that I would never again come before the bench in any capacity as a lawyer, and I meant it. I saw too many doddering old men in my day, men who barely knew how to tie their shoelaces any longer, still trying to plead a case…and some of those men were behind the bench, too! No, I'm much too old and much too tired to inflict myself on the judicial system."

Amanda immediately remembered the rumors of his ill health. "I heard that you weren't feeling well. But you look so…healthy." His color was good, his eyes bright.

He laughed shortly. "That's something I put around to keep from being bothered. Too many people read that damned book last year and wanted advice. They came at all hours of the day and night."

Amanda looked down. That was exactly what she was doing.

"I didn't mean you," he said, correctly interpreting her sudden stillness. "I'm talking about strangers, people I don't even know."

Amanda's features were tight. She should never have come here. Professor Williams was a wonderful teacher, but they had never become personal friends. Too many years and too much experience separated them. Only desperation had brought her to this point. She stood. "I'm sorry to have taken up so much of your time. You warned me in the beginning. I should have listened." She smiled, and the sweetness of her

smile had no artifice. "I'm glad that you're not ill,"
she added.

She turned to leave, but a hand stopped her. Professor Williams's expression was whimsical. "You
have something very special, Amanda. A quality
many other lawyers only try to achieve. Sincerity just
shines out of you, my dear. Stick with that, and you
won't have a thing to worry about."

The compliment was nice and Amanda appreciated
it, but she knew that sincerity alone wasn't going to
win her grandfather's case. Only hard work would do
that. Hard work and, as the situation now stood, a
great deal of luck. "Thank you," she said.

She started for the door again, opened it and was
about to go outside when Professor Williams asked,
"Would you be willing to accept me in the role of
adviser? I won't step into the well with you, I won't
talk to the judge or wrangle with Ethan Trask, but I
will give you the benefit of what little knowledge I've
managed to glean over the years. Would that be a
satisfactory compromise?"

For the first time since her grandfather's indictment, Amanda felt a spurt of optimism. She turned
back to the professor, joy spreading in her smile.
"That would be wonderful!" she said, her throat
tight.

His round face softened. "Why is it old men are
so often willing to make fools of themselves when
asked to by attractive young women?"

"I would never call you old, and I would never
dare to call you a fool. Thank you, Professor."

"My name is Peter. If we're going to work together, it should be as equals."

Amanda tried the name. "Peter," she repeated.

He nodded. "Now, you must set me straight on this case. As you know probably only too well by now, the media rarely manage to get the story right."

"Gladly," Amanda agreed.

She stepped back into the cozy room, curled up on the couch and, with cup in hand, gave her new friend an accounting of all she knew about her grandfather and the woman he was accused of murdering forty-two years before—his wife and her grandmother, Margaret Lindstrom Ingalls.

ETHAN TRASK SURVEYED the set of offices that would be his for the upcoming weeks and decided that they were beginning to shape up. Everyone involved with helping him to settle in had done their jobs efficiently and well. Desks were positioned, file cabinets provided, worktables set up. Even the secretary on loan from the local district attorney's office was already hard at work, entering something into her computer. And in one corner, packed in several boxes, was the material he would need to make the state's case against one Judson Thaddeus Ingalls. At present, he knew only the essentials. The seventy-eight-year-old man was accused of murdering his wife at their lakeside estate some forty-two years ago. The story circulated after the woman's disappearance was that she had run away, probably with another man, leaving her husband to raise their young daughter. That falsehood had been widely believed until recently, when her remains had inconveniently turned up.

Ethan placed one of the boxes on the table nearest his desk and started to empty it. He would familiarize himself with the details of the case, first by going over the police reports and then by moving through all the other materials gathered for presentation to the grand jury. He dragged a chair over to the table and sat down.

He was beginning to work his way through the initial stack of reports when the man assigned to the case from the State Department of Justice came quietly into the room.

Carlos Varadero and Ethan had worked together several times before. Ethan liked the man, admired him for both his professional ability and his tenacity. Not much slipped by the keen eye of the Cuban. As an investigator, he was first-rate.

Carlos flashed a quick smile. "I have learned something that will interest you, my friend."

Ethan pushed the papers away. "What?" he asked.

"This Amanda Baron, the woman who is to act as defense counsel for Judson Ingalls. She is his granddaughter. And…" The word was drawn out, then repeated for dramatic effect as Carlos brought another chair closer to the table. "*And* she is also the granddaughter of the deceased. There, what do you think of that? I had only to ask one or two questions. People here are interested in the trial. Many of them know Amanda Baron personally. A few know her family. More know *of* her family. They are very influential."

Ethan already knew that the Ingalls family was influential in Tyler, and it didn't surprise him that their influence carried beyond the small town's border and into the county seat. The fact that he had been brought in as special prosecutor spoke volumes. What he hadn't known was that Amanda Baron was one of them! "We have to get her off the case," he stated curtly, his mouth tightening.

"That may be hard to do," Carlos said.

"We still have to try. Her presence could prejudice the jury." Ethan crossed to the floor-to-ceiling window that overlooked the public green surrounding the courthouse. He watched as people walked to and fro along the sidewalks. "No one should be above the reach of the law," he said firmly. "No matter how wealthy, no matter how influential. Judson Ingalls thought he could get away with the murder of his wife, and if it hadn't been for a quirk of fate, he might have managed it. I'm not going to let him make a mockery of this trial."

For Ethan there was no other course. His whole life had been set along one path. It was as natural for him to separate right from wrong as it was to breathe. The pursuit of justice burned within him like a bright light, often setting him apart, forcing him to choose between what was expedient and what was just. It was a matter of pride for him that he had never backed away from a hard choice.

He turned from the window and lifted another box onto the table. "You might as well get started, too," he said, pushing it toward his assistant.

Carlos's brown eyes were amused. "I also heard that Amanda Baron is a very pretty, very determined woman. The people in the courthouse speak highly of her."

Ethan paused. "Do you think that should make a difference to me?"

Carlos shrugged. "You are a man. You will notice."

"I was sent here to do a job, Carlos."

"Do you want me to find out more about her? I could go to Tyler tomorrow and talk to some of the people there."

Ethan thought for a moment. "That might be a good idea. I'll come along, too. Feel out the atmosphere of the place."

Then he resettled in his chair and again started to sort through the material that would form his case. It was going to be a long evening.

AMANDA DIRECTED her aging MG into the wide driveway at the side of the Ingallses' big house on Elm Street. From the collection of cars, she could see that Jeff was home, which meant Cece might be there, too, and that Liza was visiting, undoubtedly with Cliff and baby Maggie.

The elation Amanda had felt on the drive back to Tyler suddenly deserted her. Even with Professor Williams—Peter—offering advice, it would still be she who would have to face Ethan Trask. She might still make all kinds of mistakes, ask the wrong questions, let important points slip by.

She looked at the huge Victorian house, whose lights were striving to hold the night at bay. The family had been through so much this past year. From the moment the body was found, rumors had started to fly. Then rumor had turned to fact, when the remains had been identified as Margaret's. From that point on, their lives had been one long nightmare. Sometimes it was hard to tell friend from foe. A few people wanted to see the Ingallses receive their comeuppance. Others remained steadfastly loyal, while still others swayed in the breeze of whatever public sentiment seemed dominant that day.

Instead of being torn apart, though, the family had grown closer—even Liza, who had once been estranged from them. They were united by the common belief that Judson Ingalls was innocent of the accusation made against him. And they looked to her to prove it.

Amanda shivered slightly in the freshening breeze, reacting to the awesome responsibility. But she soon set her shoulders, restored her confident smile and made her way into the great house that had sheltered members of her family for well over a hundred years.

Voices from the living room drew her to that section of the house. No one noticed her at first, so she had a moment to survey the scene. Her sister, Liza, sat on the floor, her long, lanky frame leaning back against her husband, Cliff Forrester. Cliff, relaxed in a wing chair, quietly combed a lock of Liza's rebellious blond hair with his fingers and listened intently as she spoke. The girls' older brother, Jeff, and his fiancée, Cece Scanlon, sat on the couch. Both looked rather exhausted from their respective work shifts at the hospital and the nursing care facility at Worthington House, not to mention the additional time each spent at the free clinic Jeff had set up in one of the empty office suites at Ingalls Farm and Machinery. For them to be off duty at the same time was unusual, as was the fact that they had chosen to spend their spare time with the family instead of away somewhere on their own. Alyssa, the Baron siblings' mother, sat in another wing chair holding little Maggie. The worried strain that had become so much a part of her beautiful features was softened by the love she felt for her first grandchild. With strands of her fine golden hair falling gracefully over her cheeks, she played with the newborn infant's tiny hand. Judson, the white-haired patriarch of the family, stood with his back to the bay window, his posture ramrod straight. He was the first to acknowledge Amanda's presence.

"Amanda," he said when Liza, too, noticed her and abruptly stopped talking. "I saw you drive up, but it took awhile for you to come inside. Are you having more trouble with your car?"

Amanda's car was the joke of the family. As it grew older, it seemed to break down almost as frequently as it ran. Still, she loved it. It had been a sixteenth-birthday present from her father, and that above all made it special to her. She smiled. "Amazingly, it's running beautifully."

"You must have placed Carl on a retainer fee," Liza teased. "I heard he closed his garage for two weeks this summer and went to Hawaii. Did you single-handedly subsidize his vacation?"

"No," Amanda retorted. "Actually, we barter. I'm going to handle his divorce, and he's going to rebuild my engine."

"Better watch out about letting him get too close to your carburetor," Jeff goaded. "I've heard he's become quite the ladies' man since he separated from his wife."

"Jeffrey," Alyssa admonished, pretending to frown while at the same time fighting a smile. "Leave your sister alone."

"Yes, *Jeffrey,*" Amanda taunted, while Liza and Cece giggled.

Even Judson managed to find a grin. The family so seldom had occasion to laugh these days, any opportunity was appreciated.

Amanda placed her purse on a small side table and claimed a section of couch nearest her mother's chair. She leaned toward the baby, smoothing a tiny tuft of fine blond hair. "And how is Miss Margaret Alyssa today? Learn any new words? Can we count past ten yet? Hmm?"

The weeks-old infant opened her eyes and blinked at her aunt, causing Amanda to feel the weight of responsibility expand to a new generation. Liza and Cliff had been through so much in their individual lives—Cliff having to learn to deal with the aftereffects of his time spent in Cambodia, and Liza at last coming to terms with one of the major tragedies of the Baron family, their father's suicide. Now the two planned to make Tyler their permanent home, and as a result, young Maggie would have to live with the outcome of the trial. She would grow to maturity among people who would look upon her great-grandfather either as an upstanding member of the community, as he'd always been, or as a convicted murderer.

Amanda shook away the thought. She couldn't deal with it at present. "What did I interrupt when I came in?" she asked.

All the smiles disappeared.

"We were talking about the trial," Liza volunteered. "About Ethan Trask. Jeff heard someone at the hospital say he arrived in Sugar Creek today."

Amanda felt her insides tighten. "He did," she confirmed.

"What does that mean?" Alyssa asked.

"It means that he's getting ready to try the case. He'll set up his office, then start talking to people."

Jeff frowned. "But I thought the district attorney had already investigated the case. The police…Karen, Brick. Why do they have to do more?"

"Ethan Trask will want to talk with everyone himself. He's coming into this new, remember? The attorney general just appointed him.''

Liza's frown was fierce. "I still don't see why Mr. Burns had to ask for a special prosecutor. It's not as if he and Granddad are best buddies. They barely know each other outside of a couple of charity events. Isn't that right, Granddad?''

Judson nodded.

"I know,'' Amanda agreed. "It's hard to understand, but the district attorney had to disqualify himself because of the way the situation could be interpreted. If Granddad is found not guilty, it might be thought that the D.A. didn't push hard enough. Mr. Burns and Granddad aren't best friends, but they do know each other.''

Liza grunted. "Mr. Burns is watching out for Mr. Burns. He doesn't want to do anything to foul up his chances of reelection.''

"That's probably true, too,'' Amanda conceded. "But it doesn't change the original fact. He had no choice except to take himself off the case.''

"So he made sure we got Ethan Trask,'' Liza complained.

"He had no say in the matter. That choice belonged to the state attorney general.''

"Remind me not to vote for him, either,'' Cliff said quietly, gaining a quick smile of approval from his wife.

"Me, too,'' Cece agreed. Jeff squeezed her hand.

Amanda decided that the time was right. She had planned to tell her grandfather the news later, but since everyone was here... "I think I gained a point for our side today,'' she announced. "Actually, a whole lot of points. Do any of you remember when I was in law school and talked about a Professor Williams? How brilliant he was, and how lucky I felt to have him as one of my instructors?'' She received blank looks all around. ''Well, Professor Williams—Peter—is retired now, and he lives at Lake Geneva. I spoke with him this evening. That's why I was late, why I missed dinner. He's agreed to advise me on Granddad's case!''

The expected excitement didn't occur. Finally, Liza questioned, ''Does that mean he's taking over?''

Oh, if only that were true! Amanda thought. But she shook her head. ''No. He's agreed to help, that's all. He's very experienced in courtroom procedure and criminal law. He was a practicing trial attorney for years before he went into teaching. He's very respected. He's even written a book—''

''Does it make you feel better that he agreed to assist you?'' Judson interrupted.

Amanda gazed at her grandfather's strong face—the high cheekbones, the commanding Ingalls nose and chin, the eyes that could be stern but were mostly gentle. ''Yes,'' she answered truthfully. ''It makes me feel better.''

''Then that's all that counts,'' Judson decreed. ''I agree with your decision. His first name is Peter, you say? My father's name. A good name for a man.''

''I think you'll like him, Granddad,'' Amanda assured him, relieved that her grandfather had consented.

Judson nodded, then turned to look outside. He'd been doing a lot of that recently—standing and looking out windows. Amanda couldn't help but wonder if he was thinking about the present or remembering something from the past.

Cliff glanced at his watch, then stood. He helped Liza to her feet as well. "We have to go," Liza said. She collected her daughter from her mother's lap. "Little Maggie needs to hit the sack…not to mention Mommy and Daddy. Cece, when you gave us all those childbirth lessons, why didn't you warn us that once babies come into the world they like to torture their parents? I thought she'd wake up only once a night to be fed, not every two hours like clockwork. And Cliff's no help. He doesn't come with the right equipment! He gets up with me, though, just to be fair."

"Remind me to put you up on the roof the next time a shingle blows loose," Cliff teased.

Liza flashed a reckless smile. "You think I wouldn't do it?"

Jeff laughed. "Liza, Cliff's been married to you long enough to know when to back off. If he's not careful, the next time it storms you'll be up on the roof replacing missing shingles, all the while suckling your newborn child!"

"I don't want Maggie to grow up with preconceived notions about people," Liza defended.

Once again Jeff laughed. "Sis, I seriously doubt that there's any danger of that! Not with you for a mom."

Cece stood up to hug Liza. "Don't pay any attention to him," she advised. "He doesn't know what he's talking about."

Jeff pretended to be hurt. "*You* can say that about *me?* You're going to have to make that up to me, my girl." He pulled Cece back down to his side and kissed her, long and with feeling. When he let her go, she was pink. Her fingers fluttered to her short, dark hair, but the secret smile she wore was a pleased one.

With her daughter cradled in one arm, Liza made the rounds, hugging her mother, her brother, her grandfather and finally Amanda. "Walk out to the car with us," she whispered in Amanda's ear. "I have to talk to you." Her smile urged Amanda not to react.

Amanda gave a short, almost imperceptible nod and kept her own smile in place.

Liza passed the baby to Cliff, who somehow managed to look instantly comfortable with the tiny burden. His quietness seemed to instill quietness in the child. Maggie gave one tiny wiggle and went to sleep. Liza smiled and went about the business of collecting the array of baby things, which she then packed away in a soft cloth bag.

"Here, let me help," Amanda volunteered. She took the bag from her sister, which freed Liza to arrange a light blanket around her child for protection against the night.

After their final goodbyes, Amanda followed them out to the car, and while Cliff put the baby into an infant-restraint seat, Liza said worriedly, "I didn't want to ask inside, but what if he wants to see me? What should I do? Can I refuse?"

Amanda knew immediately who "he" was: the man who seemed to be on everyone's mind—Ethan Trask. "Yes, you can refuse," she said. "But he'll subpoena you for the trial. He has the power of the state behind him. He can make you testify."

"But what if he comes around before that…what do I do?"

"Am I your lawyer?"

"What do you… Of course you're my lawyer!"

Liza replied, catching on quickly. "Mine and Cliff's both. Right, Cliff?"

Cliff straightened, his tall good looks emphasized by the diffuse light from the house windows. "Right," he agreed.

"If you're contacted, call me right away," Amanda said. "Tell him you won't be interviewed unless I'm present."

Liza gave a devilish smile. "I'm almost beginning to feel sorry for the man!"

"Well, don't. He knows a lot more about what he's doing than I do."

Liza sobered instantly. "I wish Cliff and I had never found the rug or that Joe Santori had never given me the bullet. I wish…no, I can't wish that. If I'd never come back to Tyler, Cliff and I wouldn't have met, and there'd be no Maggie. But if I hadn't insisted upon redoing the lodge… It's my fault, isn't it, that this has happened? Leave it to me! Leave it to Liza to screw everything up!"

"Liza…" Cliff's quiet voice cut into his wife's frustration. "No one blames you."

"It would have come out eventually, Liza," Amanda agreed. "Granddad had thought several times about selling the lodge. It was only a matter of time before he did and before someone else started renovations."

"But he looks so *old* now. What if he can't stand up to the pressures of a trial? What if he collapses? What if he—"

"You're tired," Amanda said. "A lot has happened to you over the past few weeks. You've given birth, you're trying to adjust to motherhood, both you and the baby are still chock-full of hormones. The grandfather you love dearly has been indicted for murder…just an ordinary month in the life of one Mary Elizabeth Baron Forrester.'' Amanda patted her sister's hand. ''Go home, Liza. Go home with your wonderful husband, and let me worry about Granddad. I have reinforcements now. I'm not nearly as afraid as I once was.''

''Are you telling us the truth?'' Liza demanded. ''You're not just saying that to make me stop worrying?''

Amanda crossed her heart, the sign the Baron siblings had used since childhood to signify truth telling.

Liza's face brightened, but Cliff wasn't fooled. Unlike his wife, Cliff didn't *want* to be fooled. Amanda hesitated to look at him, but she felt her gaze drawn. In her brother-in-law's black eyes she saw the truth. And she knew that *he* knew she hadn't spoken it.

CHAPTER THREE

"THIS WAY, PETER. Over here," Amanda urged. In her haste to get to the spot where Margaret's body had been found, she drew ahead of the overweight professor. She moved agilely across the gently sloping hillside, while he proceeded more slowly. As she waited for him to catch up, she double-checked the accuracy of the location. To her left was the lake and the offshore wooden swimming float that she had known since childhood; to her right stood Timberlake Lodge—a large, rambling structure that had been built by her great-grandfather to host hunting parties for his friends, and which now was part of the Addison Hotel chain. Straight in front of her was the gnarled old pine tree she and Liza and Jeff had played under when they were young and had come to the lodge for a stolen afternoon. "This is the spot where they found her. A willow tree used to stand near here, but Joe took it down when he and his men were checking the water pipes."

The professor wiped his pink cheeks. As he puffed from exertion, his alert eyes moved over the manicured lawn of the newly opened resort, then lifted to the multigabled structure that nestled at the top of the hill. "If she was running away, she didn't get very far," he said.

"No," Amanda agreed.

"Why here?" Peter asked.

"I don't know that, either."

"What does your grandfather think? Have you asked him?"

Amanda hesitated. "My grandfather doesn't like to talk about it."

Peter's answer was a displeased grunt.

"I know," Amanda defended. "I just haven't pressed him. He's coming to my office this afternoon. We'll talk then. He's promised to tell me everything he can remember."

"I hope his memory is excellent."

"It is."

She received another grunt, but this time Peter sounded more satisfied. She watched as he absorbed the quiet beauty of his surroundings. Timberlake Lodge always had the same effect on her. It was hard to believe that something as frightening and horrible as a murder could ever have taken place in such a sylvan scene.

She broke the silence that had fallen. "The police found her suitcase...did I tell you that? It was all packed and ready to go. Only for some reason, it was in the lodge's potting shed. Well, not when they found it. Actually, it had been stolen. Whoever took it must have realized they didn't have anything of value, so they dumped it on the highway between here and Belton. One of our police officers found it. It had her initials, M.L.I., and Granddad identified her clothing."

Amanda lapsed into silence again, remembering the awful moment when Karen Keppler and Brick Bauer had come to the house, in uniform and on official business. And the way Karen had looked at her grandfather...suspiciously, as if she were already persuaded to believe that he had killed Margaret.

"Rather odd that it wasn't with the body," Peter mused.

"I know. If Granddad had done it, wouldn't he have gotten rid of the suitcase, too? To make it look as if she had taken it? He knew Phil—Phil Wocheck was the gardener at Timberlake then. He knew Phil was in and out of the potting shed all the time, digging through things. Granddad couldn't have expected the suitcase to stay hidden if he was the person who put it there...which he wasn't."

"You're sure of that?"

"Of course I'm sure. I'm sure!" she repeated.

"This Phil Wocheck. He's the man you said testified before the grand jury? The man whose testimony seemed to carry so much weight?"

"I'm afraid so."

Peter frowned. "I wonder what he knows."

"We all wonder that!"

"You need all the information you can get, yet the prosecution is required to give you only your grandfather's statements to the police. If you want more, you'll have to file a motion."

"I'm working on it now."

"Good girl," the professor approved.

Amanda started back up the hill, this time making sure to go slowly enough so as not to outpace her companion. What Phil had said to the police and then to the grand jury had been the subject of much speculation, both within the family and without, for the past few weeks. But Phil, observing the grand jury's injunction not to speak of his testimony, would say nothing.

Frustration curled in Amanda's stomach. She had
so little to work on! She had no idea what the prosecution would throw at them. She had only the charge
included in her grandfather's indictment: first-degree
intentional homicide, the worst accusation the State
of Wisconsin could issue against a person.

The professor had started to puff again when two
men appeared at the top of the pathway. One was tall,
the other short. One moved with commanding assurance, the other with compact grace. Both had dark
hair. When she recognized them, Amanda felt her
breath grow shallow. She, too, might suddenly have
gained forty pounds and forty years. Instinctively her
hand reached out toward the professor, whether to
warn him or to ask for protection, she didn't know.

The professor glanced at her curiously, then he followed the direction of her gaze.

"It's him," she whispered tightly. "Ethan Trask."

"Introduce me," Peter said.

"I can't! I haven't met him yet!"

"Then you'd better introduce yourself." Peter
seemed amused by the turn of events. Or rather, by
Amanda's reaction. "He's not a god," he said. "He
puts his pants on one leg at a time, just like I do."
He glanced at the beige trousers Amanda wore. "Just
like you do."

"I sit on the end of the bed and jam both my feet
in at the same instant," Amanda replied shakily.

Peter's smile was no longer hidden. "Then that
makes you special. Introduce yourself!"

The men were almost upon them. Amanda swallowed. She had already felt the sweep of Ethan
Trask's gaze and the much friendlier estimation of his
companion. Of the two, she would much rather deal

with the shorter man. She took a step sideways, signaling a desire to communicate.

"Mr. Trask?" she said. To her own ears, her voice sounded dry, strained. She could hear the fake attempt at confidence.

Up close, the special prosecutor was even more impressive than he had been the day before. He seemed taller, more intense, more determined, more handsome. His eyes were neither black nor brown, but an intimidating combination of the two. His dark brown hair was perfectly groomed, a tendency to curl tolerated but not encouraged. His features might have been carefully sculpted to give the image of strength—straight nose, firm jawline, sturdy chin, a mouth that was at the same time sensual and austere. The cut of his perfectly tailored suit bespoke a body that was muscular, athletic.

Amanda's heart rate accelerated as he turned to look at her. Under his direct gaze she felt like a rabbit caught in a snare. "I, ah... My name is Amanda Baron, Mr. Trask, and I represent—"

Her name seemed to hit him like a lightning strike. It wasn't so much that he jolted physically, but his mind seemed to snap to attention, focusing solely on her. It was all Amanda could do to continue. "I represent Judson Ingalls. This is Peter Williams, retired professor of law at the University of Illinois. He's going to—"

"Amanda Baron." Ethan Trask repeated her name as if he had heard nothing else she'd said.

Amanda smiled nervously. "Yes. I represent—"

"I know who you represent."

Amanda shot a look at Peter, who in turn was studying the assistant attorney general. Her gaze then went to Ethan Trask's companion. She was searching for a kind word, a kind face. She found it in the shorter man when he smiled at her. Still Amanda remained confused. She didn't understand exactly what was happening. Ethan Trask sounded angry. Again attempting civility, she held out her hand.

There was a long moment before he responded, a moment that came close to insult. When finally his fingers closed over hers, they were brisk, businesslike. Amanda was quick to break contact. Her arm fell back to her side, but her hand still tingled.

"My assistant from the DCI, Carlos Varadero." Ethan Trask indicated the man at his side.

Amanda knew that the Division of Criminal Investigation was the investigative arm of the State Department of Justice. A crack unit, it provided assistance to the attorney general's office—which meant that she had been correct the first time she saw him: if he was affiliated with Ethan Trask, he was dangerous, smile or no smile.

Amanda shook his hand quickly, as did Peter. For a moment nothing happened. All of them seemed ill at ease. Then Ethan Trask said quietly, "I'm going to file a motion to disqualify you as defense counsel in this case. Since you are the granddaughter of both the defendant and the deceased, I consider your role inappropriate."

Now it was Amanda's turn to reel. She blinked at the unexpectedness of his attack. "But…that's not fair!" she cried.

"Not fair?" Ethan Trask repeated, pouncing on the word. "What you and your grandfather are trying to do is what's not fair, Miss Baron. The law does not play favorites."

Amanda blinked again. She took a step back toward Peter. What was the man talking about? *She* was the one who had resisted representing her grandfather. *She* was the one who had done everything in the world to avoid her appointment.

Peter spoke for her. "The accused has a right to the counsel of his choice, Mr. Trask."

"Ordinarily, yes. But this is not an ordinary case."

"It's a fundamental right," Peter insisted.

"We'll see what Judge Griffen has to say." Ethan Trask's attention shifted back to Amanda. "I'm filing the motion," he said levelly, scorching her with the intensity of his gaze. Then he motioned to Carlos Varadero that they should continue on their way. After a brief nod, Carlos fell into step at his side.

Amanda was still speechless once she and Peter were alone again. She watched the progress of the two men. After consulting what had to be diagrams and photographs pulled from an envelope Carlos Varadero carried, they proceeded to the spot where she and Peter had stood earlier—the site of Margaret's one-time grave.

Amanda's emotions were a jumble. Shock and amazement warred with affront.

Peter took her arm and continued to trudge up the hillside. "A rather intense young man," he pronounced.

"He's got to be six or eight years older than I am, and I'm almost thirty!" Amanda protested.

"I'm speaking from the great advantage of my years. Once a person passes sixty-five, nearly everyone seems young."

Amanda stopped, anger having overtaken all her other emotions. "What did he mean, Peter? What does he think Granddad and I are trying to do? My only goal is to mount a successful defense, to be sure that my grandfather doesn't go to jail for the rest of his life for a murder he didn't commit!''

''Obviously Mr. Trask thinks you're placing an unfair burden on the state, and he's giving you fair warning of what he intends to do. I wondered if he'd latch on to that.''

''You mean you had an idea that he might?''

''If he's as good a lawyer as everyone says, yes.''

''You might have warned me,'' she complained.

Peter smiled. ''I didn't want to frighten you unduly.''

''I'm *not* afraid of him! At least, not anymore.'' Amanda threw a look back over her shoulder toward the two men, who happened, at that moment, to be looking up at them. ''Humph,'' she sniffed, then she jerked her head around and walked proudly on.

The man had two eyes, two ears, one nose, one mouth. He was just an ordinary human being, nothing more, nothing less. All she had to do over the next weeks was to keep telling herself that!

CARLOS NUDGED Ethan's arm and pointed to the two people making their way slowly up the hillside. A slender young woman with bright chestnut hair and a portly man dressed in a rumpled suit, who walked as if his knees hurt.

At that moment, the woman turned, and for the space of a second, the distance between them evaporated. Ethan again saw those huge, dark blue eyes that seemed to fill her face. She wasn't classically beautiful, but there was something about her that was arresting. A small, straight nose, firm rounded chin, delicately carved cheeks—her features were a blend of feminine strengths. It was the look in her eyes, though, that had stopped him, forced him to notice her. Besides quick intelligence and a certain pride, there was a freshness about the way she looked at the world. A sweetness and generosity of spirit that Ethan was unused to in the people he dealt with on a day-to-day basis. Then she turned away, and he was released.

"Mmm," Carlos murmured. "It seems this Amanda Baron is everything we were told she would be."

"Keep your mind on your work, Carlos."

"Can you, my friend? Are you able to do that?"

"Easily," Ethan claimed.

The investigator shook his head. "A man must have more in his life than work. A woman, a child…"

"I don't see *you* with a woman or child," Ethan parried.

Carlos smiled. "It is something I dream of, and one day—one day—I will have it."

"Which will be a great moment for us all," Ethan returned sarcastically. "Now, do you think we can get back to the business at hand?" He lifted the police photos he had been studying. "The body was found right about here, and Margaret Ingalls's room was on the lower floor of the lodge." Ethan shuffled other photos until he found the ones he wanted. They showed a room empty of furniture and adornment, except for a painting of a woman, a wall mirror and a fireplace. On the far wall, leading outside, were French doors.

Ethan handed the photographs, one by one, to his assistant. Both had studied the glossy prints last night, staying in the Sugar Creek office until well past midnight as they tried to digest as much information as they could about the case.

Ethan said, "It's a short trip from the bedroom to this point. The gardener—this Philip Wocheck—claims to have picked her up and carried her down here. He says he 'helped her go.' Wasn't that his testimony before the grand jury?"

Carlos nodded. "He also said he saw someone run from the room. It might have been Judson Ingalls and it might not. Do you think he is covering for his old boss?"

"Considering his sudden bouts of forgetfulness brought on by intensive questioning…yes, I'd say he's covering something."

Carlos shook his head. "The man is seventy-five years old, my friend. People that old—"

"Can't be allowed to evade telling the truth! Age is a fact of life, not an excuse. Look at what's already happened. The local D.A. didn't press charges against him when, by every count, he should have—for obstruction of justice at the very least, if not for acting as an accessory."

"He did volunteer the information," Carlos reminded.

"Yes, but did he tell the whole story or did he evade?"

"The D.A. believed him."

"I know. But something just isn't right. I believe he's hiding something—like the fact that Judson Ingalls ordered him to dispose of the body. Otherwise, why would he—"

"He has no immunity. He did not ask for it."

"No, he hasn't," Ethan agreed. "And when we talk with him, I'm going to remind him of that fact."

The men moved down to the lake. This was a preliminary visit to familiarize themselves with the murder site. Each knew that they would return, probably more than once. As Carlos looked out over the water, Ethan studied the resort perched on the crest of the hill. The account he had read last night was prominent in his mind. It was a story of wealth, excessive behavior and passions gone awry, the kind of story that Ethan had seen repeated many times. He hunched his shoulders, impatient with delay.

Carlos skipped a rock across the water. "It is very beautiful here," he said, his accent as soft as his words. "It reminds me of a place I knew in Cuba, not far from my home. I was just a child, of course, but my father would often take me to the water and we would sit and talk. About nothing in particular...just talk."

Carlos lapsed into a silence that Ethan didn't break. He, too, remembered a time spent by the water, along the wharves of one of the two great rivers that formed a confluence at Pittsburgh, Pennsylvania. Only for him there had been no father to sit and talk with. He'd had no father—at least, none that he knew. And the time he'd spent on the wharves had not been idyllic.

Ethan wrenched his mind from the past—from the scruffily clothed boy who'd stood out from those around him, the boy who had never fit in because he couldn't act as irresponsibly as the others did, the boy who in the end had held himself aloof even though he'd ached to belong.... "Let's go check out the lodge," Ethan said in a clipped tone. "And this potting shed we've heard so much about.'' Then he turned away, from the lake and from his memories.

AMANDA WORKED through her lunch break. Peter had given her a few helpful directions and then had gone back to Lake Geneva. He was expecting a call from his literary agent that afternoon and didn't want to miss it. When she had questioned him as to whether he was trying to sell another volume of his memoirs, he had avoided a direct answer and escaped as quickly as he could.

With a mystified smile, Amanda had set to work, and soon was immersed in sorting through the precedent-setting cases and rules of law that she would use in writing her brief for Judge Griffen on the defendant's right to counsel. She hadn't expected to be doing this. She hadn't expected an objection to her relationship in the case.

Margaret's granddaughter. She didn't feel like Margaret's granddaughter. She didn't feel as if Margaret deserved to be any relation at all. For the family, the woman had been nothing but trouble.

Liza had grown up oversensitive to the fact that she looked so much like the hell-raising party girl from the past, and since people rarely lost an opportunity to speculate on the similarity of their behavior, Liza had eventually begun to act like her, more in a twisted sort of rebellion than because she was like her grandmother. Liza was spirited, but there was no meanness in her.

And Jeff...Jeff had married a woman just like Margaret, as selfish and as insensitive as a rhino. The family had tried to talk him out of it, but Jeff had been well and truly under her spell. Because of a secret fascination with Margaret? The marriage had ended and Jeff had pretended that it didn't hurt. But Amanda knew that it did.

Then there was their mother. Alyssa had never gotten over Margaret's abandonment of her as a child. Now it turned out that Margaret hadn't abandoned her after all, but had planned to; she had left a note. Same difference in the end. Die, walk out...their mother was still scarred for life.

Amanda's thoughts moved on to the person most hurt by Margaret's thoughtlessness: Judson. She remembered the pain that burned deeply in his eyes and remembered that throughout her childhood she had acted the fool many times in order to make her grandfather laugh.

For herself, Amanda once had thought she'd escaped untouched. She didn't look like the Ingalls women—tall, leggy blondes. She looked like her father, Ronald Baron. So did Jeff, except for his inheritance of their grandfather's commanding nose and chin. Yet she now knew that she had not escaped. For her, fate had played a delaying game. It had waited to spring her grandmother on her at a later date—to be exact, forty-two years. It was no wonder Amanda felt nothing except annoyance with the woman. Margaret was as much a troublemaker dead as she had been alive.

And Ethan Trask thought it unfair that she should represent the man accused of murdering Margaret? If anyone, it should be she! She resented the woman, just as she resented the assistant attorney general's intimation that she had planned some kind of wrongdoing.

Ethan Trask...

Amanda's fingers stopped on the pages of one of her law books as unwanted feelings fought their way into her consciousness. She had tried to ignore it earlier, but beneath all her outrage had lurked something else, the fact that on some core level, she found Ethan Trask extremely attractive. She felt herself growing steadily warmer. Then a tap on her door rescued her from further discomfort. A second later, her grandfather poked his head through the opening. "Amanda, honey?" he said. "Tessie told me to come right in."

Amanda's greeting was a little more enthusiastic than it normally might have been. She jumped up to give her grandfather a hug.

Judson smiled bemusedly as he patted her back. "I realize the situation is bad, but is it this bad?" he teased.

Amanda didn't want to let go of her grandfather's solid strength as memories of her childhood once again stirred. She'd had two men in her life then, her grandfather and her father. She had lost her father, a fact that remained like a huge gaping hole in her life even after ten years. She didn't want to lose her grandfather, too. She didn't think he would live very long in jail.

She made herself step back, more because she didn't want to frighten him than because she was ready. She forced a smile. "No, it's not that bad," she assured him. "Only a minor bobble or two." She hesitated, then plunged in. "Ethan Trask wants me off the case. He's going to file a motion with the judge. He doesn't like it that I'm both your and Margaret's granddaughter."

Judson's still handsome features settled into a frown. "Can he do that?" he asked.

"Not without a fight...and I'm going to give him one. That's what I was doing just now, working up my argument."

Judson glanced at her loaded desk. "Would you like me to come back later? I can always find something to do at the plant or the lab."

Amanda shook her head. "No, this is fine." She showed him to a chair. Her grandfather still held himself with a quiet kind of dignity, but the past year had taken its toll. It was hard for him to ignore the rumors that flashed about town, to ignore the fact that people he had known all his life might think he had killed his wife. Hard to realize that people he had helped could turn against him. His face contained many more lines than it had before; his shoulders slumped, particularly when he didn't feel on show. Amanda's heart went out to him. He put on a brave front for the family, especially Alyssa. He didn't want any of them to worry. But how could they not worry?

Amanda settled behind her desk and folded her hands on top of her paperwork. "This is something we have to deal with, Granddad. First, if I'm disqualified, we have to find you a new lawyer. Possibly Peter could be persuaded...or he might recommend someone."

"I want you, Amanda."

Amanda's hands tightened. "I know. But if that's not possible, we'll have to find someone else. We'd appeal the decision, of course, if it went against us. But a decision on such an appeal probably wouldn't be handed down until after the trial. Not unless you want to put off the trial for a number of months so that the appeals court has time to issue a decision." Amanda stopped when she felt her grandfather stiffen.

"I know. You want to see the end of all of this. So do I. So we go back to filing our appeal while the trial is held. If you lost the case, but we won the appeal, you'd have to stand trial all over again…this time with me as your lawyer." Her grandfather's face whitened. "That's not something we want, Granddad, not either of us. If I were some kind of high-powered defense attorney, I'd say yes…we'd go for that. But I'm not." She sighed. "What I'm trying to say is…if I get disqualified, I think you should find another lawyer. Someone with more experience than me. Someone we could be sure of—"

Her grandfather broke in softly, "I still want you, Amanda." Judson Ingalls was a stubborn man.

Amanda murmured, "Let's face that decision when we need to. It's still down the road, and we may not even come to it."

Judson smiled. "That's right. I think you'll win, to begin with. There'll be no need for an appeal. This Ethan Trask…he isn't infallible, is he?"

"No…" Amanda replied slowly.

"No," Judson repeated, satisfied.

From experience, Amanda knew when it was time to retreat. She moved to another subject, one she had resisted bringing up before. But they couldn't put it off any longer. "Proceeding on that assumption…Granddad, I know you don't like to talk about anything concerning Margaret, but under the circumstances, if I'm to defend you properly, you're going to have to talk to me. You're going to have to treat me as if I'm a stranger. You have to be honest with me. Not keep anything back. Tell me things you'd never tell anyone else, particularly a member of the

family. Warts and all, I have to know. Is that understood?''

Judson's white head bobbed.

Amanda continued, ''Anything you tell me will be
privileged information. It will go no further than your
defense team.''

''I understand.''

Amanda relaxed slightly. Her grandfather could
sometimes be prickly. At least they had gotten this
far.

''Where do you want me to begin?'' Judson asked.

''I suppose the night Margaret disappeared.''

A muscle pulled at the side of Judson's jaw. ''We
had an argument. I already told the police that.''

''What was it about?''

''Money, her running around with other men, the
way she ignored Alyssa…''

''When did the argument start?''

''That morning. It ran on into late evening. It
would stop and start. She was having a party—one of
her constant parties. They'd go on for days. People
were around that I didn't know…didn't *want* to
know!''

''When did you see her last?''

Judson was silent. Finally, he said, ''About six or
seven o'clock. She had some kind of special evening
planned with her friends. They were going to play a
new game—I don't know what kind. I didn't ask. *I*
sure as hell wasn't going to play!'' He paused again,
becoming lost in the past. ''She told me to get out.
She told me she hated me. So I went.'' A wealth of
feeling lay beneath the flatness of his words. Amanda,
who knew her grandfather well, could sense his suf-
fering.

"Where did you go?" she asked.

"Out. I walked beside the lake, I don't know for how long. A couple of hours? When I got back—"

"Did anyone see you while you were walking?"

Judson shook his head. "No."

"Go on," Amanda encouraged.

"When I got back…she was gone. I found a note on the mantel. It said she was leaving."

"What happened then?" Amanda prompted.

Judson looked down at his hands. "I—I went a little berserk. I picked up a perfume bottle and threw it across the room. It broke some things on Margaret's dressing table…bottles, dusting powder, face creams. It made quite a mess. Then I—" He stopped.

"Then you…what?" Amanda pressed, her voice husky.

"I cried," he admitted simply. "Like some kind of huge baby, I just stood there and cried."

Answering tears formed in Amanda's eyes, but she quickly blinked them away. If she expected her grandfather to divorce himself from their relationship and talk to her, she couldn't behave in a manner that would inhibit his confidences.

"Then what?" she asked.

"Then I went to see Alyssa. My little girl was all I had left."

Amanda allowed him time to collect himself, while she, too, did a little collecting of her own emotions. "Would you like some water?" she asked.

Judson shook his head.

Amanda continued, "These men that Margaret 'ran' with. Did you know any of them? Do you remember their names? Do you know if any of them are alive today?"

Again Judson shook his head, but the motion had grown tighter, as if the strain he was under had sharply increased.

"It would help if you could come up with a name or two, Granddad. What about that summer? Was there anyone special?" Liza had already told Amanda about the man Rose Atkins had remembered shortly before she died. Rose had been invited to a few of Margaret's parties, as she was one of the few people in Tyler Margaret liked. Liza had shown the old woman some of the photos she had found in the attic at Timberlake Lodge, and Rose had recognized one of the men. *They were very close,* Liza had reported Rose saying. *He was probably her lover.* "Does the name Roddy mean anything to you, Granddad?" Amanda asked, probing his memory.

At that, Judson jerked to his feet. "That's enough," he clipped shortly. "I have to go to the plant. A meeting I forgot. We can do this some other time. Right now I have to—" He didn't complete his sentence; his jaw clamped shut instead.

Amanda got slowly to her feet. They had barely begun their review. She needed much more detailed information. But it was evident that she wasn't going to get it. Not right now, not after striking what was unmistakably a raw nerve. She shrugged. "Sure, Granddad. We can talk again later."

"Good," he said. Then he pivoted and walked stiffly from the room, leaving Amanda to stare after him in frustration.

CHAPTER FOUR

WHEN ETHAN OPENED the front door of Marge's Diner, the hum of cheerful conversation mingled with the smell of hot coffee and cooking food. By the time he made his way to the counter, all conversation had stopped. Knowing himself to be the focus of attention, he hitched a seat on one of the red-topped stools, helped himself to a menu propped next to the salt and pepper shakers and frowned down at his choices for a late lunch. It was always like this when he came to a new town on a prosecution. He was the outsider, the stranger. As with a gunslinging lawman of old, people were both in awe of him and afraid. But Ethan was accustomed to being the outsider. It didn't bother him. Slowly conversation resumed, though at a much more subdued level.

Minutes later, the door opened again and Carlos entered the establishment. When he spotted Ethan, he came to his side and took a seat. Ethan handed him a menu.

''What've you come up with?'' Ethan asked.

''Typical stuff. The lady at the post office seems to be the gossip maven. And there is a kid—a Lars Travis—about fifteen, who delivers bits and pieces of rumors along with the local newspaper. I talked with the lady, but the kid is in school.''

''What did the lady say?''

Carlos dropped the menu and fished in his pocket for a notebook. Referring to it occasionally, he said, "A number of people in town think Judson Ingalls did the dirty deed. Most of the same number think Margaret deserved it. She did not fit in here—she was a big-city girl from Chicago who scandalized everyone with her behavior. Judson was thought to be getting the short end of the stick. He was a local war hero, not that anyone remembers much about what he did in the war. After Margaret 'left,' Judson raised his daughter, Alyssa, on his own. Ingalls F and M, the family business, has been an important part of the community almost since its inception. It employs a substantial number of the people in and around Tyler. Mr. Ingalls is very active in community affairs. He supports the local high school sports teams, especially the Titans, the football team. His daughter is on the town council and every other committee Annabelle Scanlon—she is the postmistress—can think of." Carlos paused. "I sense resentment there. She is probably jealous. The Ingallses have always had most of the money in town and most of the class."

He went back to his notes. "Alyssa Ingalls married one Ronald William Baron—who, incidentally, killed himself about ten years ago when his grain elevator business collapsed financially. The Barons had three children—Jeff, a doctor at the hospital here, Amanda and Liza, who seems to have taken after Grandmother Margaret and was quite a hell-raiser before she married. She shows up in a couple of our reports. She found the rug and turned over the bullet found in Margaret's room at the lodge."

Ethan nodded. He looked for the waitress. She was leaning against the far end of the counter, talking with a policeman. Ethan sensed that they were discussing him and Carlos, and he had the hunch confirmed when the policeman's hard gaze met his. The waitress glanced at him, too, but she made no move to come take their order. Once again she started to talk with the policeman.

Carlos replaced the notebook in his pocket. "Everyone I talked to seems to think highly of Amanda Baron. She is liked, she is respected. I heard no word against her, not even from the postmistress."

"We'd like some coffee down here, please," Ethan called, his strong voice cutting into the waitress's tête-à-tête.

Carlos smiled, amused by Ethan's direct attack.

The policeman said something, causing the waitress to push away from the counter and come toward them. On the way she nonchalantly collected a full coffee beaker and two cups. After the cups were filled, she started to walk away again, but Ethan stopped her. "We'd also like to order."

"Cook's just stepped out," the woman said, her middle-aged face set uncompromisingly.

Ethan glanced behind the serving counter into the kitchen. "Who's that in the hat?" he asked.

A flush stole into the woman's cheeks. By that time the policeman, dressed in the dark uniform of the Sugar Creek Sheriff's Department, had ambled over. He was a compactly built six-footer with squared features and a no-nonsense edge that was tempered by a friendly smile.

"Serve the men, Marge," he advised. "Two hamburgers don't commit you to one side or the other. Judson will understand."

Color still brightened the woman's cheeks. "I'm

loyal to my customers and my friends, Brick. Judson comes in here every day. And for these men to just barge in and act as if—''

''They're just doing their job,'' the policeman said. ''You serve Karen and me when we come in...and we're the ones who arrested him.''

''That's different,'' Marge claimed.

''No, it's not.''

Marge looked at the policeman for a long moment, then at Ethan and Carlos. ''All right,'' she conceded grudgingly, ''what do you want?''

Ethan glanced at Carlos, who gave a short nod. ''Two burgers. One no onion, one no tomato.''

Marge moved away, leaving the policeman to introduce himself. ''Lieutenant Brick Bauer of the Tyler substation,'' he said, extending his hand. ''I've heard you've been asking around town today.''

''News travels fast,'' Ethan remarked.

''In most small towns it does, but especially in Tyler.'' Brick glanced at the people sitting in booths and clinging to stools farther along the counter. He nodded whenever he caught an inquisitive eye. ''You're quite an object of speculation, Mr. Trask.''

''As you said, I'm just doing my job.'' Ethan introduced Carlos, who, he saw, did a quick estimation of the policeman.

Brick Bauer sighed. ''So are we all, so are we all...but it's not a nice business sometimes.'' He straightened, resting an arm on top of his holster flap as so many of his fellow officers did. ''I expect you'll be wanting to talk with me later?''

Ethan nodded. ''We'll call before we come.''

''Good. Then I'll arrange to be in.''

With another nod, he ambled off. In no hurry, he

paused to speak to people at two tables on the way out the door.

Ethan glanced at Carlos. "What do you think?" he asked.

"A fair man who can put loyalties aside when it comes to telling the truth. He will be a good witness."

"My thoughts exactly."

The two burgers were delivered with a clank of glass plate against hard counter. Marge didn't wait around to ask if they needed anything else.

Ethan's smile was wintry as he surveyed their meal. "Do you think we should really eat these?"

"We have not been poisoned yet," Carlos said.

"There's always a first time," Ethan murmured, then he bit into the piping-hot burger and instantly decided it was the best he had had in years.

AMANDA TRIED to go back to the preparation of her brief, but she just couldn't make herself concentrate. Who was this Roddy and why had her grandfather behaved so strangely at the mention of his name? Had the man been intimately involved with Margaret in the weeks before her death? What did her grandfather know about him?

She got up from her desk and went into the outer office. Tessie looked up from her computer keyboard. "I'm going out for a while, Tessie," Amanda said. "Just around the square. If anyone needs me, I'll be back in about—" she checked her watch "—half an hour. Not more than that. I need some fresh air."

Her secretary nodded and went back to work.

The day was unusually warm for the latter part of September. Sunlight rained through the leaves of the huge old oak trees and onto the grassy square. Even the fall flowers, nicely kept in their beds, seemed to be especially colorful this day. It was as if Nature was giving everyone a second chance at summer before the frigid winds of winter came to call.

Amanda sat down on a wooden bench in one of the sunnier sections of the park and watched as a few young children played nearby. The upcoming trial was like the worst threat of winter to her: an impending time of darkness and cold. That is, if she were allowed to assume her rightful place at her grandfather's side.

She sighed and, made sleepy by the unusual warmth, let her eyes shut. Mere seconds passed, however, before a huge shaggy dog came lumbering across the lawn to jump on her. "Samson!" Amanda laughed, snapping to attention as the friendly white dog continued to try to lick her cheek, her chin, her nose, her mouth.

"Samson, down!" Pam Kelsey called, hurrying to contain him. She made a grab for his collar. "Sorry, Amanda," she apologized, once she had gained control. "He's just been groomed and thinks he's king of the hill."

Amanda grinned as she rubbed a fluffy head. "That's okay. I think he's king of the hill, too. Any dog this sweet deserves a little spoiling."

"Actually, we had to get him groomed today because he spent all of yesterday trying to dig his way out of the backyard. I don't understand why he's started to do it, but he has. He's twelve years old. He should know better!"

"Maybe he's lonely," Amanda suggested. "You should get him a friend. No, seriously. With both you and Patrick at school all day, and then with you coaching the football team and Patrick helping you…Samson probably feels as if he's lacking attention."

"What kind of friend?" Pam asked carefully.

"Another dog. Preferably a female, neutered, of course. Unless you want to have puppies."

"Good heavens."

Amanda laughed. "Samson has a few good years left in him. He's probably not ready yet to hang up his spurs in that department. He could still be a father."

"Why not get another male and not have to worry about it?"

"Because introducing a male dog at this stage might make matters worse. They might not like each other."

Pam tilted her head, her brown eyes curious. "How do you know so much about it?" she asked. Then she remembered. "Oh, that's right. You once wanted to be a vet, didn't you? Patrick told me."

Amanda smiled wryly. "Right now, I wish I'd stuck with it."

Pam's pretty face lost its smile. "I heard that Ethan Trask and his assistant were asking questions around town today. I took off from school during my free period to collect Samson, and I ran into Annabelle outside the post office. She said a man named Carlos something-or-other had talked to her for almost an hour. So you know what that means…they now know almost everything there is to know about Tyler."

"By the time this trial is through no one will have any secrets left."

"Do you really think it will be that bad?"

Amanda looked at Pam and saw her genuine concern. Not for her own sake—Pam wasn't involved. She hadn't moved to Tyler until late last summer, around the time Margaret's body had been found. She had no connection to the town's past except through her marriage to Patrick Kelsey, the Kelseys having been in Tyler since its founding, just as long as the Ingallses had. Amanda shook her head. "No, I'm exaggerating. I'm feeling a little frustrated right now, so I'm acting theatrical."

Pam reached out to clasp her arm. "If there's any way Patrick and I can help, you just let us know. We don't believe Judson could have done a thing like that. We may not be able to be in court with you because of our commitments at the school, but we'll be with you in spirit. Tell Judson we support him, okay?"

"Okay," Amanda agreed. Her spirits lifted just a little. Their family did have friends—the Kelseys, the Bauers...and there were others.

Samson woofed at Amanda, as if to say goodbye, then he jerked, ready to move away.

Laughing, Pam whipped out a leash and connected it in one smooth motion. "He got away from me earlier before I could get this on. I think he spotted you sitting here. Animals like you, don't they?"

"Usually, yes," Amanda admitted.

Pam's brown eyes moved over her. "I think they trust you."

Amanda shrugged. "They probably see a soft touch."

"No, I think they sense something more. You're a lot like your mother, Amanda. The same pure heart."

Amanda wondered if Pam would still think that if

she could see the photo of Ethan Trask in her office, the one with the dart sticking out of his nose.

ETHAN COUNTED OUT the correct amount tallied on the waitress's check and added a few dollars more for a tip. Service hadn't been exactly wonderful, but the woman *had* come back to refill their coffee cups. As they left the diner, he noticed that most of the same people who had been present upon his arrival remained. Their eyes followed him to the door. Once outside, he wondered whether, if either he or Carlos were to surprise them by opening the door again, they would all be talking at once about the same subject.

They walked to Ethan's car, a sleek black luxury model that he had allowed himself. As he opened the driver's door, he asked, "Did you find out anything about the ring?"

Carlos shook his head. "Nothing, my friend. No one knows anything about it."

Ethan frowned as they settled into their seats. "Judson and Margaret were married in 1941. The ring found with the body is engraved 1941—at least, the segment we can read says that. It has to be his."

"As far as anyone knows, Judson Ingalls never wore a ring."

"Keep asking. You may turn up something with one of the older people you talk to. Someone who knew the two of them way back when."

Ethan started the car and backed out of the parking slot onto the street.

"What about you?" Carlos asked when they pulled forward. "What did you learn?"

"That Judson Ingalls started talking seriously about selling Timberlake Lodge shortly after the body was found. And he sold it to the Addison Hotel Corporation for less than market value."

"Was the buyer spooked because of the body?"

"Not according to the assistant manager. Addison would have gone higher, but Judson Ingalls didn't ask it. I think he wanted the place off his conscience."

"That would not make his troubles go away."

"Out of sight, out of mind? Remember that painting of Margaret Ingalls in her bedroom? He didn't ask for it, either. And years ago, after he'd ordered the room locked up, he moved to his house in town and never went back. The man's pretty good at ignoring what's unpleasant."

"He cannot ignore a court date."

"No." Ethan smiled. "He can't."

Ethan looked away from the street for a second to glance at Carlos. The next thing he knew, Carlos was yelling for him to stop. Ethan's reactions were quick. Without asking why, he jammed on the brakes and the car rocked to a halt. It was then he saw Amanda Baron. She was inches away from the front grill. She looked back at him, stunned.

Ethan expelled a long breath and made himself get out of the car. "Are you all right?" he asked, hurrying toward her.

Huge blue eyes looked up at him. "I know you want me off the case," she whispered. "But I didn't think you'd be willing to go this far."

Ethan was in no mood for sarcasm, even if it sprang from shock. He answered stiffly, "I assure you, I've never yet had to resort to killing the competition."

"Perhaps I should check your police record."

"I don't have a police record."

Carlos, who had exited the car as well, smiled as

he leaned lightly against the front fender. "It is true," he said. "He is not a wanted man."

Amanda sent Carlos a look that made his smile grow. Ethan saw that while fright warred with anger in her expression, humor at the situation was beginning to dawn. Her undecided gaze returned to Ethan, and once again he felt himself physically stirred. He was aware of everything about her. The way the beige slacks fitted her slender hips and legs; the way her ribbed scoop-necked top, dyed a dusky rose and worn beneath a casually loose beige jacket, settled against small, but nicely rounded breasts. The way her bright chestnut hair shone in the sun...her flawless skin, the beautiful blue of her eyes, her soft, kissable mouth. He jerked his thoughts away from such undisciplined chaos.

"You stepped out in front of me!" he accused.

"I did no such thing! Look where I am. How did I get this far across the street if I'd just stepped out?" She was standing in front of the driver's side, not the passenger side closest to the sidewalk. "You were speeding," she countered.

Ethan shrugged the logic away. It was important for him to keep the upper hand. He had to stay in control. "No, I wasn't. I never speed. Not in a town."

"Then you admit you sometimes speed on a highway."

"I didn't say that."

"And if you speed on a highway, it means you might drive over the limit elsewhere...like in a town!"

"Check the skid marks," Ethan parried. "They don't indicate high speed. No, you didn't look. You were in the park, probably distracted—you do have certain things to be distracted about. You decided to go back to your office…'' He indicated the sign on her office directly across the street. ''So you started off without looking. You were probably walking rather quickly, thinking about all the things you had to do. You didn't see the car.''

Again, a blend of emotions crossed Amanda Baron's pretty face. For an instant she looked as if she were about to confess, but her fighting spirit returned, and she taunted, ''Prove it!''

Ethan had sensed victory, but before he could return her taunt, a series of claps came from the man who had witnessed their exchange. Ethan looked around. He had forgotten that Carlos was there.

The investigator smiled broadly. He straightened away from the car even as he continued to clap his hands. He looked first at Amanda Baron and then at Ethan, his dark eyes dancing. ''Bravo!'' he approved. ''Magnifico! A wonderful performance! But you are both forgetting. There was a witness, a highly experienced observer—me! I saw everything, and I say you owe each other an apology.'' He pointed at Amanda Baron. ''You stepped out.'' And at Ethan. ''And you were not watching where you were going. No one wins, no one loses, no one was hurt. No debate.'' Carlos shook his head. ''Lawyers,'' he grumbled amusedly to himself. ''You will argue with a tree!''

Amanda Baron stared at him for a few seconds, then she, too, started to laugh. She was beautiful when she laughed, Ethan thought. Her entire face lighted up. He continued to hold himself stiffly. A smile never cracked his lips.

''I suppose,'' she said, ''since we do have a highly

experienced witness, I'll have to admit to some responsibility. I *was* thinking of something else, and I didn't see the car.'' She looked at Ethan, waiting for him to make a similar concession.

Ethan felt Carlos's eyes come to rest upon him, too. Finally, he allowed, ''I agree. It was my fault as well.''

Carlos approved. ''Ah, that is good. An understanding!''

In the silence that followed, Amanda Baron shifted slightly and glanced again at Ethan. All Ethan wanted to do was get back behind the wheel and drive away. He was uncomfortable standing in the street with her. Uncomfortable with the unexpected strength of his feelings. All he could think of was that it was a good thing he had filed a challenge against her as defense counsel. He would have hated to go to trial and try to maintain an adversarial role. It would have played havoc with his concentration.

Because he had confidence in the justness of his argument to Judge Griffen, Ethan let a tight smile slip into place even as he maintained, ''But I wasn't speeding. I hold my ground there.''

Several cars passed them and then paused, drivers and passengers curious about what had happened. Amanda Baron returned the salute of one group and called hello to another. She glanced toward her office.

Ethan took the onus onto himself. ''If you're sure you're all right,'' he said, ''we'll be on our way. I'm sorry for any fright you may have experienced.''

''So am I,'' she said. Then, surprising him—actually, surprising both of them—she thrust out her hand. She looked down at it blankly, as if the appendage weren't hers.

Ethan took it. Her hand felt warm and capable, very feminine, very soft. He held it a moment before letting go.

Amanda Baron threw Carlos a quick smile, murmured goodbye to both of them, then hurried the rest of the way across the street and disappeared inside her office.

Ethan had no idea how long he stared at the closed door, how long before Carlos called him back to awareness. It couldn't have been more than a few seconds. Yet from the way the investigator grinned once Ethan had resettled in the driver's seat, it might have been hours.

"I think you have noticed her, my friend," Carlos teased, referring to his earlier comment.

"I tried to kill her, you mean," Ethan corrected.

"And I think she noticed you."

"Don't be ridiculous."

Even, white teeth flashed. "I only say what I see. I make nothing up."

Ethan started the car. "She hates my guts. I'm here to send her grandfather to jail."

Carlos's shrug was expressive, silently holding to his statement.

"Naa," Ethan denied.

Carlos's answer was another shrug.

Ethan laughed shortly. "I think you'd better have your eyes examined when we get back to Madison. Now, to return to business. This Joe Santori, the building contractor who found the body and the bullet—is he willing to see us tomorrow?"

"I arranged a time in the afternoon. I thought you would want me to do a little more digging around here in the morning."

Ethan nodded. "You're right. Besides doing a little more probing about the ring, check into Judson and Margaret's marital troubles. They fought about her having affairs with other men, but see if there was anything else. Also, nose around about the possible police cover-up, both then and now. Let's see where we stand in that regard. We don't want any surprises."

"Do you think any evidence might be tainted?"

"It's doubtful in this case, but witnesses might be. Who are the two ex-police chiefs? Zachary Phelps and Paul Schmidt?"

Carlos nodded.

"We may need to have both testify. If we do, I want to know which way they'll go. Also, I'd like you to do a little checking on Philip Wocheck. See what people have to say about him. You might try your postmistress again on that."

As Carlos nodded again, he started writing reminders to himself in his notebook.

Ethan carefully checked the street for both traffic and inattentive pedestrians before he accelerated. As he did, he glanced across the wide street toward the office that had Amanda Louise Baron, Attorney-at-Law emblazoned on the door. He had known from the beginning that this was going to be a difficult case. Forty-two years had passed since the murder occurred, the accused was a well-respected, wealthy, influential man in the community and the evidence was mostly circumstantial...all hard enough strikes to overcome. But he hadn't counted on having to deal with someone like Amanda Louise Baron, or her unwanted effect on him.

AMANDA WATCHED the car pull away. It certainly had taken them long enough! What were they doing? What were they talking about? Her? Her grandfather? The case?

She moved away from her spy's perch in the corner of the room, letting the vertical blind swing back into place. As usual, Tessie had made the necessary adjustments to keep the afternoon sun from interfering with her computer screen.

Tessie sat at her desk, a silent witness to her employer's antics from the moment she'd entered the door and scurried to the corner. At last the secretary's silence came to an end. "We had a call while you were out," she said. "Judge Griffen wants to set the disqualification hearing for tomorrow morning. You know him—he doesn't like to let grass grow under his feet. They want a callback as soon as possible."

Tomorrow morning! Amanda thought of her laden desk. Could she possibly be ready by tomorrow morning? She checked her watch. She had the rest of the afternoon and tonight, and if she made judicious use of every second... "Tell him I'll be ready," she said. "What time?"

"Eight-thirty. He has a trial scheduled at ten."

"Right," Amanda said. "I guess I'd better get going." As she started into her office, she felt her secretary's eyes follow her. Pretending to an innocence she didn't feel, she paused to ask, "What is it? What's wrong?"

"May I ask what that was all about just now? Or is it some kind of deep, dark secret?"

Amanda shrugged. "Oh, nothing. I just..." She stopped. Tessie would see through her in a second. "I ran into Ethan Trask," she admitted wryly. "Literally! Well, I almost ran into him. Actually, we almost ran into each other. Neither of us was watching where we were going—him driving, me walking.''

Tessie lifted an eyebrow at her unaccustomed inarticulateness. To complete her humiliation, Amanda felt herself flush. And she was a person who *never* flushed.

Tessie's eyes widened. ''I've heard that he lives up to his reputation. Plus he's even better-looking than his picture. Must be true,'' she decided.

''It's not that at all,'' Amanda declared. ''He almost ran me down in his car just now! Anyone would be upset.''

''Would anyone peek out the window to see what he did next?''

''I was merely—''

''Watching to see what he did next?''

''My behavior is strictly in the best interest of my client. Ethan Trask is the enemy. I was conducting a little surveillance, that's all.''

''Did you learn anything?'' Tessie asked dryly.

Had she learned anything? Amanda couldn't answer truthfully. How did she explain that despite the man's determination to prosecute her grandfather, she found him fascinating? He was so self-contained, so controlled. He barely ever smiled, and when he did, his lips made only the faintest movement, as if they were unaccustomed to the motion. His decisive intensity acted on her like a magnet, drawing her to him. When he first jumped out of the car to see if she was hurt, she had seen genuine concern in his eyes. But the hard, no-nonsense edge had soon returned. Which was the real man? she wondered. And should she care?

"He signaled properly before pulling into traffic,"
she murmured in answer to her secretary's challenge.

"That must have been a big disappointment."

"Not really," Amanda claimed. "Not when I'm
looking for keys to his psyche."

Tessie rolled her eyes. "That's a bunch of baloney
and you know it."

"It never hurts to be prepared."

Tessie snorted as she twisted back around. She
hadn't believed Amanda, hadn't believed anything
she'd said. Amanda recognized the fact and knew that
she would have to live with it. Just as she knew that,
whether she liked it or not, every time she went near
Ethan Trask something seemed to happen to her in-
ternal balance wheel, and her equilibrium went right
out the window.

So...how was she going to spend the next eight to
ten hours? By preparing an argument that she hoped
would allow her to continue to pit herself against him
in a courtroom. Did that make sense? No. But these
weren't ordinary times. And it was her grandfather,
not to mention the rest of her family, who would pay
if she allowed any kind of reckless emotion to get in
the way of what she had to do.

Reckless emotion! Her? Amanda almost laughed.
She had always been the steadiest of the Baron crew.
The middle child. The one who had never caused anyone a moment's worry. Good, steady Amanda.
Amanda, who had suffered quietly when her father
had committed suicide. She still sometimes felt as if
she'd never get over his death, yet she hadn't gone
off the rails like Liza and Jeff. *Reckless emotion?*

Amanda closed herself into the pseudowomb of her
office. This was her domain. In here, she was in

charge. She had hung every picture, arranged every book.

Her gaze drifted to the newspaper photograph of Ethan Trask. Since she had left the room earlier— how long ago was that, a hundred years?—the dart had fallen from his nose. Gravity had pulled it to the floor.

Gravity, magnetism…

Amanda snatched the photograph from the wall and crumpled it in her fist.

CHAPTER FIVE

THE CONFERENCE ROOM was quiet as all the players involved waited for the court stenographer to load the shorthand typewriter with a long, thin strip of folded paper on which he would record the hearing. The judge, the Honorable Eustace D. Griffen, sat on one side of the long table, while Ethan Trask and Amanda sat on the other.

Amanda's throat was parched, her palms sweaty. She had talked to Peter before leaving Tyler for the courthouse in Sugar Creek, and he had assured her that her arguments had strength. Still, sitting there, she wasn't as sure. At her elbow, Ethan Trask looked formidable and efficient in a dark suit, his handsome features serious. He had murmured her name in greeting when they met in the hall and hadn't said anything to her since.

The court reporter nodded to the judge. Judge Griffen was one of only two jurists who presided over the judicial system of Sugar Creek County. He and Judge Bolt took turns sitting for criminal and civil suits. October was to be Judge Griffen's month to hear criminal cases. He was a long, thin man with a deeply lined face. Heavy bags hung beneath weary-looking brown eyes, giving him the sad appearance of a basset hound. But anyone fooled into thinking Judge Griffen indolent was in for something of a shock. He tolerated no nonsense in his court, and his mind was as sharp as a razor.

His gaze took in both Ethan and Amanda. "I've read your briefs," he said. "Now I want to hear your arguments. Mr. Trask, you first."

Ethan stood, accidentally brushing against Amanda's arm. No one except them took notice of the contact or was aware of the way both instantly withdrew, as if from an electrical shock.

"Your Honor," Ethan began, his voice giving no hint of his being disconcerted. "It is not the state's contention that a defendant be denied representation by the counsel of his or her choice. The right to choice of counsel is a vital part of our system of justice. It is the state's contention that in *this* instance the defendant's choice can harm the people's ability to present their case. It is out of the norm. Amanda Baron is the granddaughter both of the defendant and of the deceased.

"As prosecutor, I am of the firm belief that this representation will place an unfair burden on the state. To have her sit in court day after day at the side of the defendant would influence the jury to believe that she, a member of the family, believes him innocent. By her mere presence she presents herself as a character witness—but a witness I cannot cross-examine.

"In no way is she unique, except as this silent witness. She is not a criminal defense lawyer of any repute. In fact, she has never before been involved in a case of this magnitude. The simple truth is that the defendant has purposely set out to gain a lawyer who would make improper use of the familial relationship, and the state requests that he be directed to choose another."

The judge nodded and turned his mournful-looking eyes on Amanda. Shakily, she stood as Ethan sat down. She reached for a glass of water to loosen her vocal cords. She was afraid it was all over. The logic of his argument seemed unbeatable. It didn't matter that she and her grandfather had not planned the situation as he suggested. If it looked as if they had— as it did now—the judge would rule against them. It was up to her to change his perception.

"As counsel for the defense, it is not my job to make the prosecutor's job easier." Her voice sounded tremulous. She cleared her throat to make it stronger. "My duty is to defend my client to the best of my ability under the law. It is the law which states that the accused is to be represented by counsel at all stages of a criminal proceeding—counsel of his or her own choosing. As Mr. Trask has so aptly conceded, such representation is one of the defendant's most fundamental rights.

"No other relationship is as uniquely trusting as that of lawyer and client. The two must work together under a set of exceptional pressures, especially in a case that involves a criminal trial for a serious felony. The defendant *must* be free to choose the person he or she has most confidence in.

"It is true, Your Honor, that I am both the accused's and the deceased's granddaughter. But as you've read in my brief and as will become apparent during the trial, it wasn't possible for me to even know my grandmother. She died thirteen years before I was born. She is like a stranger to me. When my grandfather first asked me to represent him, I attempted to dissuade him because of my relative inexperience. However, I am the counsel of his choice.

Not for any of the nefarious reasons Mr. Trask presumes, but because of the trust that exists between us. Therefore, as the judicial system of this state prepares to put my client through the ordeal of a trial for the most serious crime known to society, the state *must* honor the rights that are unalienably his.''

Amanda sat down. She was afraid that her inexperience had shown all the way through her argument. She worried that she had become too passionate in the course of her defense, and that, especially at the end, the thread of her logic had become lost and weak.

She chanced a quick glance at Ethan Trask. He sat very still, watching the judge. She, too, looked at Judge Griffen. The judge studied the papers set before him, the written arguments that both had sent to his office earlier that morning. Eustace Griffen liked to start the day early. He wasn't a man to let half the morning go by before he started to move.

The judge looked up. He tapped his fingers against his lips. Finally, he said, ''I'll have a decision in half an hour. No more, no less. Be in the courtroom.'' Then he got up and left the small room. The court reporter, carrying his machine with him, was at his heels.

Amanda and Ethan were suddenly alone. It was like the deafening quiet after a storm. They might have been two statues—unmoving, unfeeling. Then Ethan stood and started to gather his papers. Amanda followed suit. Her hands trembled, her body was icy cold. A piece of paper fluttered to the floor. As she reached for it, she felt his gaze sweep over her. There was no expression in his eyes. He merely watched as she retrieved the errant sheet and replaced it on her tiny stack.

She gave a wavery smile. She had never before experienced such an excruciatingly awkward moment. What did they do? What did they say?

She tapped her papers on edge, unnecessarily straightening them. Finally, unable to stand the tension, she said, "I expected this to take longer."

Ethan snapped shut the black leather briefcase he'd produced from the floor by his side. "Sometimes it does," he replied.

Amanda placed her papers in the tapestry satchel her mother had given her for Christmas. Alyssa had never approved of the worn old briefcase her daughter had used through law school, and she had ensured Amanda's acceptance of a new one by making it a gift. Amanda latched the case shut and gave the buckle a pat. Then she looked at her watch. She didn't know what to do with twenty-five minutes. She was much too anxious to sit and wait.

Ethan started out the door, but paused to ask, "Is there a snack bar nearby?"

Amanda brightened. "Yes. I'm going there myself. I'll show you." Then she wished she hadn't volunteered, because his face seemed to freeze before he gave a jerky nod.

As she preceded him down the hall, Amanda's own face burned. Twice in two days she had found herself blushing, and both times the cause was Ethan Trask. If he hadn't wanted to be seen with her, why had he agreed? It was not a legal impropriety as long as they didn't discuss details of the case. Not that she blamed him for his attitude—she didn't exactly feel easy about being in his company, either. For more than one reason.

On the middle floor of the three-story structure, in an alcove around the corner from the main stairway and just to the left of the central bank of elevators, a tiny snack bar was open to the public. There were no tables, only a couple of benches without backs. At one bench, an old woman held a sleeping child on her lap, while another child knelt on the floor and used the seat as a roadway for a tiny car. At the other bench a couple of jurors, identified by their badges, were finishing a coffee break. Seconds later they walked past Ethan and Amanda, who had stopped.

"Well," she said, "this is it. Has someone shown you where the cafeteria is?"

Ethan nodded stiffly. "Yes."

"Good." Amanda shifted the tapestry briefcase in front of her and held on to it with both hands. "Well…" She glanced at her watch for something to do. Twenty minutes to spare. Her gaze shifted to the short line at the snack bar.

Ethan motioned for her to go ahead of him. Amanda acquiesced, her stride stilted. She was wholly aware of the awkwardness of the situation, aware of the man behind her—aware that she *was* aware. She remembered the accidental contact as he had stood up in the conference room, remembered how quickly they both had pulled away. She ordered a coffee, and once it was delivered, crossed to the now-empty bench and sat down.

The hot, black liquid tasted wonderful. She needed it. She tried to pretend that she didn't notice Ethan Trask as he, too, stepped away from the counter, hold-

ing a steaming cup. She felt his glance slide over her
and then move away.

She tried to pretend that her mind was occupied
with other things—the outcome of the hearing, the
upcoming trial. She didn't want Ethan Trask to think
that she wanted to indulge in conversation, particularly if he didn't want to. It would be a long time
before she forgot his frozen look. She watched the
child at play, then let her gaze drift to the people
walking by in the nearby vestibule, but all the time
she was sensitive to his movements. She knew when
he set down his briefcase, when he took a sip of coffee. Most of the time he looked away from her. He
studied the floor, the opposite wall. Then his gaze
moved to her again and, unable to help herself, she
looked up. The attorney general's Avenging Angel
shifted uncomfortably as their gazes touched.

ETHAN FELT like a fool. They were acquaintances
even if they weren't allies. And for the two of them
to persevere in this charade of avoidance—even if he
felt that it was his safest option—was ridiculous. He
could at least talk to the woman. She wouldn't bite.
Neither would he.

"I trust you had no ill effects from our near-
accident yesterday?" he said.

She seemed surprised that he would speak to her.
"Only an injury to my pride," she answered wryly.
"I'm normally a very cautious person."

"So am I," Ethan assured her.

The conversation shriveled. Ethan checked his
watch; so did she. They both drank more coffee.

After a moment she said, "I would have hated to
dent your car."

Completely out of character for him, Ethan heard himself chuckle lightly and say, "I can just see the headlines: Local Lawyer Lamentably Lacerated by Passing Public Prosecutor."

A quick smile of appreciation broke over her attractive features. "Oh, I like that," she said. "That's good! Did you just make it up?"

Ethan shrugged. If any of his associates in Madison had heard him say that, he would have been horrified. He worked hard to perpetuate a certain image, one that wouldn't conform to a dalliance in alliteration.

"My family loves to play word games," Amanda continued. "My granddad most of all. He—" She broke off abruptly as she remembered where she was, why, and whom she was with. She looked down at the paper cup held tightly in her hands.

Ethan glanced away. One moment she had been beaming, enthused, the next crushed. Uneasily, he accepted the fact that he was the cause. More for something to do than actual need, he checked his watch again. "Ten minutes. I think I'll start back." Yet he hesitated. He didn't want to walk back with her, but he couldn't just leave her, either. He schooled his features to mild inquiry and murmured, "You coming?" with just the right amount of unconcern.

"I'll—I'll be along in a minute or two. I just want to finish..." She didn't complete the sentence but lifted her cup instead. Her features, too, were now carefully controlled.

"Right," Ethan concurred. He downed the rest of his coffee in two quick gulps and added his paper cup to the growing mound in the trash can. Then he walked away, his back straight, his mind disciplined.

AMANDA WATCHED him leave. For the space of several seconds she had forgotten everything. She had forgotten her family, her duty, the decision she was waiting to hear.

Her stomach tightened as she castigated herself. She was here for one purpose and one purpose alone: to fight for her grandfather's continued freedom. The grandfather that she loved dearly. She wasn't here to respond to the unexpected charm of a very handsome man. She had to keep reminding herself that he was the enemy!

The short trip upstairs allowed Amanda the time necessary to pull herself together. She was a professional; she had to act like a professional. On the way she saw several people she knew and each gave her a thumbs-up sign, including Larry Richardson. Of course, Larry felt obliged to comment on how nice she looked that day. But even his usual skirting along the edge of sexual harassment was in itself reassuring at a time when Amanda felt a strong need to have nothing in her life change.

The courtroom the judge was using that morning looked cavernous as she walked up the short aisle and slipped into a seat at the defense table. Ethan Trask was already in place. He gave a tight nod when he caught her glance. Amanda looked away. This was serious business.

The judge entered through a door in the corner. As he strode to the bench, a court officer called out, "All rise."

Amanda and Ethan clambered to their feet. The judge nodded to the court reporter and received a nod in return.

Amanda's heart thundered in her chest. If she were

successful, this moment would be a preamble to the trial. A cowardly part of her wanted the judge to reject her argument. If he did, the intense pressure would lessen. She could be a part of her grandfather's defense team but not have all the responsibility rest on her shoulders. The more noble part of her believed strongly in what she had said to the judge and felt that her grandfather should be granted all his rights. She held her breath as she waited for Judge Griffen to finish shuffling papers and tell them his decision.

The judge looked up. ''The question before the court is a serious one,'' he intoned. ''It involves the right of an accused individual to choose his own counsel and whether the choice of that counsel would work an unacceptable hardship on the prosecution of this case. Both arguments were well pleaded. Mr. Trask, Ms. Baron, well done.

''When duty is cited, it is a reminder that I also have a duty to carry out. In this court, I am the final arbiter, and I take that assignment seriously. It is what I am paid to do, and it is my moral obligation. I am often called upon to make hard choices.

''If I am to err, it has to be on the side of the defendant, because that individual must be given every latitude to make his case. Therefore, Mr. Trask, I am going to deny your motion for disqualification…with certain conditions.'' He looked from Ethan to Amanda. ''First, Ms. Baron, at no time during the course of this trial will you be permitted to refer in any way to your relationship to the defendant or the deceased. The same goes for you, Mr. Trask. Also, there will be no comment to the media by either of you in this regard. Second, because of the widespread media interest in this case and the probability that it will only increase when the trial begins, I am going to direct that the jury be sequestered once it is empaneled. Third, as the jury is selected, challenges for cause by the prosecution will be endorsed freely by me if it is shown that the prospective juror has been influenced by Ms. Baron's relationships.''

The judge shuffled papers again. Then he said, ''Now, I'd like to set the date for this trial to start in three weeks, the second Tuesday in October. I'd also like for it to be completed no later than October 31. We should be able to finish in that amount of time since this is to be a straightforward endeavor. I want no dilly-dallying or fancy footwork from either of you. No unreasonable delays. The jury are not to be kept from their jobs or their loved ones for any longer than is necessary. Do either of you have a problem with what I've just said?''

Both Amanda and Ethan shook their heads.

The judge continued, ''Can you be ready in that time, Mr. Trask? Ms. Baron?''

In turn, both agreed. Amanda did so with a sinking heart. Three weeks! Actually, two days short of three weeks! She had to build her case, line up witnesses....

''Good,'' the judge said approvingly. ''Adjourned,'' he decreed, before leaning over to confer with his assistant.

Amanda sat motionless. She had won.

Ethan Trask pushed away from the prosecutor's table. People were starting to file in for the ten o'clock trial. One of the defense lawyers for that trial came up to the table where Amanda still sat. She stood up slowly, apologized for her delay. As she turned, she met Ethan Trask's dark eyes.

He was incredibly handsome. A part of her

couldn't deny it even as she reeled from the shock of her argument's success. His strong features were set. He had lost.

Amanda's heart skipped a beat. He gave a curt nod. "Congratulations," he said stiffly. She mumbled something, she wasn't sure what, but it must have been appropriate. Then she watched as he walked away—up the short aisle and through the oversize swing doors into the hall.

When Amanda left the courtroom some minutes later, she was met by several reporters. They had learned of the hearing and wanted Amanda to comment on the outcome. She could tell by their questions that Ethan had honored the judge's stipulation. She did, too. "I have no comment," she said, and continued down the hall with them trailing along behind her, shouting questions.

THE FIRST PERSON Amanda called when she stopped at a pay phone was her grandfather. He was at the F and M on the outskirts of Tyler, and he sounded relieved at the news. He had refused to go to the hearing, waiving that right to Amanda. The restrictions didn't seem to bother him. Neither did the unexpectedly close trial date. "I knew you could do it, girlie," he said, using the endearment he reserved for her. "And I know you'll do your best in court."

"We have to talk again, Granddad. Today. When would be a good time for you?" She heard her grandfather sigh. Cradling the phone closer to her ear, she said, "I have to start planning your defense. We don't have much time. These next nineteen days are going to pass very quickly."

"All right, all right. I'll make it my business to be home by the time you get there. Will that do?"

He sounded irritated, but Amanda couldn't help it. She nodded. "That's great! The sooner the better. I'll be home in twenty minutes. I'm leaving the courthouse right now."

The second person Amanda called was Peter Williams. The professor answered after the first ring, as if he had been waiting for the call.

"We won, Peter!" Amanda exulted.

"Ahh, that's fine...fine."

"I'm back to being afraid," Amanda admitted.

"Well, don't be! You took on Ethan Trask and won. You've shown that you're his equal. You've shown *him* that he's not infallible in this case. That's a major victory."

Amanda knew that Peter was trying to bolster her confidence. She also knew that she was in no way Ethan Trask's equal in trial experience.

"What you have to do now," Peter continued, "is get to work on those discovery motions. He's not going to want to give you anything, while you want everything! Statements of witnesses, police reports, a listing of the physical evidence, photos...the works. You want to get everything you can that pertains to the case. Strike while the iron is hot. The judge ruled in your favor this time. He probably will again. How much time do you have before the trial starts? Did he set a date?"

"It starts in nineteen days."

"Ouch!"

"Not much time, I know," Amanda agreed. "I'm on my way now to meet with my grandfather. We hit a slight snag the last time we talked. This time we won't.''

"From what you've told me, he's a very strong-willed man."

"I'd like for the two of you to meet as soon as possible. If you're going to be working closely with me—''

"Amanda…" She heard the hesitancy in the professor's voice. "We have a little problem. Do you remember that call I came home to take last night? From my agent? Well, I didn't tell you, but it concerned a novel I've written. He's found a publisher for it. Only…the editor wants me to make some changes. And he wants me to do it right away. I'm not going to have as much time as I thought." There was a tiny silence, during which Amanda wondered what to say. Peter hurried on, "I'm not going to bail out on you completely. I'll still help. I wouldn't do this to you, Amanda, except it's something I've wanted all my life. My memoirs only whetted my appetite. If I turn down the publisher now—''

Amanda cut in. "Of course you can't turn him down. I wouldn't want you to, Peter."

The older man's voice brightened. "I'm so relieved you understand. I meant it when I said I'd still help. The major restriction I'll have is that I won't be able to come to Sugar Creek to sit in on the trial as frequently as I'd like. You'll have to tell me what happens. Just as we'll have to consult more often over the telephone during your trial preparation."

"I understand. Listen, Peter, I have to go. My grandfather…''

"Of course…of course," he murmured. "Amanda, I truly am sorry."

"Don't think about it another second," she answered. "I do understand. And as long as you're still willing to help…"

"I'll help you all I can. Though you're much more capable than you think. You have good instincts, Amanda."

Amanda tried to smile, but her lips were too tight. "Thanks," she murmured and hung up.

She tried not to panic as she hurried out of the courthouse, but waited until she slid into the little red MG. It was there she let herself fall apart. "Oh, God. Oh, God. Oh, God," she murmured, almost like a chant. "What am I going to do? What am I going to do?" She wasn't angry with Peter—he couldn't help it. Nor was she upset that she had won her argument. That was what she'd wanted, wasn't it? It was the combination of the two events that did her in. Together they were like an avalanche roaring down a mountainside to crush her. Amanda dropped her head onto the steering wheel and held on for all she was worth.

A tap sounded on her partially rolled-up window. She looked up to see Ethan Trask standing outside her car. He'd had to bend over to look at her. When she recognized him, she wanted to dissolve into the floorboards.

"I thought that was you," he said, frowning. "Are you all right?"

She tried quickly to rearrange her expression. "Oh, I'm fine. Thanks." To her own ears her voice sounded strained. To his? She could only hope that she'd fooled him. "I, uh…" Her fingers were curled around her key ring. "I just dropped my keys, that's all. I was trying to find them."

His dark eyes refused to release hers. He knew she was lying. But then a child would know she was lying. She wasn't very talented in that department. To strengthen her case, Amanda waved the keys.

He straightened. "If you're sure." He seemed hesitant to move away. "Are you going back to Tyler?" he asked.

"Yes."

"So am I. I'll follow behind you for a way. You still look a little…pale."

If that was indeed a fact, it lasted only a moment. Amanda felt her cheeks grow warm. She made another desperate try. "I'm fine…really."

"I'll still follow you," he insisted.

Amanda watched as he settled into the sleek black car sitting beside the MG. It started efficiently, smoothly. The MG did not. She had to make several attempts before the contrary little engine caught, and as she drove away, her cheeks were an even darker shade of pink than before.

About halfway to Tyler, the black car moved into position beside her. The passenger window slid effortlessly down. "Still okay?" he asked.

Amanda nodded and waved. A moment later the bigger car pulled into the lane ahead of her and accelerated down the road. She didn't blame him. She had kept a full ten miles per hour below the speed limit, not because the little MG couldn't handle more, but because she hoped Ethan Trask would grow tired of driving so slowly and would want to hurry on. Her ploy had worked.

She released a heartfelt sigh once she was on her

own. Of all things…for them to be parked next to each other *and* for him to see her in such a state!

Amanda shook her head. Three strikes and you're out—wasn't that the saying? All she needed now was for the MG to go on strike!

CHAPTER SIX

THE LITTLE CAR purred all the way home. Well, not exactly purred—it was more of a low growl. Still, Amanda pulled into the driveway without incident. As the Wisconsin winter grew harsher, she usually parked the MG in the garage and leased a more serviceable vehicle. But each year she held off for as long as she could. The MG symbolized freedom to her, independence.

She hurried into the house. She was long past the twenty minutes she had promised her grandfather—actually double it. As she moved through the kitchen, the housekeeper, Clara, was already at the stove starting lunch. Amanda veered from her intended path to filch a carrot round. Grinning, she popped the bite-size vegetable into her mouth.

"You know better than that, my girl." Clara pretended disapproval.

Amanda and her siblings had grown up with Clara Myers. Their mother had grown up with the woman as well. Clara and her husband, Archie, had worked at the Ingalls mansion since shortly after Judson's marriage. At sixty-seven, Clara was a round, sunny woman whose face was a road map of wrinkles—wrinkles that only increased when she smiled. Amanda thought her beautiful.

"You know I can't resist your cooking," Amanda teased as she reached for another carrot round.

"If you don't leave a few, I won't have anything left to cook!"

Amanda pretended contrition. She left the piece of carrot—one of many—where it was. "Is Granddad here, Clara? I'm a little late, so I'm hoping he was, too."

"He's in his study. And I think he's tired of waiting. He came out just a few minutes ago to roar for coffee."

Amanda pushed away from the counter. "Then I'd better not keep him waiting any longer. Is his coffee ready? I'll take it with me as a peace offering."

"Two shakes and it will be. All I have to do is pour."

Amanda added a second cup to the tray, and once Clara had filled a decorative china pot with fresh brew, she took it down the hall.

Her grandfather was pacing back and forth across the book-lined room.

"Sorry for the delay, Granddad," she apologized and immediately stopped to pour his much needed coffee.

"Was it that fool car of yours?" he demanded. "Did it leave you stranded on the side of the road? Honestly, Amanda, that thing could be a real danger to you. You never know who might come along. A maniac, a—"

Amanda handed him the cup of coffee and wordlessly directed him to drink some of it.

He ignored her. "The world is a much more dangerous place now. Things happen in broad daylight that used to not even happen at night. Sugar Creek certainly isn't the same place it was. Neither is Tyler, for that matter."

He was winding up for a long tirade. Amanda stopped him by saying, "Actually, the person who came along was Ethan Trask, and he's far from being a maniac. He followed me in his car most of the way to Tyler."

"What did he do that for?" her grandfather asked, his eyes narrowing.

"Because he felt like it? I don't know. He just did." She quickly brought the topic around to the subject she wanted to discuss. "Granddad, I know that talking about the past upsets you…but you have to understand. I'm not being nosy. You have to give me all the information you can in order for me to build your case. Ethan Trask isn't going to offer a plea bargain—not that we'd want him to, because we wouldn't accept it. But he's not even going to *offer* one, which means that he feels his case against you is strong. Whereas we—we don't even have the beginnings of our case yet. We can't go to court like that! You say you don't know who killed Margaret, except *you* didn't. Well, someone did! We have to talk to people…people who were at the party, if possible. We'll have to locate them, try to see what they remember."

"They're probably all dead," Judson said.

"You aren't. Some of them won't be, either. Then there's Phil Wocheck. What does Phil know that he was asked to testify to before the grand jury? Do you have any idea? That's the kind of thing we need to talk about, Granddad. Something for me to work on. I'm going to try to get as much information from the prosecutor's office as I can, but with only these few

short weeks, I can't afford to wait to get started.
You're my main source of information, Granddad.
My main *resource*."

Her grandfather had been keyed up when she'd entered the room. He had been gruff with her when he
was rarely gruff. Sensing that he was still upset, she
made her voice softer. "It might be a good idea for
us to hire an investigator, Granddad. Someone to find
these people when we come up with a list of names.
Someone to talk to them first, see what they remember, what they know."

"How much would that cost?" Judson asked.

Amanda frowned. This was the first time she had
ever heard her grandfather ask that question. "They
don't come cheap," she said. "Not the good ones."

"Then we may have to pass."

Her grandfather had moved to look out the window. As usual, he held himself ramrod straight, his
white head proud, but this time Amanda could see
how much effort this action took. She moved closer
to him. "Granddad, it would be a good investment. I
don't want to frighten you, but you have to understand that if you're convicted…you could be sent to
jail for the rest of your life! Even if you lived to be
150, you'd still be in jail, because the judge could
order no parole, no time off for good behavior. That's
why I wanted you to find someone who's an experienced trial attorney. This is really serious, Granddad.
Since you won't agree to that, at least let me hire an
investigator. It could make all the difference to our
case. If we were to find out who really killed Margaret, there wouldn't *be* a case! You wouldn't have
to go through the ordeal of a trial—"

"Amanda," her grandfather interrupted, turning to

face her. She had never seen him look so somber, not even when he had learned that he was to be indicted.

"What?" she whispered, sensing that she wasn't going to like what he had to say.

"I don't have enough money to do as you ask. If I did, I'd give it to you, but I don't."

"You don't…" Amanda couldn't complete the sentence. She'd known that the F and M had been going through hard times. She'd known that they were facing the third layoff this year. As a member of the Ingalls/Baron family, she'd known all along that they weren't as rich as everyone in Tyler thought. Jeff was a doctor, but he put most of his money into the free clinic he'd founded. Liza was barely making it on her newly conceived decorating business. Alyssa…Alyssa had never worked a day in her life! Not that she didn't contribute. Almost everyone in town would suffer if she didn't give of her time. But she didn't bring in any money. And herself? Amanda had managed to put some cash aside, but she donated a great deal to Jeff's clinic and to other projects, not to mention frequently acting as attorney at little or no fee for people who were in need.

"The only way I could raise any spare money," Judson said quietly, "is to start selling the contents of this house."

"We could do that," Amanda agreed.

Her grandfather's jaw tightened. "No. I won't do it. This house has been handed down from one generation of Ingallses to the next. I will not sell even the smallest part of it."

"But, Granddad…"

"I won't! Your mother has been through enough. I refuse to give her more pain!"

"But she—"

"No!"

Amanda subsided. Then her gaze settled on the Van Gogh drawing that held pride of place over her grandfather's desk. She brightened. "Granddad, what about the drawing? We could sell it. You bought it yourself—it wasn't passed down to us. It's got to be worth a great deal of…"

Her grandfather's shoulders slumped. "It's a reproduction. I sold the original at the beginning of the year when the plant started getting into trouble. There's no money left from the sale of Timberlake, either. All of that went into the plant, too. If the F and M goes down, so do a lot of people in this town. I *have* to keep it operating." He looked at her sadly. "I have no extra money of my own, Amanda. I barely have enough to pay my bills each month."

Amanda was silent, then she asked quietly, "Is that why you wanted me for your lawyer—because you know I'd work for free?"

Her grandfather's face changed. It was obvious that the idea hadn't occurred to him. He strode over to her and wrapped her in his arms. "Of course not! I want you as my lawyer, Amanda, because I don't think anyone else in this world would defend me with as much fire. When I tell you I didn't kill your grandmother, you believe me!"

Being so close to his familiar strength warmed the ache in Amanda's heart. So did seeing the truth in his face. It helped her to know that his faith in her was real.

"Does Mother know about this?" she whispered.

Judson shook his head. "No, and I don't want her to. I've tried to protect her from many things over the years. In some instances I've succeeded, in others I haven't. This is something I *can* control. I don't want her to know anything about it. We'll ride it out. And after the trial…after the trial, I'll get everything put to rights.''

His words were brave, but Amanda sensed the tension beneath them, both about the outcome of the trial and about the F and M's financial resiliency. She leaned away from him. ''You're underestimating her, Granddad. She's a much stronger person than you think.''

Amanda remembered a conversation she'd had with her mother earlier in the month. Alyssa already knew of the F and M's financial difficulties. She also knew that her father was considering a foreign offer to buy the company, a move she was against. Alyssa had a much better head for business than Judson gave her credit for. If pressed, she would probably even make a good manager for the firm. Still, as upset as her mother was about the upcoming trial, Amanda didn't know how well she would receive the news of Judson's additional financial difficulties.

When her grandfather remained silent, Amanda sighed. ''Well,'' she said, ''we'll just have to make do.'' She would hire the investigator herself, using her savings, she decided. As for other expenses—the day-to-day bills, the fees for expert witnesses—when or if that time came, she would confide in the other family members and among them, they would find the money. They'd have to!

''Here,'' she said, ''let me pour you a fresh cup of coffee. I don't mind taking the one that's cooled. In fact, I rather like cold coffee. At the office the phone always rings or someone comes in. I never seem to get to it when it's hot.'' She rattled on, hoping to help her grandfather relax. She handed him the other cup and watched as a little color came back into his cheeks when he took a sip. Finally, she prodded gently, ''We have to start sometime, Granddad. Are you ready?''

A muscle jerked in Judson's cheek, but he nodded.

Amanda plunged right in. ''The gun that the police say murdered Margaret...is it really yours?''

ALYSSA WANDERED about the house. She knew Amanda was in the study with her father and that in all likelihood they were talking about the case. If she had the courage, she would knock on the door and ask to come inside. But she didn't have that kind of courage. Not at the moment.

She stepped out onto the screened porch at the back of the house and settled into one of the twin walnut rocking chairs that had been old when her father was an infant. She started to rock, the back-and-forth motion quick rather than relaxing. Her body was tense.

What was going to become of them? Jeff and Cece; Liza and Cliff and little Margaret Alyssa; Amanda, herself, her father? Their world seemed to be hanging from a single string, which at any moment could break. If it were within her power, she would make all their troubles go away. She would wave her magic wand and everything would return to the way it used to be. Margaret's body wouldn't have been found, her father wouldn't have been arrested...she wouldn't be having those dreams!

Alyssa's stomach tightened, causing her to feel slightly ill. The dreams. Sometimes they seemed so real! She wanted to run from them, hide from them, but they seemed to be gaining strength. Her mother, a man, herself, a gun…a gunshot. Were they real? At times she thought they were, at other times she didn't. Seeing the images was like fighting through a maze filled with gauze. Spiderwebs of the mind. She had confided their existence sparingly—to her father, to Edward Wocheck. But she hadn't told Amanda. Should she? Would they have any bearing on her father's trial? Alyssa didn't know what to do. She wanted to help her father, but she was afraid. She believed him when he said that he hadn't killed Margaret. She did! He'd sworn it! But then who was the man in her dreams? She jerked to her feet. *Not her father!*

A car on the street in front of the house backfired and Alyssa reactively froze, her mind growing numb. Seconds later, when she came back to reality, she found herself rubbing the inside of her right hand. The skin tingled, burned.

A sob tore from her throat, and she hurried back into the house. Not walked, ran…as if she were escaping from a terrifying nightmare.

ETHAN LISTENED to Carlos with only half his attention. His thoughts kept returning to earlier in the morning, when he had come upon Amanda Baron slumped over the wheel of her small sports car. He recalled the way, when she raised her head, that her beautiful blue eyes had looked so tragic, her features so ravaged by doubt. His training told him to ignore any sympathy he might feel for his adversary. One gladiator could not be sorry for another—not without opening himself to defeat. But on a human level, he couldn't help but wonder what was wrong. She had won the decision on his challenge. Why had that upset her? Or had she been upset by something else?

"My friend." Carlos nudged him. His tone held light amusement, as if he had repeated the phrase more than once. A smile tugged at his lips. "Ah…now I have managed to get through. To lose is very hard, but in the end I do not think it will matter that Amanda Baron sits across from you in court."

Ethan stirred himself. "It's not that," he denied. "I was thinking of something else. Something I—" He stopped. It would be unlike him to confide. He worked the muscles of his shoulders. "I think I'm tired. The day started too early this morning."

"For me as well. But it was productive. Where did I lose you?"

"Um…you went to some kind of retirement home?"

"Worthington House. I thought that a logical place to start, since the people who would know most about Judson and Margaret Ingalls would be of that age. I was correct. I found several individuals who remember the Ingallses' marital problems. Margaret was a 'bad girl' by Tyler standards. She had fast friends from Chicago. Judson did not like her friends or the fact that she kept inviting them here. Neither did his mother. Particularly when he was off in Europe during the war. Margaret started spending more time in Chicago after he came back—to be closer to her socialite friends, to get away from Tyler? Probably both. When his mother—Alberta Ingalls, incidentally, the woman the public library is named after—remarried and moved away, Margaret came back. But she soon started inviting her friends to parties at the lodge again, and the marriage went downhill. People here did not like her, and she did not like them very much either.

"No one can remember Judson Ingalls wearing a ring. One woman—" Carlos referred to his notes "—a Martha Bauer, states for a fact that he never had one. She said she remembers, because she always admired his hands. They are like a musician's hands. Long, artistic."

Ethan snorted.

Carlos grinned. "It seems our Judson could have had his pick of the women around here. Instead, he fell in love with Margaret." Shaking his head, Carlos lamented, "Love, it is not an easy thing."

Ethan snorted once again, only this time not so softly. "You're getting soft, Carlos," he chided dryly.

"I have always been soft…on the inside."

"I meant in the head. Come on, what else did you learn?"

"There was possible police culpability early on, but nothing that can be proved. When Margaret was first reported missing, Zachary Phelps was the police chief. He was a good friend of Judson's. I found him at the Kelsey Boardinghouse on Gunther Street, a couple of blocks from the town square. Zachary says Judson told him Margaret was gone, showed him a note he said was from her, and that was that. Zachary did not question it. I asked him why he did not look into it further, and he said he did not need to."

"Did he say what happened to the note?" Ethan asked in interest.

"He does not know. He never saw it again."

"The same note that Philip Wocheck says he saw."

"Which gives us confirmation of its existence."

"I'd still like to have it."

"I will ask around, see if anyone knows where it is."

Ethan checked the time. It was too early for their appointment with Joe Santori. "Let's have lunch, then find this ex-chief Schmidt. He might have a few interesting things to tell us."

They didn't make the mistake of going to the diner again. Instead they stopped off at a Dairy King drive-in on the outskirts of town. It didn't draw the same local crowd as the diner, and Ethan quickly discovered why. His hamburger was greasy, his fries limp and his milkshake watery. All in all, it wasn't a wonderful dining experience.

Carlos was stoic as they crawled back into the car. When he wordlessly offered Ethan an antacid tablet, Ethan took it.

CHIEF PAUL SCHMIDT lived in a comfortable frame home a few miles outside of Tyler. He was a man of middle height and middle weight, with a heavy brow over eyes that were still sharp despite his sixty-some years. He invited Ethan and Carlos into the den.

"What can I do for you gentlemen?" he asked, his tone friendly but cautious. He knew who they were.

"We have a few questions concerning the Ingalls case," Ethan said. "If you can spare a few minutes?"

Chief Schmidt gave a hearty laugh. "Spare minutes are all I have these days. My wife actually orders me out of the house at times—says I get in her way. Can you believe that? *I* get in her way?" After receiving polite smiles, he invited the men to sit down. "What can I do to help you?" he offered.

Ethan came straight to the point. "In your testimony before the grand jury you said that you and

Lieutenant Bauer were the first officers on the scene when the body was discovered at Timberlake Lodge. You set up a police line and called in the crime-scene people—all standard operating procedure. What I'm curious about is why it took so long to identify the body. The remains were found August 6th. You knew almost right away that it was an adult female, and you knew Margaret Ingalls was missing. Yet it wasn't until the following December that anyone even started to look for her dental records in order to check identification. You retired the first part of December, didn't you? So the search didn't begin in earnest until after you left. Could you possibly explain that, Chief Schmidt?''

Ethan's tone had been formally polite, but Paul Schmidt's edge of jocularity crumbled. He immediately became defensive. ''But that wasn't the first time someone looked for the records!'' he declared. ''Brick Bauer had looked for them, under my direction, just as soon as we seriously began to consider the idea that the body might be Margaret Ingalls's. He found the name of her dentist in Chicago, but the man was dead! No one knew what had happened to his records. His partner had moved on, and the office was closed. What were we supposed to do? Manufacture them?''

''Decidedly not. But why didn't you keep looking?'' Ethan remained cool, professional. His tone neither condemned nor excused.

Paul Schmidt couldn't stay seated any longer. ''You have to understand. We had other cases. We'd recently found a drifter beaten to a pulp on the edge of town. He had no ID, so we printed him while we waited to see if he'd live or die. We found out he was wanted for questioning about a murder in Michigan—he was the prime suspect. We also were co-operating with the sheriff's department in Sugar Creek on a countywide con game some people were operating. We're not that big a police force. At least, we weren't back then. We weren't with the sheriff's department like we are now. We had only our own resources, and they were stretched pretty thin. That's why we finally had to merge with the county force. We did the best we could.''

''But surely one man—''

''One man's a lot when you only have fifteen people to cover all shifts. That's what we had back then—fifteen people!''

Ethan was not visibly affected by the man's excuse. He merely nodded once and stood up. ''I believe that's all we have to talk about for now. Thank you for answering our questions.'' He held out his hand, and with reluctance, Paul Schmidt took it.

Ethan gave a small smile, and he sensed Chief Schmidt relax slightly. The man knew that Ethan had the power to indict him if he thought there was enough evidence to support a case of police malfeasance. He must have felt that he had given a good account of himself.

As they walked down the gravel drive to the car, Ethan said, ''He feels pretty safe, but he knows he's vulnerable. He'll tell the truth on the stand.''

''While still protecting himself, of course.''

''Of course.''

''Do you think he held up the investigation?''

''He was Judson's good friend, and he had a handy excuse. I'd say yes, he did.''

"Not to mention that he was ready to retire and be completely out of it."

"That, too."

Once inside the car, Ethan checked his watch. "Now we meet Mr. Joe Santori. Then I think I'll head back to Sugar Creek. What about you?"

Carlos shrugged. "I think I will stay around Tyler a little longer. See what I can see."

THE GARAGE next to a small yellow-and-white, gingerbread-trimmed Victorian house bore a large sign that read Santori Construction. A battered pickup with miscellaneous building materials piled in its bed was parked in the driveway.

Ethan and Carlos got out of the car and were met at the garage door by a tall lanky man with black hair, black eyes and wide, powerful shoulders. He was dressed in worn jeans, a faded flannel shirt and heavy boots. His strong Italian features were creased into a smile. He immediately thrust out a hand to each man in turn.

"I hope you don't mind if we have our meeting out here. My wife has a friend visiting."

"Not at all," Ethan replied. Already he liked the looks of the man. He had an open, honest face and a direct way of speaking.

The interior of the garage had been converted into a combined workroom and office. The sweet aroma of newly cut wood lent the place the smell of a forest. Long wooden planks leaned against a worktable where modern cutting equipment held pride of place.

Joe Santori offered them each a stool. Carlos lifted a piece of unfinished work from a nearby bench. The flat wood had grooves and notches and had been freshly sanded. He examined the piece with interest. "Very nice," he approved. "My grandfather made cabinets in Cuba. He would have loved your tools. He would also have enjoyed your talent."

Joe shrugged off the compliment. "I play around with a few pieces in my spare time. My main job is general construction. I repair roofs, refinish floors, build spare rooms—"

"Renovate lodges," Ethan suggested.

Joe Santori looked at him. "That, too. But the big boys came in when the Addison chain bought Timberlake. They wanted their own crew for the addition."

"But you were there long enough to find Margaret Ingalls's body."

"*I* didn't find the body. One of my men did."

"But you were there," Ethan insisted.

"About fifty feet away."

Ethan nodded. He started to ask another question when Joe Santori stood up. "Would you two like something to drink? Some coffee?"

Ethan shook his head. Carlos did, too. Joe looked uncomfortable. He glanced at the door.

"Is something the matter, Mr. Santori?" Ethan inquired.

"No. I just…I was waiting for someone to get here before…"

The rough growl of a sports car's engine grew loud in the driveway and then shut off. Joe looked instantly relieved. He went to the door to greet the visitor, just as he had greeted Ethan and Carlos. Only this time his welcome was warmer.

Ethan immediately knew the newcomer's identity.

He recognized the sound of the engine. A second later, Amanda Baron appeared in the doorway.

"I'm sorry I'm late, Joe," she said. "I had a delay at the house." Then she flashed a smile that was enough to take Ethan's breath away.

Her blue gaze searched him out. She'd known he was there! She wasn't surprised! Ethan moved uneasily on the wooden seat.

"You all know one another?" Joe Santori asked.

"Yes," Amanda said. She didn't look tormented now. She looked bright-eyed and bushy-tailed and ready for battle. His memory of her in the car earlier that day might have been of another woman entirely.

Ethan got slowly to his feet. "What's going on here?" he demanded.

Joe said, "I've asked my lawyer to be present while I'm being questioned."

"Your lawyer?" Ethan echoed. He didn't like this. He didn't like it one little bit. His back stiffened.

"His lawyer," Amanda Baron confirmed.

"Since when?" Ethan's voice was like the crack of a whip.

"Since—" she looked at Joe "—since I first set up practice in Tyler. Joe was one of my earliest clients."

"I don't believe this," Ethan complained angrily. "This is attempted interference with the prosecution's case."

"In what way? I'm here to represent my client as he's being questioned. It's perfectly within his rights."

"Don't play games with me, Counselor," Ethan grated. "You know precisely what you're doing. You're here to insert yourself in my case."

"I'm filing for discovery anyway."

"Which you might not get! The judge won't necessarily allow it."

Both Joe and Carlos had backed away. The argument was between the two lawyers.

"You wish!" Amanda retorted. "Let's wait and see. I won against your challenge."

"Don't let it go to your head!"

Amanda smiled again, seemingly unrepentant.

While maintaining her defense, she had moved across the room and now stood just inches away from him. Face-to-face, Ethan found both her attitude and her behavior outrageous. In his mind he started to compose his formal letter of complaint to the governing board of attorneys. Audacity, presumptuousness and culpability were just a few of the words woven into the text. Then, subtly, his focus altered, and instead of wanting to report her, he found himself wanting to kiss her. Kiss her until she wouldn't challenge him anymore. Kiss her until that defiant little body melted against his in an energetic display of complete abandon.

As he realized the direction of his thoughts, he drew back. But he couldn't break the thread that held their gazes. Did she know what he was thinking? What was *she* thinking? Something had changed in her eyes as well.

Ethan forced himself to turn away. "Come on, Carlos," he barked. "We'll pass on this interview. We already have Mr. Santori's testimony on record."

As Carlos hastened to his side, Joe Santori tried to placate him. "I don't mind talking to you, Mr. Trask. I have nothing to hide. Judson Ingalls is a friend to my family. I don't believe he murdered his wife. Anger of that sort isn't in the man. But my belief doesn't stop me from telling the truth.''

''I'll speak with you again in court, Mr. Santori.''

Ethan settled in the car, waited for Carlos to close the passenger door, then backed quickly out the drive, being careful not to sideswipe the little red sports car that sat obstinately out of place. Just like its owner, he grumbled angrily to himself. Then he thought again of dark blue eyes, and he gunned the engine to get away.

CHAPTER SEVEN

JOE TURNED AWAY in confusion. "I don't understand what just happened," he said. "Mr. Trask didn't seem very pleased."

Amanda felt detached, oddly disturbed. The trial and its ramifications seemed a great distance away at this moment, for a fire had started deep inside her body. It was tiny now, but she knew that if left untended it could grow to at least a three-alarm blaze, possibly more. She and Ethan Trask had been glaring at each other. He had looked so angry, as if he wanted to strangle her...then his look had changed. Amanda wasn't widely experienced, but she knew sexual interest when she saw it. She also knew when she responded. Which she had. Just now.

"Amanda?" Joe prompted.

Amanda shook herself from her abstraction. "What? I'm sorry. What did you say?"

Joe repeated patiently, "Ethan Trask. He didn't seemed very pleased to have you here just now. Did I do something wrong?"

"Not at all," Amanda assured him. She made herself smile. "I'm your lawyer. I'm here to look after your best interests. It was all perfectly legal."

"That's what Liza said when she called. She said she was telling all your clients to call you if Ethan Trask asked to talk to them."

Liza! Amanda hadn't meant for Liza to spread the word to everyone! "When did she call, Joe?" she asked.

"Just before I called you. About an hour after lunch. I knew Ethan Trask was coming, so I thought I'd better hurry. I meant what I said before, Amanda—I don't believe your grandfather did it. And I'll do anything I can, short of lying, to help him."

Another friend. Someone else to remember when any of the family began to feel alone and depressed. "We'd never want you to lie, Joe. We wouldn't want anyone to. The strongest ally Granddad has is the truth. And that's what we're going to tell the jury."

Joe nodded approval. "Would you like to come inside? Nora's here. She's visiting with Susannah."

Amanda shook her head. "No, actually I have to go out to the boathouse to see Liza. Tell them hello for me, though, and tell them I'll call. No, better not do that. I don't know when I can keep the promise. Just—just tell them I said hello."

"They'll understand," Joe said seriously, then he broke into a huge grin. "Unlike a certain prosecutor."

Amanda had started walking toward the door. At Joe's last remark, she stopped. The problem was, Ethan Trask understood only too well. If she showed up every time he tried to talk to a witness in Tyler, he might come to think that the townspeople were in collusion against him. A nice thought, but not highly ethical. She started to correct Joe's impression, but changed her reply to an answering grin and a shrug. Joe had been making a joke.

THE BOATHOUSE WAS LOCATED a short distance from Timberlake Lodge. The year before, just like the lodge, it had been uncared for and musty. When Judson sold Timberlake, he had kept a small strip leading to the boathouse so the family could retain one small claim to the land they had owned for so many years. Together, Liza and Cliff had redone the place, and using Liza's gift for interior design, they had created a comfortable home on the upper floor of the structure.

Liza must have seen Amanda coming, because she whipped open the door just as her sister arrived at the landing. It was doubtful if an impartial observer would ever notice a close relationship between the two women. Liza was tall and blond with long, slim legs, while Amanda was shorter, more rounded, with darker hair and darker blue eyes. But differing physical characteristics barely touched the differences in their personalities and outlooks. Liza was a tad on the wild side; Amanda was contained, steady. Liza liked to push people to the breaking point just to see what they would do next; Amanda tried not to disturb the status quo. The personality of each woman seemed to have been set from birth.

In spite of their differences, though, the two had always managed to get along. The only time Amanda had been seriously angry with her sister was when Liza had hurt their mother so deeply by rejecting her after their father's unexpected death. But that was in the past. Liza and Alyssa had made up their differences, and with the arrival of little Maggie, the sharp sting of Liza's need to strike out at everyone had abated. Loving and living with Cliff had also helped. For the first time, Liza felt needed.

"Amanda," she said hurriedly, "what's up? Did Joe reach you? Ethan Trask is meeting with him this afternoon. Joe wants you to come over to his place and—"

"I'm just coming from Joe's," Amanda interrupted.

Liza breathed a sigh of relief. Then she grinned. "Well, all right! It worked! How did it go? How did Ethan Trask take it?" As Liza closed the door, she pushed a tangle of hair away from her face, and her blue eyes sparked with excitement.

"Not particularly well," Amanda said, dropping her purse onto a white canvas couch. She didn't want to throw cold water on her younger sister's enthusiasm, but she felt she had to say something right away. "Liza, when I said for you to call me if Ethan Trask asked to talk with you, I didn't mean for you to broadcast that message to the world. I meant for *you* to call me. You or Cliff."

"Are you saying I've done something wrong?" Liza demanded.

Amanda sighed. "No. But I wish you'd have asked me first."

Liza tossed her head. "I took a little initiative. There's nothing wrong with that, is there? If it was all right for us to call you, why not other people?"

"How many have you called?" Amanda asked.

"I've put the word out fairly well. To our friends."

"What did you say?"

"Are you cross-examining me?"

"No, I just need to know."

The tiny mewing sound of a newly born infant made both sisters turn toward the back of the house.

"Did we wake her?" Amanda asked guiltily.

Liza shook her head. "No, it's time for her afternoon snack. Wait here, I'll go get her."

Amanda waited in the nicely turned-out room. Her sister's slightly bizarre taste had been given free rein, but the resulting combination of colors and textures was pleasing to the senses.

Liza came back carrying a tiny bundle. She let Amanda kiss the downy blond head in greeting before she sat down on the couch and adjusted her blouse and bra to accommodate the hungry baby. "Now," she said briskly, as if she had been a mother all her life—as if anyone would have pictured her doing this quite so happily a few years before!—"what have I done that's so wrong? Are the police going to come arrest me or something? Are Granddad and I in danger of being put in adjoining cells?"

Amanda couldn't help herself. She laughed. Liza was always so outrageous. Nothing about that aspect of her personality had changed. "No," she said, settling on the couch herself. "It's just that I have to decide how far I want to push this. Ethan Trask was none too happy to have me there this afternoon. In fact, he left. He didn't talk to Joe."

"Good. Maybe we can have that happen with everyone."

"That's just it. If I show up everywhere he goes, he'll have grounds to file a complaint against me with the lawyers' grievance committee. I'll have to be careful."

"You mean he could have you disbarred?"

"That's doubtful, but a complaint wouldn't look good on my record."

"I don't like this Mr. Ethan Trask."

When Amanda lowered her gaze, Liza took her silence as agreement. Liza looked down at her baby for a few long seconds, a loving softness touching her slightly uneven features. But the gentle moment was soon replaced by something else: worry. Finally, she said, "Amanda...pull open that drawer in the table next to you. Inside, there's a leather book. Take it out."

Amanda did as her sister directed. She examined the book curiously. It was old, covered in rust-colored suede, and the clasp was tarnished. "What is it?" she asked.

Liza hesitated, then she said, "Margaret's diary. Cliff and I found it shortly after we met. It was in one of Margaret's tall chests in the attic at the lodge."

Amanda looked at the book again. It didn't seem quite so insignificant any longer. "Margaret's?" she echoed.

Liza nodded.

"Have you read it?" Amanda asked.

"Not past the inscription. I said I was going to, but I just couldn't do it. I know! Everyone thinks I'm fearless. But...I just couldn't do it. I was afraid." Liza stopped. Her gaze dropped back to the baby. She played absently with a tiny hand.

Amanda's heartbeat increased. She, too, was afraid of what she'd find. She placed her finger against the tiny metal button and pushed. The clasp released.

"No!" Liza said quickly. "Not here. Not..."

Amanda's fingers halted. Her sister didn't want her to open the book in the baby's presence. Maggie might be named after the original Margaret Alyssa, but that was as close as Liza seemed to want her to come, at least to her great-grandmother's darker side.

Amanda slipped the diary into her purse. "I'll let you know," she said quietly.

A grateful smile touched Liza's lips.

WHEN AMANDA ARRIVED back in her office that afternoon, there was a message from Peter asking her to call.

"I haven't heard from you all day," he complained gruffly. "I wondered if you were still angry with me."

Amanda set her purse on her desk. Inside was the diary. What might it contain? she wondered. Incriminating information against her grandfather that she would be bound to turn over to the court? Or might it reveal the real murderer's name? It had taken all the willpower Amanda had not to pull off the road and tear into the book. But she had restrained herself. She wanted complete privacy when she looked at it.

"Definitely not," she said, answering the professor's query. "I've been busy, that's all."

"How are things going?" he asked.

"Frankly, Peter, I don't know. I talked to Granddad. He's given me a little more information, but there still seem to be huge gaps. I don't think he's purposely hiding anything. He's given me a few names of people who attended the parties Margaret used to have at the lodge. He can't remember Roddy's last name, though, and that's the person I'd most hoped he'd remember. He gets all uptight when he talks about him. I think the man was one of Margaret's lovers, possibly the man she was leaving Granddad for...but his first name is all Granddad seems to know. That's all Rose Atkins knew, too. She met Roddy at one of Margaret's parties, but she couldn't associate any other name with him—according to what she told Liza before she died. Rose recognized him in some of Margaret's old photos. Oh!

And she also said he was a good dancer, which isn't much to go on.''

"Have you hired an investigator yet?" Peter asked.

Amanda's hand tightened on the phone. "Not yet. There's a small problem. Do you know anyone good who would be willing to work at a cut rate?"

Peter was quick to pick up on the undercurrent of her question. He didn't probe. Instead he replied, "If you don't mind taking on another pensioner, I do. Leo Stein worked for me several times in my practice. He called just the other day. He's retired and lives in Madison, doesn't like the wife of the son he's living with and is looking for something to do."

"Would he be willing to go to Chicago? That seems to be where most of these people came from. A few might still be living there."

"He loves Chicago."

Some of the brittleness peeled away from Amanda's heart. She had felt abandoned by Peter. But he hadn't abandoned her. "Tell him to call me, then. Oh—and Peter…thanks."

"Nothing to it," Peter said.

Amanda slowly replaced the phone. Then she told Tessie not to disturb her for any reason. She took the diary from her purse and placed it on her desk. She straightened it. Then she straightened it again. What surprises might it contain? she wondered, fascinated by the prospect. She'd seen a sample of her grandmother's handwriting before, on a birthday card her mother had kept all these years. A card that Alyssa both loved and seemed oddly frightened by. Her mother had never put her feelings into words, but Amanda had been quick to sense her mixed reactions.

What would it be like to see her grandmother

through the woman's own thoughts? Through her own words? Was it that prospect that had frightened Liza away from reading it? Amanda slid the clasp free and opened the book to the first page.

An hour and a half later she put down the diary, her emotions in a tangle. Margaret Lindstrom Ingalls had been horribly egotistical. Everything in the diary concerned her wants, her desires, her comforts. She demanded the best creams, the best powders, the best perfumes, the best clothes, and she kept a record of where and when she'd found them. At her parties, Margaret served only the best foods, unconcerned about the cost. Not one word had been written about her child or her husband. The diary was a testimony to self-indulgence. On behalf of Alyssa and Judson, Amanda seethed with indignation. Yet at the same time, she felt there was a certain tragedy involved in such excess. Margaret had not been a happy woman. She'd seemed to keep striving for something that remained just out of reach.

Amanda sighed and rubbed her forehead. The diary had revealed nothing that would either help or hinder their cause. All the trepidation had been for nothing.

Weary in both body and spirit, she reached for the telephone once again. She had to let Liza know what she'd found. If her guess was correct, her sister hadn't even begun to settle down since seeing her off to town.

ETHAN WORKED steadily through the rest of the afternoon in his new office in Sugar Creek, going over the various segments that, put together, began to form his case: grand jury proceedings, witness statements, police notes, notes and memos made by the local district attorney's office, the information that Carlos had worked up. He prepared a list of people he still wanted to speak with. Only by burying himself in his work could he keep from thinking about Amanda Baron. Keep from dealing with the uncomfortable questions he had no answer for. Keep from thinking about those wide blue eyes....

"You look tired, my friend," Carlos murmured as he came into the room.

"It's been another hard day," Ethan said, stretching. His long arms reached high above his head.

Carlos pulled up a chair. "I have discovered more interesting information."

Ethan's interest was immediately caught. His arms came down. "What?"

"You are not so tired anymore," the investigator teased.

"Spit it out, Carlos."

"I have found a woman who used to work as a maid in Timberlake Lodge at the time of Judson and Margaret's marriage. She lives in Belton, the town nearest to Tyler. I have talked with her and she has agreed to see us. She remembers an argument the night Margaret Ingalls disappeared and the way Judson Ingalls behaved afterward. Also, I went to the library in Tyler, and by checking the newspaper accounts of that time, I learned the names of some of Margaret Ingalls's party guests." He withdrew several sheets of paper from his pocket. "I made copies."

Ethan examined them. "Have you been able to locate anyone yet?"

Carlos shook his head. "No. All are from Chicago except, in this instance—" the investigator pointed midway down one column "—the woman named Rose Atkins was from Tyler. She died last December."

"I thought Margaret didn't like anyone from Tyler."

"She seems to have gotten along with a few people. None are alive for us to talk to, though. The list was pretty short."

"Who told you this?"

Carlos smiled at Ethan's perception. "Actually, it was the postmistress, Annabelle Scanlon. She was seventeen when Margaret disappeared. She never went to the parties herself. She was too young, but she knows who did…at least who from Tyler."

"Looks like you get a trip to Chicago."

"One name stands out in the clippings toward the end of spring."

"Who?"

"Someone named Roddy. No last name. Unless that *is* his last name. No one seems to have called him anything else."

Ethan considered the situation. "Did the Ingallses keep a guest register at the lodge?"

"I have already thought of that. I stopped off on the way back to Sugar Creek. No one in the hotel's business office knows. I asked if I could look around, and I ended up in the attic. There were some files up there in boxes, mostly registers and logs from the years when Peter Ingalls—that is Judson's father—brought his friends to Timberlake Lodge to hunt and fish. Nothing from Margaret's time. I looked around some more, but I could find nothing else. She probably did not keep records. She does not seem the sort."

"When did the former maid say we could come see her?"

"She is free anytime we wish."

Ethan gathered the materials he had been working on and swept them into a file drawer, which he then locked. "Let's get to it," he said, and he strode out of the room with Carlos close behind.

In the hall Carlos said, "One more thing I learned from Annabelle Scanlon. Philip Wocheck has the reputation for being very old-fashioned in his beliefs, in the way he thinks. If he was ordered to do something by someone in authority, he would do it—no matter what it was."

Ethan nodded shortly, his mouth set in a grim line.

AMANDA WAS TAKEN UNAWARE by a sudden, huge yawn as she let herself into the house. It wasn't that late, barely after nine o'clock, but she had completed her written motion for discovery, asking that the prosecution give her copies of all materials pertaining to her grandfather's case. Specifically, she asked for a list of the prosecution witnesses, along with their names and addresses. She'd asked to review the statements of witnesses and all police records. She'd asked for information regarding the physical evidence and copies of any photographs taken. She'd tried to think of everything. Tomorrow morning she would hand-deliver the application to the judge.

The house was quiet. Clara and Archie had gone off to their quarters; her grandfather was nowhere to be seen. Even her mother was out. A note said she was at a school board meeting.

Amanda had bent over to check the contents of the refrigerator, curious to see what kind of meal Clara had left for her that evening, when the door was suddenly swept out of her hand and a large body attempted to push her aside.

"Get out of the way, thief! You ate my dinner the other night, and I had to go to bed hungry!" a male voice cried.

Jeff! Amanda pushed back with her hip, trying to stand her ground. "I never ate your dinner!" she declared. "If Clara didn't leave you any, it was because she didn't know you'd be coming home hungry. She knows I always do!"

The struggle continued, as if they were children. Then Jeff resorted to unfair tactics. He lunged at her, dragging her off her feet, then carried her fireman fashion across the kitchen to a chair in the breakfast alcove. Both were laughing all the way.

"Brute!" Amanda accused.

Jeff fell into a chair alongside her. A shadow of stubble marked his jaw and chin, and his rich chestnut hair needed cutting. He was dressed in jeans and an unremarkable plaid shirt, a look not at all in keeping with the probable next chief of staff at Tyler Memorial Hospital. At the moment, though, he was head of Emergency Medicine and had the red-rimmed eyes and telltale droop of exhaustion to prove it.

They continued to share the joke, then slowly resumed their adult demeanor. Jeff straightened. "Go ahead, eat your dinner. I've already had mine. Cece stopped off before she went to the clinic to teach her prenatal class. We actually managed to eat a meal together."

"You two need to get married."

"We're working on it. In fact..." He paused. "Amanda, how do you think everyone would react if we decided to do it before the trial? I know it's short notice, but Cece and I don't want a large wedding. Just immediate family. And if we wait until after..." He stopped, not wanting to put his thoughts into words.

"I think you should do whatever you want, Jeff. You know everyone in the family will support you."

"But I don't want it to look as if we think—"

"It would make Granddad happy. He likes Cece. He thinks the two of you are good for each other."

"Unlike my previous choice." Jeff shook his head at the memory.

"Cece's right for you. You're right for her. The two of you always have been, even when you were in high school."

Jeff rubbed his face. "I'm exhausted. We had a bad accident that involved two vans. One, with a bunch of kids on board, flipped over."

Instantly alarmed, Amanda asked, "Was anyone hurt badly?"

"None of the kids, thank God. Only cuts and bruises and a couple of broken bones. Two of the adults didn't fare so well, though. It was really touch and go for a while, but I think they'll both make it. I checked on them before I left."

"Were they from around here?" Amanda asked.

Jeff shook his head. "Happened on the highway. One group was from Madison, the other from Casner."

They lapsed into silence. As Jeff toyed with the fringe of a place mat, Amanda thought about the children and their parents, and the families of the injured adults, and she felt a certain kinship. Her life, too, had been altered by the occurrence of a single, shattering event. All their lives had been.

Jeff shifted in his chair, drawing her gaze to his face. Beneath the fact of his obvious exhaustion lay the less apparent damage of long-term tension. Exhaustion could be cured by rest. Fear and worry sometimes had no cure. Anxiety was starting to leave its mark on all the members of the Ingalls/Baron family.

To alleviate some of her brother's concern, Amanda said softly, "I'm doing the best I can for Granddad, Jeff."

Jeff was startled that she had read his mood so accurately. "I'll have to watch myself around Mom. If you can see through me so easily, so can she."

"Mom's not doing so well herself right now. She's getting worse, Jeff. She's so brittle, so tight. It's as if she's going to break into a thousand tiny pieces. She pretends that she's not, that she can handle anything that comes along, but when you look into her eyes…"

"I'm worried about her."

"Me, too."

"What can we do?"

Amanda shrugged unhappily. "Win Granddad's case?"

Jeff reached out to cover her hand. "That's a tremendous burden we're putting on you."

"I'll manage," Amanda quipped.

"That sounds like something Mom would say."

Another quiet moment passed before Amanda asked uneasily, "Jeff, do you remember ever seeing Granddad's gun?"

Her brother's body tensed as he sat back. "His gun?"

Amanda nodded. "A revolver with ebony handles and his initials inlaid in silver."

"Why?" Jeff snapped. He could be just as prickly as their grandfather sometimes.

"I remember seeing it," Amanda admitted quietly. "When we were children, Granddad showed it to us once. It was in a fancy wooden case. There were two molded gun rests lined with velvet...but only one gun."

Her brother hunched his shoulders, his features dark. "I don't see what that has to do with anything. So there was only one gun. So what?"

"You remember then?"

"Yes! I remember! But I still don't see where—"

"The police think Margaret was killed with the missing gun. They're both thirty-two caliber...the same as the bullet Joe found in Margaret's room at Timberlake Lodge. Anna Kelsey called yesterday. She rang to ask me about something else, but before hanging up, she apologized for all the trouble she'd caused us. Naturally, I asked what she was talking about. She explained how Brick had found the gun the police are holding because she'd asked him to move some things around in Phil's closet. Since she thought Phil would probably leave Worthington House and be back in the room soon, Anna wanted to freshen it. When Brick moved one of the boxes, the bottom collapsed and the gun fell out. They must have done tests on it and found that the markings match."

Jeff sat forward, his surliness forgotten. "So the rumors were true!" he exclaimed. Then he frowned. "But why did *Phil* have the gun if it was Granddad's?

And if it was used to murder Margaret, wouldn't that mean that Phil—''

''The grand jury didn't indict Phil.''

''Why not?'' Jeff demanded.

Amanda shrugged. ''The district attorney must not have thought him guilty.'' Then she added, ''Anna also said something else. She said that Mom was there when Brick found it. Mom and Edward Wocheck.''

''You mean…Mom knew about the gun?'' Jeff reacted with surprise, just as she had when first informed.

''Apparently,'' Amanda confirmed.

''Why didn't she say anything? And Edward! I can understand why *he* wouldn't say anything—he wouldn't lift a finger to help Granddad. But *Mom?*''

''I have no idea.''

Jeff heaved a great sigh as he rubbed the back of his neck. ''Did you talk to Granddad?''

''He's the one who reminded me about the presentation set.''

''Does he know what happened to the other gun?''

''He said the last time he saw it, he'd put it in a safe in Margaret's room at the lodge. She was worried about prowlers. He said he'd given it to her more for her peace of mind than expecting that she'd ever have cause to use it.''

''But Phil…why would Phil have it?''

''When I get the discovery information—*if* I get it—we'll know. We'll know exactly what he said to the grand jury, and then I'll question him.''

''Do you think he was blackmailing Granddad, like the rumors also said?''

Amanda shook her head. ''Granddad denies it. In fact, hearing that makes him angry.''

Jeff hesitated, then he asked softly, "Do you believe him?"

Understanding the workings of her older brother's mind—older by only one year—had always been easy for Amanda. She knew him almost as well as she knew herself. And now, as she surveyed his downcast gaze and the tight way he held his lips, she realized that his question went much deeper than if she believed what their grandfather had said about Phil's possible extortion. He was asking if she believed their grandfather when he swore that he was innocent of Margaret's murder. Jeff would fight the world to protect their grandfather. He would even give his life, if called upon. But it was clear that he had some misgivings...some doubts that he was too ashamed to admit.

Amanda took her turn at offering comfort. She placed her hand over her brother's much larger one and whispered huskily, "I believe him."

CHAPTER EIGHT

JUDSON SAT BLINKING in the bright afternoon light as
Amanda settled into the comfortable driver's seat of
her grandfather's car. They had just run through the
gauntlet of reporters assigned to the courthouse.
Questions had been shouted at them, flash photos
taken—only a sample of what was to come.

"You okay, Granddad?" Amanda asked, concerned about the paleness of her grandfather's com-
plexion.

"Is that all there is?" Judson asked slowly.

"It should be, until the trial starts. We won again,
Granddad! We'll get everything we asked for."

"But what was it the judge said about an exception?"

"He was talking about a ruling by the State Su-
preme Court that says a prosecutor's files are an exception to the open records policy." Amanda started
the engine. "That means when we're granted discovery information, we can't have *everything* the prosecutor has. For instance, we can't have information
that's sensitive and has no bearing on this case—gossip, in other words—or statements by witnesses
who've been promised confidentiality and who won't
be testifying. We also can't have the prosecution's
working papers, memos, their notes on strategy…things like that. But we *can* have everything

else that's relevant. And, believe me, Granddad, that's a lot!''

"When will we get it?" he asked.

"Hopefully, soon. If it's not in my office by tomorrow afternoon, I'll be giving Mr. Trask a call." Amanda put the car in reverse and backed out of the parking slot.

As they started to move forward, Judson said quietly, "I'm very proud of you, Amanda. I'm not sure if I've ever told you that before, but if I haven't, I should have."

Amanda felt a warm rush of gratitude. "Thank you, Granddad."

"And I want you to know, whatever happens—"

"Granddad—"

"I appreciate everything you've done for me. So does your mother. We're not a family to wear our hearts on our sleeves. We don't talk very much about our feelings. That might be a good thing and it might not. But that's the way it's always been and probably always will be. At least, among the older generation. Maybe with you young people, things will change…I don't know."

"You sound so solemn, Granddad. I tried to tell you earlier…don't let the courtroom or the judicial procedure weigh you down. I know it's frightening— all these people you don't know looking at you, talking about you…people who are going to have a direct influence on your life. But you come into court an innocent man. The prosecution has to *prove* you guilty. We don't have to prove you innocent."

"The media seem to think I'm guilty. Have you read some of the stories? Have you heard the TV commentators from Madison and Milwaukee? They already have me tried and convicted! They don't say so outright, but they twist things so out of shape that…'' He couldn't continue.

"I've heard them,'' Amanda answered grimly.

"And now they're going to be in the courtroom, too!''

"Only one camera, and it's in a fixed location.''

"I don't like it.''

"I know, Granddad. I tried to make the judge's decision go the other way.'' Her grandfather's good name meant everything to him. She had used every argument she could think of, but the judge had ruled against them. To his credit, Ethan Trask wasn't over-joyed with having the trial televised either, but the lawyer from a local-access cable station in Madison—a station also received in Tyler—had prevailed.

"Rob Friedman has never written anything against you,'' she said, reminding her grandfather of the local newspaper publisher.

"Thank heaven for small favors!'' Judson grumbled.

Her grandfather's sarcasm was not in keeping with his personality. It was a sign, one of many, of the strain he was under from the fast-approaching trial.

Amanda tried to concentrate on driving, but the events of the past few days crowded into her brain. She hadn't had the option of sitting around and wait-ing to see if she would be granted the discovery ma-terial. She had hired Leo Stein, the investigator Peter recommended, set him to work, then made appoint-ments to talk to Brick and to Karen. Brick had told her what he could about the case, while Karen, cap-tain of the Tyler substation, was closemouthed. Brick had grown up in Tyler and felt a certain loyalty;

Karen was a relative stranger and a cop who went totally by the book. The evidence against Judson looked really bad, Brick said. The prosecutor had a strong case.

The prosecutor…

Amanda's grip tightened on the steering wheel. She hadn't been sure what she'd feel when she met Ethan Trask at this morning's hearing. She'd just about convinced herself that she had imagined the whole thing between them, then she'd looked across the vaulted courtroom and seen him standing at the prosecution table, tall and aloof and achingly attractive. Of course, nothing had shown in his eyes, dark as night when they met hers. But she hadn't expected anything. He had murmured her name formally, ''Ms. Baron,'' and had continued to assemble his notes. His voice was wonderful—rich, melodious. It played along her nerve endings like the sweet sounds of a cello. She'd tried to concentrate on her notes, tried to keep her eyes from straying to his table. But she hadn't been very successful. He sat alone, a man of strong character, armed only with words and the set powers the court system allowed him—a force against the world's evil.

Feeling her inadequacies, Amanda had turned to her grandfather and taken his hand. An observer might have thought she was giving reassurance. In reality, she had gained it. Her grandfather wasn't evil. He was a wonderful man who had given unselfishly of himself to his family, to his town and to his country, and she had to keep her mind focused in order to show that to the jury. She couldn't let any personal feelings she might have toward the man who was her grandfather's sworn enemy get in the way. But even

now, driving away from Sugar Creek, she still felt
Ethan Trask's magnetic presence.

She glanced at her grandfather, hoping that they
might talk. But Judson was in no mood for further
exchange. He sat hunched in his seat, a scowl on his
aristocratic features, withdrawn from her and from the
world.

AFTER DROPPING her grandfather off at their house,
Amanda went back to the office. An hour later, Tessie
knocked lightly on her door, stepped out of the way
and allowed a man who was carrying a box to enter
Amanda's office. The man was Carlos Varadero.

"Miss Baron," he said, smiling graciously. "The
first installment. I will bring the rest after copies have
been made. Ethan hopes that this will satisfy you for
the time being."

Amanda struggled to her feet.

"Put it over here," Tessie directed, quickly clearing a place on a side table.

"Thank you," Amanda said. "I didn't expect to
see you so soon. I thought—"

"I am to tell you that Ethan will not, in any way,
act to delay the order of the court."

"That's—that's very good of him," she stammered
in surprise. "But he was so angry the other day."

"He is a fair man."

"He didn't think *I* was behaving fairly."

Carlos shrugged. "We are confident in our case."
He placed the box on the table, then bowed with old-
world charm and left the room.

Tessie stared after him. "*Who* was *that?*"

"Carlos Varadero. Ethan Trask's investigator."

Amanda tore open the box. "He's from the Division of Criminal Investigation."

"Hmm. I love a man with an accent."

"Tessie! You swore husband number three was going to be it."

Tessie sniffed. "I can't help it if I've outlived them all. Maybe I should try a younger man next time."

"He's the enemy, remember?" Amanda cautioned, using the same logic on her secretary as she had used on herself.

"Forbidden fruit. That makes him even better!"

Amanda looked up from the papers she was riffling through. *"Tessie!"* she admonished, shocked. She hadn't thought of it like that...and she didn't really want to!

"Oh, keep your shirt on. I was only teasing," her secretary grumbled. Then she closed the door with a little snap.

Amanda blinked, then started to laugh. She had no idea whether to take Tessie seriously or not.

"WHAT DID SHE SAY?" Ethan asked, once the investigator arrived back in Sugar Creek.

Carlos's brown eyes gleamed. "She was surprised."

Ethan frowned. "That I'd sent the material?"

"That you sent it so promptly. She expected you to delay."

"Maybe I should have."

"I told her you are a fair man."

"That probably went over well. What did she say? No, don't answer that. Why should I care? Let's get back to work." He frowned down at the papers that had been occupying him before Carlos's return, but he glanced up as Carlos seated himself. "What are you smiling at?" he demanded.

"The two of you," Carlos replied. "She asked me questions about you, too."

"Wha—" he started to ask, then clamped his mouth shut. He was already behind this afternoon, and there was only one reason: persistent thoughts of Amanda Baron. He wasn't going to let her take up any more of his valuable time!

Carlos's grin widened, but he didn't say anything.

Ethan ignored him. "I've made arrangements for us to meet Philip Wocheck tomorrow afternoon. Will you be free at two o'clock?"

"Two o'clock," the investigator confirmed.

"It should be interesting," Ethan promised.

Carlos nodded. "I still cannot find anyone who remembers Judson Ingalls wearing a wedding ring. I asked the people in Chicago and they cannot remember one, either. I hate to say this, but I doubt that we are ever going to make a connection. Just as we could not connect Judson to an extramarital affair. The people in Chicago laughed in my face when I even mentioned it. They said he was too straitlaced, too proper."

"But they remember hearing arguments."

"Frequently. Almost every weekend when they were guests at the lodge. Of course, they have all taken Margaret's side. I have been told that the arguments had something to do with finances."

"And not her lovers?"

"Well, that, too."

Ethan frowned. "Finances," he mused. "She was spending too much money, that kind of thing?"

"Someone said something about his business—the one in Tyler—being in trouble."

Ethan straightened. "The F and M?"

"That is what this person said."

"Who?" Ethan demanded.

"Marsha. Marsha Dare."

"She's reliable?"

"Mind like a steel trap. She claims to have been Margaret's best friend."

"Didn't she find it curious when she stopped hearing from Margaret?"

"She said she always thought Judson had killed her—either him or someone else. She did not think Margaret would live very long. She did not think she would, either, but she is celebrating her seventieth birthday next week."

"Did she ever report her 'best friend' missing?"

"No, she did not trust the police."

"The Tyler police?"

"Any police."

Ethan sighed. "What did she say about Judson's financial troubles?"

"Only that he kept pestering Margaret to sign something. Marsha did not know what. I will check with his bank in Tyler."

Ethan nodded. He mulled over the possibilities Carlos's information might lead them to, then said, "Abigail Simpson's daughter drove her in today. She signed her statement and brought Margaret's note." He reached into a manila envelope and withdrew a folded piece of lilac-colored paper. The ghostly scent of expensive perfume drifted in the air. "As she said, she kept it pressed between the pages of a book, but she couldn't remember which book. She and her daughter found it last night.''

Abigail Simpson was the maid who had once worked at Timberlake Lodge. Ethan and Carlos had gone to talk with her several evenings before. She was a small, nicely dressed woman, with a good memory for most things, but a little hazy on others. Still, Ethan thought that she would make a credible witness, and he intended to put her on the stand.

Carlos opened the scented sheet. The handwriting was bold, very feminine. It stated clearly the writer's intention to leave. And it was signed *Margaret.*

Ethan slid the note back into the envelope and set the clasp. ''Another nail,'' he said calmly.

''They are lining up.''

''Yes,'' Ethan agreed.

AMANDA PUSHED away from her desk with a sick heart. She'd had to stop more than once during her first perusal of the material. She couldn't believe it. Everything looked so bad. And this was only the first installment!

The mystery of Phil Wocheck's involvement had been solved: he had heard an argument all those years before, then a gunshot. When he'd hurried to Margaret's room, he had found her dead. Then he'd buried her! Phil! Amanda was shaken. All those years...Phil had known! He'd also seen a man run from the room, but he couldn't identify him. He would not say that it was Judson, but he wouldn't say that it wasn't. He admitted taking the gun; he also admitted hiding Margaret's suitcase. But he wouldn't say why. In his testimony before the grand jury, his explanations were fuzzy, rambling.

Amanda continued to reel from shock. *Phil? Why? Why had he done it?* Unless *he* thought Judson had killed Margaret. There was no love lost between the two men, and as far as Amanda knew, there never had been. In the town's eyes, Phil was of the Old World. He had emigrated from Poland shortly after the start of World War II to escape the horrors that were taking place there. He had come to work at Timberlake Lodge as the gardener and handyman. From the little Amanda had learned from her grandfather, Phil had clung to rather feudal ideas concerning employer and employee. He'd felt he had his place, and he never strayed from it. Not until years later, when Judson had refused to allow a marriage between the young Alyssa and Phil's son, did the feudal element erode enough to allow resentment to take its place. Everyone in town knew about Judson's rejection of Edward, and Phil's deep, burning anger. This included Amanda and her siblings. So why would Phil bother to protect Judson? It didn't make sense.

Amanda walked across the room. Her grandfather had denied the rumor that Phil was blackmailing him, and she believed him. It wasn't in Judson's character to allow himself to be blackmailed, and it wasn't in Phil's character—what she knew of him—to do such a thing. Phil had kept quiet all those years because... Because of an old-world loyalty to the man he had once worked for? Because it was part of his code? No. Amanda dismissed the idea immediately. Such a thing might have applied when Phil found the body, but didn't now.

Yet there was not one word of accusation against Judson in his testimony. No matter how hard the district attorney had tried to get him to admit a connection, Phil had stuck to his story.

Her phone rang. Almost in a daze, Amanda answered it. When she heard Peter's voice, her spirit reached out to him. "Oh, Peter! I'm sorry I didn't call to let you know. We won this motion, too. But, well…"

"But you've seen some of the evidence, and it looks pretty bad."

Wordlessly, forgetting that she couldn't be seen, Amanda nodded. "Yes," she finally whispered.

To her surprise, Peter chuckled. "You'll survive. The malady is strictly temporary."

"What? I don't understand," Amanda said. She felt ridiculously near to tears, ridiculously near to collapse, and Peter was laughing?

"That sinking feeling you get when you see the state's evidence for the first time. If you're a drinking person, pour yourself a stiff drink. If you're not, brew yourself a strong cup of tea. Take a few long gulps and sit down. Then look at it all again. I promise, the next time you see it, it won't look half as bad. You'll start to see maneuvering room, you'll start to see holes."

"It all looks so…convincing. And I only have part of it. The rest will come in the next day or two."

"Be glad you have what you have."

"Oh, I am." Amanda sank into her chair. She looked at the stack of material and tried to feel as confident as Peter said she should.

"Did you get the list of witnesses yet?" Peter asked.

Amanda lifted a set of papers. "Yes."

"Anyone you weren't expecting?"

Her eyes ran down the list. They ranged from Joe Santori and the dry cleaner who'd found blood on the rug taken from Margaret's room, to a series of expert witnesses who would be called upon to confirm the various physical evidence involved in the case. "Not really. Liza's listed as a state witness. She's not going to like that. No, wait. There are a couple of names I'm not familiar with. An Abigail Simpson from Belton and someone named Marsha Dare from Oak Park, Illinois." She looked through the stack again. "I don't have either of their statements yet."

"Hmm," Peter murmured. "Oak Park is a suburb of Chicago."

"I've already considered that."

"Have you heard from Leo yet?" Peter asked, referring to the investigator he'd recommended.

"Not yet. He said he'd call as soon as he found something."

"Maybe he's already come up with her on his own."

"He's only been there one day."

"It doesn't usually take Leo long." Peter sneezed. "Sorry," he apologized, "allergies." She waited while he blew his nose. "Now, for the real reason I called," he said. "Have you started to formulate strategy yet? I'll have a couple of hours free this evening, from about seven to nine, and if you'd like for me to—"

"I'd like!" Amanda interrupted.

Peter chuckled again. "Then come over. I've got to get away from this manuscript for a while. It's starting to drive me crazy. Writing it was one thing, rewriting it is something else entirely. I keep changing parts that change other parts that change other parts...."

"What kind of book is it?" Amanda asked curiously.

"A crime novel. But more like a Joseph Wambaugh than a Mickey Spillane. The hero is an ex-cop."

"Will you autograph a copy for me when it comes out?"

"Of course. One of the first."

After Amanda hung up, she felt better. For no real reason, she just did.

She spent the rest of the afternoon pouring over the sworn statements of the state's witnesses. As Peter had promised, a second and third reading gave her room for hope. Doubt could be raised in many instances.

The skeletal remains had been in pretty bad shape when discovered, both from tree roots and from the disruption by the backhoe. Then ten months had passed before the cause of death had been determined. The excuse, Amanda knew, was that the State Medical Examiner's laboratory had been functioning with a short staff and an overwhelming work load. Pertinent though that excuse might be, it opened several doors for her. The eventual finding could have been rushed; it might even be incorrect.

Also, Margaret could have died from a cause other than a massive blunt trauma to the head. She might have had a stroke or a heart attack, then fallen and hit her head. That kind of information couldn't be found in a study of bones. And just because a gunshot had been heard didn't mean that Margaret had been hit by a bullet. From the evidence Amanda had seen so far, there was no ironclad proof of a connection between the gun, the bullet and Margaret's death, although the prosecution was sure to imply that there was.

Amanda sat back and rubbed her temples. Her grandfather's case rested on the standard of reasonable doubt. For every point the prosecution made, she'd have to show an inconsistency or an alternate explanation. She'd have to build defects into the state's presentation, raise questions in the minds of the jurors—so that, in the end, they would be able to pronounce no other verdict than not guilty.

BY THE TIME Amanda left the office shortly after five o'clock, all she wanted to do was find a nice quiet corner at home and let her mind rest for an hour...preferably in her room, in bed. But the first person she met as she came into the house was her mother.

Alyssa made no pretense about the fact that she'd been waiting for her. "Amanda...I have to talk to you. Edward called. He said that Ethan Trask has made an appointment to see Phil tomorrow afternoon. Why would he do that? I thought Phil had already testified. I assured Edward that you'd be there. That you wouldn't let that horrible man do anything he shouldn't." Alyssa's features were twisted with worry, her movements jerky. "Isn't it bad enough that he's torturing Father? Does he have to torture everyone else, too? What kind of man *is* he?"

Amanda drew her mother to a chair. "He's just doing his job, Mom. In other circumstances, you'd be one of the first to support him. You believe in law and order, remember?"

"You're *defending* him?" Tears began to fill Alyssa's eyes.

Amanda dropped to her knees at her mother's side. "Mom, I *have* to defend him. He's an officer of the court, just like I am. A charge has been brought against Granddad. We both have to do our part to see that justice prevails."

"But your grandfather—"

"Will have a fair trial."

Alyssa searched her daughter's face, and what she saw must have reassured her. Some of the strain left her delicate features; some of the worry disappeared from her eyes. "I'm sorry," she whispered, wiping her cheeks, "but sometimes I feel so…"

"We all do," Amanda soothed.

"Liza called today, too. She told me Ethan Trask wanted to talk to her, but she refused to meet with him. She said you'd told her that was her right."

Amanda nodded.

"Could Phil do that, too?"

"Anyone can. No one is compelled to talk with him until he puts them on the stand."

Alyssa's blue eyes widened. "Will he do that to Liza?"

"I'm afraid so."

"Oh, dear."

Amanda laughed lightly. "She's not going to be easy for him to question."

"No," Alyssa agreed, giving a quick grin. But the grin soon faded. "Amanda…do you think he'll want to talk to me?"

Amanda sat back on her heels. She hadn't considered that. She frowned. "Why? Do you know something that might be pertinent to the case?" She

thought of the news she had recently received—that
Alyssa had been present at the Kelseys' when the gun
was found and hadn't told anyone about it. Did her
mother know something else? "Because, Mom, if you
do…please tell me. I need all the help I can get. If
you know anything, anything at all—"

Alyssa stood. She crossed to the mantel and
reached with long, sensitive fingers to adjust a flower
in an arrangement. "No, I don't know anything," she
denied, but Amanda noticed a tightening of her voice.
"I just wondered, that's all. Ethan Trask and that man
who works for him seem to be talking to people all
over town," Alyssa continued. "I thought possibly…they might ask to speak with me."

"You were only seven when Margaret disappeared.
I doubt he thinks you'd know anything relevant."
Amanda hesitated. "Mom, again, if there's anything
that you—"

Alyssa wheeled around. From somewhere she'd
found a bright smile. "Come on," she said. "Enough
of this. You must be starving. Did you eat lunch today, or did you skip it? Clara told me how she prac-
tically had to force you to eat yesterday." She pulled
Amanda to her feet and, linking arms, guided her toward the kitchen. "She made the most wonderful
vegetable soup today."

Alyssa continued to talk, but Amanda had the uncomfortable feeling that her mother's determined
chatter was a cover for something else.

CHAPTER NINE

ETHAN STRETCHED OUT between unfamiliar bed sheets. As in many hotel rooms, the furniture was functional but not particularly comfortable. That went double for the bed. His six-foot-one-inch, 182-pound frame seemed to find every hard spot in the mattress. He moved about, searching for a more comfortable position, but only managed to make the situation worse. Uttering a mild curse, he sat up.

The room was dark except for a tiny strip of light admitted by the too-narrow window curtains. Traffic noise from the street outside was muted, but still audible. The stale, slightly plastic smell of the room mingled with the tang of antiseptic cleansers. Home, he thought wryly. Yet it could have been worse. The state was economizing. The latest joke to make its way around the attorney general's office was that state assistants would next be asked to pitch a tent whenever they went off on a case!

Ethan rubbed a hand over his jaw, feeling the stubble. He'd left the office earlier than usual to get some rest, but it didn't seem to be working out. He was all keyed up. His mind was full of information about the approaching trial.

Carlos had come back to the office that evening with more news about the financial troubles surrounding Ingalls Farm and Machinery. It seemed the business was experiencing the same kind of difficulties today as it had forty-two years ago, a short time after Judson had taken over management following his father's death. Carlos had talked to the manager of the bank that handled the F and M's account. It turned out the manager had been a clerk at the same bank all those years before, and with a little memory jogging, he had remembered the earlier troubles. The F and M had almost gone under, he'd said. Then a sudden infusion of cash had put it back on its feet—an infusion that had come just after Margaret Ingalls's disappearance. Judson Ingalls had walked into the bank one day with Margaret's signature on the bonds they jointly owned.

Carlos had also made tentative contact with the F and M's longtime accountant, who confirmed what the bank manager had told him. Tomorrow he and Ethan were going to talk formally with both men and take their statements.

Ethan swung his legs over the side of the bed and stood up. The line of light momentarily highlighted his nudity, clinging to his nicely contoured muscles. His body was long and lean, slim hipped, wide shouldered, athletic. Then he moved away from the light, going into the dressing area to pull on some clothes. He couldn't just continue to lie there. He was too restless. Gathering his keys, he thrust them into his pocket as he let himself out the door.

The case against Judson Thaddeus Ingalls was growing stronger. Ethan had no doubt at all that the man was guilty. As he settled behind the wheel of his car, his intent was to go back to the office; there was so much work to do to organize the case. But as the car rolled out of the hotel parking lot, it turned in the direction of Tyler.

"YOU NEED TO MAKE the prosecutor work for everything he gets," Peter said after examining the discovery information Amanda had brought with her. "Ethan Trask will want to control the courtroom. He'll try to make your grandfather look as if he has no feelings, as if he killed his wife, then went back to life as usual, behaving as if nothing untoward had happened. He'll say that Judson made no attempt to locate Margaret in all those years because he knew exactly where she was. What you'll have to do is supply an answer for every question Mr. Trask places in the jurors' minds. Give them a logical and innocent reason for everything that happened. You'll need to show your grandfather as a caring, compassionate man who loved his wife more than anything in the world. How he tried to keep the marriage together…he did do that, didn't he?"

Amanda nodded. She sat curled on the couch opposite Peter, who sat in a chair. "He did everything he could," she said.

"Then show it. Find witnesses who knew Judson and Margaret. Get them to tell the story."

"There aren't many left," Amanda reminded him. "Forty-two years is a long time."

Peter lapsed into silence, then he asked, "Have you thought about putting Judson on the stand? I know that's an extremely dangerous move…but sometimes it's necessary, particularly in a case like this."

"I've thought of it."

"How do you think your grandfather would hold up?"

"It would be hard on him, but he could do it."

"Do you think he'd agree?"

Amanda smiled slightly. "I think he'll insist."

Peter again paged through the witness statements, pausing to read here and there. Finally he looked up. "The prosecution always has something to prove," he stated. "Something they don't express outright because they can't—the judge wouldn't allow it. They manage to get it across, though. What do you think Ethan Trask might go for?"

Amanda answered without hesitation. "Judson Ingalls is a man of privilege, and because of that privilege, he thought he could get away with murdering his wife. Now it's up to the jury to show him that he can't."

"Class warfare," Peter murmured.

"In a way. That's what I'd do if I were him."

Peter smiled. "Maybe you should go into the prosecutor's office yourself. It sounds as if you've missed your calling."

"No, thank you," Amanda exclaimed. "I like what I was doing before all this came up. I like to help people with the little things of everyday life—setting up wills and trusts and executing contracts."

"Maybe this case will change your mind."

"I doubt it."

Peter moved in his chair, settling his pudgy body in a more comfortable position. "All right," he said, "now for the defense. Who is the defense going to put on trial? Margaret seems the logical choice. You show what kind of person she was—how she ran around with other men, playing fast and loose with everyone. You show how easily she could drive other

people to distraction. And how one of them—someone at the party?—could have easily murdered her."

"The person Phil Wocheck saw running from the
room."

"Exactly."

"I don't know if Granddad would like that. He
won't want me to besmirch Margaret's name."

"It's already going to be besmirched. It already *is*.
Ethan Trask, if he's worth his salt—and I think he
is—is going to play up Margaret's wanton behavior.
He'll show that Judson was wildly jealous, and that
on that final evening, Margaret pushed him over the
edge."

The weight crushing Amanda's spirit seemed to
grow heavier. She felt attacked from all sides.

A hand touched her shoulder. When she looked up,
she saw that Peter had come across the room. "The
hardest thing for you to do will be to keep your emotions from getting in the way. You claim that Margaret means nothing to you…but she's still your
grandmother. Your grandfather loved her. She bore
him a child, your mother. Her blood runs in your
veins. It's going to be more difficult than you think
to divorce yourself from that fact."

Moisture slid unwillingly into Amanda's eyes. So
many interwoven threads were needed to make a
whole. Her family history was one-quarter Margaret's. She could not ignore so large a part of herself
even if she wanted to. She had tried to, had tried to
pretend that Margaret was just a name from the past.
But she was more than that. Much more.

Amanda glanced at her watch. It was well after
nine o'clock. She had taken up far too much of the
professor's time. "Thank you, Peter," she said, stand-

ing up. "Thank you for everything. If I didn't have you, I don't know what I'd do."

"You'd do just fine," he insisted. "In actual fact, I'm helping very little—a few telephone calls, a few brief consultations. You're doing all the hard work, making the difficult decisions. I told you from the beginning that you have good instincts. Now all you have to do is learn to trust them."

Amanda leaned forward to kiss her old professor's cheek. "Still..." she murmured, giving him a sweet smile before gathering her things to hurry out to her car.

THE NIGHT WAS COOL, with a touch of the approaching winter in the air. It was crisp, quiet. Few people were on the road. Amanda didn't bother to put the top up on her little sports car, deciding instead to ride along with the wind blowing through her hair. She loved nights like this one. Stars by the thousands twinkled in the sky. The moon was a tiny sliver. The low, rolling pastureland zipped by on either side. For a few blessed moments she could forget.

Then up ahead she saw a car slewed to one side of the road. Huge forms were in both lanes, lumbering about. A man was in their midst, making what was doomed to be an inadequate attempt to herd them. When he saw the lights of her approaching car, he trotted toward her, waving his arms.

The growl of the MG's engine shifted from high to low as Amanda responded. Several black-and-white Holstein cows ambled past. She killed the engine and jumped out, ready to help.

"I'll cut around behind them," she offered. "If you'll stand over there and keep them going

straight…'' She stopped, the words dying on her lips.
The man wasn't just anyone. He was Ethan Trask.
Ethan Trask!

He looked just as taken aback as she was, just as
startled. What were the odds of two people—two people as different as they were, but as irrevocably
linked—meeting in such a place, in such a time?

He wasn't wearing a suit. He was wearing jeans…
jeans. And his cream-colored sweatshirt was unzipped
at the neck. If anything, the casual look magnified his
attraction. His dark hair was mussed, a shadow of
beard darkened his cheeks, his carved features somehow seemed more rugged. His obsidian eyes reflected
the night. Amanda felt frozen in place but not in body.
In her body, all kinds of amazing things were happening.

A second set of cows ambled past, breaking the
humans from their trancelike state. Ethan Trask said,
''I've been trying to get them back inside the fence
for the past ten minutes. They don't want to go.''

Amanda grinned to cover her alarm. ''Well, would
you, if you'd had a taste of freedom?''

''I'm afraid a car will come along and hit one, and
in the process hurt the driver. No one's been by,
though, except you.''

''This road is fairly isolated. How did you find it?
Were you talking to someone in the area?'' Amanda
glanced at the cows farthest from the break in the
fence, the pair that had gone past her. She started to
circle around them. ''You were lost, weren't you?''
she challenged.

Ethan did as she'd directed earlier. He stood aside,
ready to keep the cows from veering right as she
drove them forward. ''Actually, I was,'' he admitted.

The cows were occupied with the business of finding grass. Amanda walked up to one and waggled her hands. Then she clapped and waved her hands again. One cow raised her head, looked at Amanda and started to turn around. As it lurched away, so did a second, then a third. The fourth continued munching. Amanda kept after the moving cows. "Come toward them," she instructed. "Aim them toward the break. Make some noise," she added.

Ethan looked at her, then clapped his hands as she'd done. The cows continued to move, and soon they were back in the pasture. Ethan showed her the fence post. It was sheered off at the ground.

"We'll have to tell the farmer," Amanda said. "Any makeshift repairs we come up with won't hold."

They used the same procedure on the remaining cows, six in all, then went back to the recalcitrant cow that was still eating grass. She rolled her eyes toward them and stubbornly kept her head down.

"This must be the ringleader," Ethan decided. "What do we do with her?"

"Well, we can't leave her here." Amanda sighed and looked over at the others, which for the moment were content to remain inside the fence.

"Can we push to get her started?" Ethan asked.

"We can try," Amanda said.

She pushed from her side, and after getting no results, Ethan pushed from his. He was able to move her, but only a couple of steps. He started to go around back, but Amanda stopped him. "Not there," she said. "She might kick you."

Amanda bent down and gathered a generous handful of grass. She waved it in front of the animal's nose, then started to talk soothingly, rubbing the strong, muscular neck. After a moment, it had some effect. The cow shifted position and reached for the grass in her hand. Ethan quickly pulled up more grass. The cow reached for that, too. Amanda signaled for him to move back slightly, encouraging the cow to walk toward him. She did, causing Ethan to flash a quick smile. Together he and Amanda coaxed the cow in with the others and mended the fence as best they could.

Once they were done, Amanda pushed her hair away from her face. A light sheen of perspiration clung to her skin, dampening the tendrils. She laughed victoriously. "Well, we did it!"

Ethan ran a hand through his own hair. "I'm glad you came along. Otherwise I'd still be out there waving my arms and yelling."

"Something like this is hard for one person to do. Particularly for a city boy."

"How do you know I'm a city boy?"

She shook her head in mock pity. "It's *obvious*. You are, aren't you?"

"Pittsburgh."

Amanda grinned. "See?"

His dark eyes moved over her face, and Amanda felt a sudden shift in atmosphere. Her body tensed, tingled.

He broke eye contact. Shrugging, he looked out over the nighttime landscape. "This is definitely different from Pittsburgh."

"Do you like it here?" she asked, finding herself curiously short of breath.

"I've been away from Pittsburgh for so long...."

"You didn't answer my question."

He looked back at her. After a moment he said, "Yes, I like it here."

A curling sensation made its way through Amanda's core. They weren't just talking about the difference between Pennsylvania and Wisconsin. It was something else, something more elemental. She couldn't make herself look away.

"Do you find the people here...friendly?" she asked.

"Yes, for the most part."

"We pride ourselves on making visitors welcome."

He said nothing, merely continued to look at her.

Amanda was alive to everything about him. She knew when he breathed, when his heart beat. She could see a tiny pulse in his neck, just above a fine spray of dark chest hairs that didn't dominate so much as intrigue. She wanted to reach out and touch him, stroke the fine hairs, stroke the tiny pulse. Her hand moved, but she jerked it behind her back, anchoring it with the other.

What was the matter with her? Had she gone mad? She looked away, looked at anything but him. *She had to remember who he was!*

BLOOD POUNDED in Ethan's ears. He knew he should walk away. He knew what he was about to do was stupid in the extreme. She was his adversary, for God's sake! But a power greater than himself seemed to take hold of his hand and bring it to her cheek. Her skin felt like the softest of satin...smooth, creamy. Suddenly warm. Under the light of the stars, her eyes looked huge, startled. But she did not pull away. He could sense her heart flutter. His eyes dropped from her face to her small, rounded breasts. They strained against the soft material covering them. ''I don't—'' he started to say, strangling on the words.

His gaze caught hers again. She was the most beautiful woman he had ever seen. There was something about her, something...

His hand moved from her cheek to her hair, his fingers twining in the silky strands. Her eyes fell shut, her face lifted...and he could hold back no longer.

WHEN HIS LIPS touched hers, Amanda thought her heart might burst. She was out of breath, fighting for life. But she no longer needed oxygen, she needed him. She pressed her body close against him, seeking his warmth, seeking completion.

Her action excited him, causing the kiss to deepen. Her hands lifted to his neck, her fingers spreading in his hair. The springy strands slid easily over her skin. His body was strong, hard, the muscles tensed... working, pulling her even closer, straining to make her a part of him.

He gasped for breath when their lips eventually parted, his eyes glittering like the multitude of lights in the sky above. Then he came back for more, his mouth burrowing into the hollow of her throat, his tongue tracing a line of fire along the sensitive skin. One hand cupped a breast, fondling the soft flesh, teasing the hardening tip.

Amanda trembled. Her fingers fumbled with the zipper of his sweatshirt. She tugged on it, wanting to set him free, but it caught, wouldn't release.

She groaned in frustration, and the sound of her own voice, filled with such extreme emotion, brought

her back to the realization of what she was doing. Of
whom she was kissing with such abandon. Of whom
she was pressed against so ardently. Little about him
was left to her imagination. She wanted him, just as
he wanted her. But this wasn't right! Not between
them! They were on opposite sides of the upcoming
contest. Bitter enemies. Sworn foes. And they
couldn't just...

She jerked away, almost pulling him off balance as
she wrested herself from his arms. She then became
witness to his own realization, watched as thoughts
similar to her own played across his face.

His breathing was hard, ragged, in concert with
hers. He looked at her, and she could still see desire
deep in his eyes, just as she could feel it deep within
herself. If circumstances were different... But they
weren't different. Both were locked into a certain future, a future in which they were diametrically op-
posed.

"I didn't..." he started to say, his voice husky with
strain.

"Don't say anything," Amanda breathed, still
fighting for control.

She slipped as she tried to move away from him.
His hand shot out to offer assistance, but she wouldn't
take it. His hand slowly dropped away.

Amanda burned with embarrassment. How could
she have let such a thing happen?

ETHAN DIDN'T KNOW what to do next. Usually he had
more control over himself...*much* more control. He
didn't reach out and take what he wanted where
women were concerned. The few relationships he'd
had in his life had been ongoing, with women who

knew their minds as definitely as he knew his and who were equally fastidious. He didn't sleep around. He didn't give in to the quicksilver unreasonableness of passion. Except for just now.

The idea that he had done such a thing unnerved him. He glanced at her. She looked just as disquieted as he felt. He experienced a sudden need to protect her, and that, in its own way, was just as enervating. He didn't understand what was happening to him! She seemed to touch something in him that he didn't want touched. He thought about her when he didn't want to think about her. Now he had kissed her when he hadn't wanted to kiss— He stopped himself. Under oath, he would have to admit the truth. He had wanted to kiss her. He had wanted it like hell. And he still did! Her body had been just as he imagined it, all soft and warm and pliant, melting against him, making him delirious with his need for her.

Ethan clamped a tight lid on that line of thought. He was becoming aroused again, and if he just continued to stand there, next to her, he might… He straightened, adjusting his sweatshirt, checking the zipper that went only partway down the front.

NO WONDER! Amanda mocked herself. No wonder she couldn't get the darned thing down. Yet she should be grateful that she hadn't! What if the zipper had slid down easily? How far would they have gone before one of them called a halt? She looked at the cows, which had started to move toward the barn in the distance. Their moment of adventure was over. So, too, was hers.

"I'll stop by the farmhouse on the way back to town," she volunteered tightly. "If you keep on this road, you'll come to the highway to Sugar Creek. Go left when you get to it." She started for the MG.

"Should you do that by yourself?" he asked.

"I'll be a lot safer with Matthew Treager than I am with you," she snapped. Then she winced. She hadn't meant to give the impression of continued vulnerability.

"You have my word," he said stiffly, "it won't happen again."

"Good," Amanda returned, relieved that he had mistaken her reply. "Maybe then the judge won't have to rule you out of order for leaping over the defense table to get at me."

"Is this a new tactic?" he demanded. "Seduce the prosecutor if you think you have a weak case?"

Amanda spun around to face him. "My case isn't weak. Not in the least. For the simple reason my grandfather did *not* kill his wife!"

"I wouldn't be too sure about that if I were you, Counselor."

"Well, you're not me, Mr. Trask."

"Thank heaven!" he returned.

Amanda glared at him as she settled into her sports car. The engine started right away, and she quickly kicked it into gear. But before zooming off, she spared him one last look.

From where she sat, Ethan Trask's face was in shadow, his long, lean body taut. It didn't take much for her to remember being held against that hard form, to remember his mouth drinking thirstily from hers, to remember his searching hands.

And as she looked at him, she realized something else: no matter how many dueling words might fill the air between them in an attempt to obscure a mutual attraction, the attraction still existed. And there was precious little either one of them could do about it.

CHAPTER TEN

ETHAN WAS in a foul mood the next day. So much so that his temporary secretary found numerous excuses to leave the office, and even Carlos gave him a wide berth.

If anyone looked closely, they would have seen the ravages of a turbulent night. It had been hours before he'd gone to sleep, hours in which he'd had to fight every natural inclination he possessed. Both his body and his mind seemed disinclined to forget Amanda Baron, no matter how hard he tried.

And his mood hadn't been helped when he'd awakened this morning from a dream of her. They'd been in a crowded courtroom, with the judge on the bench, the jury in its box. He'd been involved in a direct examination of a witness…when the witness transmogrified into her. Suddenly she was sitting in the witness chair, looking both virginal and seductive, denying in front of everyone the attraction that had sparked between them. Unable to stop himself, he'd kept pounding away at her, trying to make her admit it. The judge had banged the gavel…and she was the judge! Then he'd looked at the jury, and all the members of the jury looked like her!

Was it any wonder that he felt more than a little ragged as he tried to get through the day?

Shortly after lunch, Carlos quietly entered the office. "It is time," he said.

"Time for what?" Ethan growled.

"Our appointment with Philip Wocheck. You said two o'clock."

Ethan tossed down his pencil and uttered a mild expletive.

Carlos offered, "Would you like me to change it to another day? A day when you feel more like—"

"Let's get the damned thing over with," Ethan said grouchily. "How about our interviews with the people at the bank and the F and M? Were you able to arrange a meeting for later this afternoon? We might as well make only one trip out there."

"They are both agreeable."

"Good. Then let's get going."

This time they took Carlos's car to Tyler. Ethan made no protest when the investigator offered to drive. Instead, he shielded his eyes from the bright afternoon sun and waited for the trip to be over.

Philip Wocheck was a temporary resident of Worthington House, Tyler's local retirement center and nursing home. After breaking his hip badly the year before, the old man had been forced to move from his usual quarters at Kelsey Boardinghouse. But soon, according to the administrator, he would be healed enough to move back.

Ethan and Carlos entered the old Victorian house that had been converted to a residence/care facility, and Ethan was impressed by the look of the place. It was very clean and homey, and the people he saw looked happy. Ethan had seen worse. In fact, he had once been part of an investigative team that had looked into the quality of care in the states' nursing homes. Most had been very good. Some had not. A few had had charges filed against them and the administrators had been brought to court.

A nurse directed the two men to Philip Wocheck's room. Carlos knocked on the door and they were told to enter. As they did so, Ethan was surprised to discover a small gathering of people there.

His glance took in the members of the group...only to stop at Amanda. His immediate scowl was a reaction to the chaos of his thoughts. She held his gaze, but didn't look comfortable.

A nicely dressed man with slightly graying dark hair stood up and offered his hand. "Mr. Trask, I'm Edward Wocheck, Philip Wocheck's son."

Ethan took his hand.

"My father has requested that I be present while you question him. He has also requested the presence of his lawyer. I believe you already know Amanda... Amanda Baron."

"I know her," Ethan said stiffly.

"And this is Amanda's brother, Jeff. Jeff is one of my father's doctors."

Ethan met the younger man's hostile look. He was tall, well-built and easily identifiable as Amanda's brother. They had the same chestnut hair, dark blue eyes and many of the same features. The doctor didn't offer his hand.

Ethan's gaze moved to the man who sat in a straight-backed chair. His face was strong, stubborn, his sharply angled features weathered with age. Bushy white eyebrows matched a full head of bristly white hair. He was a proud man and met Ethan's appraisal look for look.

Ethan offered his hand to Philip Wocheck, as did

Carlos. The old man's grip was firm even though his hands were gnarled from years of hard work.

"I didn't expect this to be a conference," Ethan said quietly. "In fact, I prefer that it not be."

Jeff Baron moved out of his chair. "What you prefer, Mr. Trask, and what you get might be two very different things!"

"Is there a reason Mr. Wocheck needs to have his doctor present?" Ethan countered, cold in the face of Jeff Baron's anger.

"I requested his presence, Mr. Trask," Edward Wocheck intervened. "My father has been through a trying time this past year, and I thought it best that he—"

"It is my understanding that your father is to be released from care within the next few weeks."

"He is, but—"

"And that he has given testimony before the grand jury. Was his doctor present then?"

"No, but—"

"Then I see no reason why he should be present now. We are in a hospital setting. If Mr. Wocheck should need emergency care, I'm sure that he would receive it. But I also see no reason why that should happen. All my colleague and I wish to do is speak with Mr. Wocheck." Ethan looked directly at the son. "Neither is your presence required, sir."

Edward Wocheck seemed at a loss for words, a circumstance that must have been unusual for such a high-powered individual. Ethan knew who he was— head of the worldwide Addison Hotel chain and in- strumental in the purchase of Timberlake Lodge. He also knew the man's history with the Ingalls family, of the early rejection of his suit for Judson Ingalls's daughter. This sudden collusion of families was suspicious.

When Edward finally started to sputter, Amanda stood up. "Mr. Wocheck, Jeff...please. It would be best if you let Phil talk to Mr. Trask alone. I know you're only trying to help, but—"

"I wish everyone except Amanda to leave," Phil Wocheck said quietly, speaking for the first time. A touch of his native Polish still flavored his words. "I have no fear of this man. This is not the old country, where people disappear. He wishes to talk, I will talk."

"But, Dad..." Edward protested. Ethan could sense fear in the younger man. Did he think his father might say something to incriminate himself? What did *he* know?

"I will talk!" Phil repeated stubbornly.

Amanda placed a hand on Edward Wocheck's arm, and Ethan experienced an unreasonable jolt of anger. The man was old enough to be her father, but he was also well preserved. It wouldn't be the first time an older man and a younger woman...

Edward's reply cut into Ethan's thoughts. "All right. We'll leave," he agreed, "but only because you ask us to, Dad. If you should need anything, anything at all, we'll be in the activity room down the hall." He then pushed out of the room, brushing past Ethan and Carlos without a word. Jeff Baron followed, but as he passed Ethan, he threw him a look that had nothing to do with the Hippocratic oath.

When Ethan turned back, he saw that Amanda had moved closer to Phil Wocheck. He didn't want her here, either. But after last night, his reasons were more complicated than they once might have been.

"Miss Baron," he said. "May I speak with you in the hall?" Carlos turned to look at him. "Carlos…if you would keep Mr. Wocheck company?"

"Certainly," Carlos murmured.

Ethan motioned for Amanda to precede him.

AMANDA WALKED with her head held high, her back straight and her knees quaking. She had tried to prepare herself not to react when she saw him again, but it had done little good. Her heart had leaped almost out of her chest the moment he'd walked through the door. Her body might have been on fire. She could barely sit still and listen to the jockeying that went on about her. She knew Jeff was angry; he seemed to be angry a lot these days. And she knew the cause—his own fearful doubt of their grandfather's actions. She had less of a handle on Edward's problem; she knew him only slightly. But her practiced eye saw that he was extremely worried. About something his father might accidentally say?

She and Ethan rounded the corner into an empty hall, away from the voices coming from the activity room. When he turned to confront her, his dark eyes moved over her face. Amanda did her best to show no reaction.

"You're interfering with my case again, Miss Baron," he said tightly. "Exactly how long have you been Philip Wocheck's lawyer?"

She lifted her head. "Length of time doesn't matter."

"It might if I take you before the Board of Attorneys."

"Is that another threat, Mr. Trask?"

"It's a promise, Miss Baron. They frown upon a

defense lawyer banding people together to protect a defendant. That little scenario in there just now…was it your idea?''

"Of course not!''

"I'm supposed to take your word for that?''

Amanda's blue eyes sparked. "Since everything I do seems to you to be suspect, probably not. But it's the truth. There are only two lawyers in town, Mr. Trask—myself and Marty Reese. Mr. Reese has his practice, I have mine. Some people prefer him, some prefer me. Tyler isn't a big city like you're used to. People have only a limited choice if they don't want to travel far from home.''

"It's odd, don't you think, that so many of the people involved in this particular case have you for their lawyer?''

"These people are my friends, Mr. Trask. I grew up knowing them. They know me.''

"It's still extremely convenient.''

Amanda fell back against the wall, shutting her eyes in exasperation. "Believe what you want, Mr. Trask! You will anyway!''

She waited for him to reply, to make another charge. When he didn't, she looked at him, and what she saw made her breath catch in her throat. Gone was the angry prosecutor, suspicious of everyone's motives. Suspicious, specifically, of her. In his place was the man beneath the polished surface—the elemental man, his passions exposed. The man she had seen last night…and responded to so uninhibitedly. Naked desire blazed in his dark eyes, igniting an answering desire inside her.

They might not have been in the corridor of a nursing home. They might not have been in the town of

Tyler. They were man and woman, caught in an attraction that was aeons old.

A nurse came out of a nearby room, startling them. "Oh! I'm sorry," she apologized, startled somewhat herself. She carried a fresh set of sheets and a lightweight blanket over her arm, on her way to a resident's room.

Amanda recognized her immediately—Juanita Pelsten. She knew her face was flaming when she said, "Juanita," in greeting, but she couldn't help it.

"Hi, Amanda," the older woman returned. Her eyes had widened as she took in the situation, and they widened even more when she recognized Ethan Trask.

Ethan nodded coolly, instantly snapping back to his professional demeanor.

Both of them watched as Juanita continued down the short hall, and both tried not to notice how the nurse glanced curiously back at them before disappearing from sight.

Amanda pushed away from the wall. "Well, that will be all over town before dark," she murmured.

Ethan frowned. "What do you mean?"

"Gossip. Surely you've heard of it."

"There was nothing for her to see," Ethan denied stiffly.

Amanda threw him a skeptical look.

"There wasn't!" he grated.

Amanda sighed impatiently. She didn't intend to argue about it with him. She knew Tyler much better than he did—let him find out the hard way. She was going to have a tough enough time on her own trying to explain. "Do I take it you still want to question Phil Wocheck?" she asked formally.

"Yes," he snapped.

"Then shouldn't we…" She flicked a hand toward Phil's room.

Ethan's body was rigid as he turned away. Was he angry with her, with the situation or with himself? she wondered. Was he angry that every time they came near each other something seemed to vibrate in the air between them, something that caused them to forget the barriers set so solidly in the way?

Amanda shivered as she fell into step at his side. She wasn't angry; instead she felt confused, unsettled, disjointed. She had never reacted to a man the way she reacted to Ethan Trask. This instant awareness, this instant attraction, this instant disregard for what she should do…if he were anyone else, if this were any other time, she might have a name to ascribe to her feelings. But not now. Not with him.

She wouldn't let it happen!

ETHAN PACED across the room like a panther on the prowl. The old man watched him steadily.

"You say you saw someone run from the room, yet you can't identify who that someone was. Why not?" Ethan demanded.

"Many years have passed. My memory…"

"Your memory seems perfectly in order when it comes to other things. You remember working in the grounds at Timberlake Lodge, you remember digging a hole to plant a tree, you remember hearing an argument, you remember hearing a gunshot, you remember going into the room, you remember finding Margaret Ingalls's body, you remember finding her note to her husband, you remember picking her up, you remember burying her…but you *don't* remember who you saw run from the room. Now that's a little farfetched, don't you think?''

Phil Wocheck shrugged. He seemed not at all upset by the prosecuting attorney's ire.

"What did the man look like?" Ethan asked.

"He was in shadows."

"How do you know it was a man?"

Phil snorted. "I can tell the difference."

"Was he tall, short, fat, thin?"

"Tall," Phil agreed grudgingly. "I told the police this before."

"You're telling me now."

"Average," Phil said.

"Average what?" Ethan asked.

"Average weight."

Ethan exhaled. He switched to another tack. "Tell me why you took the gun."

"I do not like guns."

"I didn't ask whether or not you like guns. I asked why you took it."

Phil shrugged.

"You'd seen it before, hadn't you?" Ethan pressed the question.

"I had."

"Where?"

"Around the lodge."

"Where 'around'?"

"I don't remember."

"In Margaret Ingalls's room?"

Phil shrugged again. He didn't say anything.

"You saw it there that night, isn't that correct?"

"Yes."

"The night you found Margaret Ingalls's body."

Phil nodded.

"Where was it?"

"On the bed."

"Who put it there?"

"I have no idea."

"Did you put it there?"

"No!"

"You also saw a suitcase."

Phil shrugged again.

Ethan shot a glance at Amanda. "I suggest you advise your client to talk to me. If he gets on the stand and continues to evade…" He turned back to Phil, his gaze burning. "Who told you to bury Margaret Ingalls's body?"

"No one! The whore wanted to go, so I helped her go!" Phil immediately reached out to touch Amanda's hand. "I am sorry. I do not like to speak ill of the dead, but your grandmother had already caused enough trouble. I did not want her to cause more."

Ethan didn't let up. "You expect me to believe that, without a word from anyone, you picked her up, took her out to the grounds where you'd dug the hole for the tree, and put her in it? Then you hid both the gun and her suitcase, and never said a word for forty-two years? And you did all this on your own? Give the state a little credit, Mr. Wocheck. Why would you do that? What would you have to gain? Money?"

"I wrapped her in a shawl I found on her bed," Phil said stubbornly.

Ethan frowned. "You wrapped her in a shawl?"

"The dead must be shown respect, even if they don't deserve it."

Ethan glanced at Carlos, who sat beside the tape machine, recording the interview. Unspoken communication passed between the two men. Amanda thought she recognized frustration.

Ethan came to stand near the chair Amanda had pulled close to Phil. She couldn't prevent her heart rate from quickening.

He seemed not to notice her, instead concentrating all his attention on the older man. "Do you realize that the statute of limitations never runs out on a person accused of being an accessory to a murder? That at this moment, for your part in what occurred all those years ago, I could charge you with such a crime? You buried the body, you had possession of the gun. That doesn't look good, Mr. Wocheck. I've successfully prosecuted murderers on a lot less evidence. You pulled wool over the eyes of the local D.A., but you haven't pulled it over mine. You have no immunity—you didn't ask for any. If you don't tell me the truth and tell it to me now, the minute I walk out of this room I'll start proceedings against you. One last time: *did* Judson Ingalls order you to bury the body?"

Amanda jerked forward. "Now wait just a minute. My client has agreed to speak with you. He has not agreed to subject himself to such gestapolike tactics!"

Ethan turned on her. "Your *client*—" he emphasized the word to underscore his doubt "—is withholding information. He's protecting someone. I want to know if that someone is Judson Ingalls."

"*My* client—" she emphasized the possessive pronoun "—is withholding nothing. He's told you everything he knows! As you said, he's asked for nothing. He voluntarily spoke with the police and testified before the grand jury. He didn't have to do either! In fact, I would have advised him not to, not without some assurances on your part.''

''Then it's a good thing for the prosecution that you've come to represent Mr. Wocheck only recently.''

Amanda glared into his dark eyes, eyes as uncompromising as the blackest night. She was getting the first inkling of what it would be like to sit across from him in a courtroom. And, in confirmation of his reputation, he was impressive.

Phil Wocheck shifted position, breaking the buildup of tension between the two lawyers. ''Why would I want to help that man?'' he asked. ''He did me no favors. I worked hard for him. I did my best. But he was not my friend. He was *never* my friend.''

Ethan motioned sharply for Carlos to shut off the tape recorder. But before the investigator could follow through, he lifted a hand again, temporarily stopping him. ''When you found the body,'' he asked, ''was there a lot of blood?''

''A lot of blood,'' Phil agreed.

''How much?'' Ethan asked.

Phil shrugged.

''A pint? A gallon?'' he demanded, his tone showing his skepticism of the older man's selective memory.

''Mr. Trask!'' Amanda broke in.

Ethan did not appreciate her intervention. ''From one wound? Or from others?'' he asked.

''Blood was on her hair, her neck, her shoulder. I did not look further.''

Ethan again signaled to his assistant, and then stepped in front of Phil. ''Think about what I said, Mr. Wocheck. If you change your mind, call me.''

He did not offer to shake either of their hands, and Amanda was glad that he didn't.

Once the two men were out of the room, Phil Wocheck's head sagged in exhaustion. Amanda poured him a glass of water. "I know this must be hard on you," she murmured.

Faded gray eyes focused on her. "And for you, too. You remind me very much of your mother when she was small, *malushka*. Like her, you are kind and sweet and gentle. Such people have many difficulties in this world. They must be watched over, cared for, protected...."

At that moment, Jeff burst into the room, with Edward following close behind him. "We saw Ethan Trask and his henchman leave. Are the two of you all right?"

"Of course we're all right," Amanda assured him, slightly put out with her brother for thinking they might not be. "The man isn't a fiend."

"He looked like some kind of fiend to me!"

"You're prejudiced."

The beeper Jeff wore on his belt went off, and he reached down to silence it. "I knew this couldn't last," he murmured. "Cece's just coming off duty. We were going to have coffee."

"Tell her I'll take your place," Amanda called after him as he hurried through the door. His quick backward wave told her that he'd heard and would comply.

Edward went to crouch at his father's side. "Is everything all right, Dad?" he asked.

Phil nodded.

Amanda stayed for only a few more minutes, sensing that father and son wanted to talk in private.

IF ANYTHING, Ethan's mood was worse as they got back into Carlos's car. He snapped his seat belt into place and stared into the distance. His mind was a thundercloud of dark thoughts.

So far, the day had been a huge zero. The only new thing he'd learned was that Phil Wocheck had wrapped Margaret Ingalls's body in a shawl before burying it. And that did him no good at all because no one cared, with the possible exception of Amanda Baron and her family.

Ethan wrenched his thoughts away from the defense lawyer. He couldn't take the time now to examine what was going on between them. He had to pull himself together. He couldn't let a physical attraction get in the way of the job he had to do. He was here to try a case to the best of his abilities. He couldn't let anything—*anything*—interfere.

He felt Carlos look at him once they had pulled out onto the street.

"This is Elm Street," Carlos said.

"So?" Ethan retorted grouchily.

"So that house...over there...is the Ingalls mansion."

Ethan looked in the direction Carlos pointed. He saw a huge, elegant Victorian, its front porch gracefully lined with colorful pots of geraniums. The car slowed to give him a good opportunity to view it.

"Judson Ingalls lives there," Carlos continued. "So does his daughter and her children."

Ethan's interest heightened. "They all live there together?" he questioned.

Carlos nodded, accelerating when a car came up behind them. "From what I could find out, Alyssa Baron came to live with her father after her husband killed himself. Having financial problems seems to run in the family, although everyone here seems to think they are rich. Alyssa had an inheritance from her mother's side that she spent trying to keep her husband's grain elevator open after he died. The elevator was eventually sold, but she realized no profit. Both Jeff and Amanda were in college at the time. Judson Ingalls kept them in school, then helped them, when he could, through their various graduate schools. They are a very close family.''

''Still…'' Ethan murmured.

''People in town think Alyssa Baron wants to keep her family close. They think it has something to do with her mother leaving her at such an early age. She is afraid of being abandoned.''

''Her youngest child doesn't live with them,'' Ethan pointed out.

''No, but her youngest child never seems to have done what her mother wanted.''

''Or what we want,'' Ethan said, thinking of the barely civil turndown of his request for an interview with Liza Forrester.

''Jeff Baron married a few years after he finished medical school, but the marriage did not last, and he moved back home. Now he is about to marry a woman who works at Worthington House—Cece Scanlon Hayes, Annabelle Scanlon's daughter. Annabelle thinks he is quite wonderful. She also admires Amanda. She says she is one of the nicer, more worthwhile people in town.''

Ethan suddenly grew suspicious. ''Why are you telling me this, Carlos?''

''I thought you might like to know. You seemed…interested.''

"I'm only interested because she's my adversary. I didn't like having to reveal part of my case to her today, especially when it concerned Philip Wocheck."

Carlos nodded. He didn't say anything.

"That's all it is, Carlos," Ethan stated, feeling the need to repeat himself.

Again Carlos nodded, and again he didn't say anything.

Ethan ground his teeth. The only thing left to do was change the subject. "Phil Wocheck is holding something back. I know he is. I can taste it."

"He will not be an easy man to break," Carlos agreed. "He has nothing to lose."

"Except his freedom. He could spend his remaining years in prison."

"He knows you will not do such a thing. You want the person who killed Margaret Ingalls, not the person who buried her. Philip Wocheck did not kill her," Carlos concluded with instinctive certainty. "He did not even help. There is a reason he did what he did, but he will go to his grave before he tells it."

Ethan massaged his forehead. This was proving to be one of the longest, most difficult days he had spent in a long time. It rivaled his first days on the job in the district attorney's office in New York City, when he had come fresh from law school to idealistically save the world...and had instead been crushed by the caseload and by the confusion at the Criminal Justice Building.

Carlos was right. He needed Phil Wocheck. Without the testimony of the only person who had heard the gunshot, his case lost merit. But it irked him that that same witness was holding something back, something that undoubtedly concerned the past criminal behavior of his old employer, Judson Ingalls.

"Do we have time for a quick cup of coffee before we meet with the bank manager?" he asked.

With an understanding smile, Carlos nodded.

CHAPTER ELEVEN

THE NEXT MORNING, Amanda received the remaining materials from the prosecuting attorney's office. Again, Carlos Varadero was the agent. His smile was wide as he delivered the second box. He dug in his pocket for a brown envelope. "Something else," he murmured, placing it on top.

Amanda, who had been feeling rather raw since awakening shortly after daybreak, accepted the information with a dispirited nod. She knew she should pretend total confidence, but adequate confidence would just have to do. She didn't possess the energy or the enthusiasm for more. "Thank you," she said.

Instead of hurrying away as she expected, the investigator propped himself on the edge of the table next to the box and took a moment to inspect her office. His gaze finally settled on her.

"I, too, come from a small town," he said. "A place where people grow up knowing one another. Where one person's problems are the problems of everyone else. In Cuba. Before Fidel."

Amanda watched him with interest. His uneven features were infused with the power of his personality, a strong will buttressing an affable sense of humor.

"Where people gossip easily," he continued, "telling many tales. I understand a place like this. Ethan does not.''

He paused, waiting for Amanda to say something.

Amanda looked down at the papers she had been studying before his arrival. ''Oh?'' she murmured.

''Ethan has been deprived. He trusts no one except himself. That is the lesson life has taught him.''

Amanda twirled a pencil. ''Surely he trusts you.''

''To a degree.''

She looked up. ''Are you making excuses for him?''

''I make excuses for no one.''

''Then why are you telling me this?''

Carlos smiled, as if he had been asked that question before. ''Because I believe you to be…interested. He is a good man beneath all the harshness. I would not wish you to see the one thing and miss the other.''

''He's prosecuting my grandfather for murder, Mr. Varadero.''

The investigator shrugged.

Amanda marched across the room and opened the box. If she gave him the idea that she was busy and wanted him to leave, so much the better. He didn't take the hint; he stayed where he was, watching her. She flashed him an angry glance. ''What do you want me to do?'' she demanded. ''Thank him for it? Thank him for turning all our lives upside down?''

''Just remember,'' he said softly. ''He did not choose this case. It chose him.''

''That's drawing an extremely fine line, Mr. Varadero.''

''But an important one.'' Straightening, he pushed away from the table. After giving her a small salute, he left the office in just as unassuming a manner as he had entered it.

Amanda made her way back to her desk and sat down. She stared at the door but didn't truly see it. He knew! He'd either guessed at the attraction that sprang up between her and Ethan Trask each time they met, or he had heard something through Tyler's grapevine. No one from town had said anything to her yet, but she was sure Juanita wouldn't have kept all to herself such a juicy tidbit as the scene she'd interrupted at Worthington House.

Exactly what had Carlos been trying to tell her? That he approved? Ethan Trask…deprived. He certainly didn't look deprived! No, this had to be a prosecution trick. Ethan was always accusing her of using some kind of chicanery. Maybe *he* was the one using his undoubted sexual appeal to undermine *her*. Maybe he had sent Carlos Varadero to unsettle her, to gain her sympathy. Well, it wasn't going to work! She could harden her heart against him as well as the next person; she could control her salacious instincts. She could… Amanda called a halt to her thoughts.

That wasn't Ethan Trask's method of operation. From everything she had heard and seen, he was a very straightforward individual, very direct. Trickery was not a part of his personality.

So Carlos Varadero truly had been trying to tell her something. Something that she had previously shied away from. Something she *still* didn't want to look at too closely.

She went back to the box and dug into the contents, busying herself with what she found. There were numerous photographs and diagrams of the lodge, of

Margaret's old room, of the burial site. Photographs of Margaret's skeletal remains...

A shudder passed through Amanda's body as she held up the last series of glossy prints. She'd known this was coming. She'd known that one day she would see Margaret in such a state. It couldn't be avoided. But the actual shock of it drove everything else from her mind. She forgot about Ethan; she forgot about Carlos Varadero and what he'd said. She forgot about everyone and everything except her family. How were they going to react when copies of these prints became state's evidence?

AT HOME THAT EVENING, Alyssa watched her older daughter with brooding eyes. Perhaps the family had put too much pressure on Amanda. She was the instrument of all their hopes, but her shoulders didn't look strong enough. Alyssa better than anyone knew her daughter's strengths. She was proud of her for what she'd accomplished, proud of her for the person she was. But she didn't want Amanda's sense of duty and loyalty to crush her in the end. To break her spirit.

Early the next morning, she tapped lightly on Amanda's door. "Good morning," she said, after receiving permission to enter. "I've brought you some tea, some oatmeal and a piece of toast. And I want you to eat every bite."

She waited as Amanda struggled to sit up, pushing her wavy hair away from her face. "What time is it?" Amanda asked, peering at her from still-sleepy eyes.

"Seven o'clock."

"Oh my gosh!" Amanda cried, throwing the covers off her legs. "I'm late! I wanted to be in the office by seven. There's so much to do, so much to—''

Alyssa placed a firm hand on her shoulder. ''First you eat, then you work. Remember the rule?''

Amanda grinned ruefully. ''Mom, I'm all grown-up now.''

''A person never outgrows good eating habits. Adjust the covers. I want to put this down.'' She indicated the tray she carried.

Good-naturedly, Amanda did as she was instructed. ''But I'm not hungry,'' she protested.

''I won't take no for an answer.''

Amanda took one bite and then another, warming to the task. ''What about you?'' she asked after a moment. ''Have you eaten?''

''I don't have any meetings this morning. I thought I'd enjoy a nice leisurely brunch after everyone leaves.''

''But you will eat,'' Amanda persisted.

''Of course.''

''There's no 'of course' about it. If I have to eat, you have to eat. Promise?''

Alyssa couldn't repress a smile. When her daughter looked at her like that, it reminded her so much of Amanda as a child—the same earnest little face, the same steadfastness. Amanda was not a person to give her heart freely, but when she did, it was forever. Luckily for all of them, her affection for her family was firmly grounded. ''I promise,'' Alyssa assured her.

Amanda returned to her meal, finishing it in short order. Then she sat back to sip her tea. ''Mom,'' she said after a moment, ''I've been thinking. Maybe when Granddad's trial comes up, you should consider going away for a while.''

Alyssa froze. ''Why?'' she breathed.

''Because…it's not going to be easy. Things are going to be said. About Granddad, about…your mother. It might be easier for you not to hear them.''

''You think I haven't already?''

Amanda hesitated. ''The trial will be worse.''

Alyssa looked deeply into her daughter's eyes, then she turned away. Panic spread through her. *The dream.* Again she saw herself…saw herself *seeing* herself…heard a voice whisper reassuringly. Then there was still more pain and fear…. Drawing in a ragged breath, she stood up. Her instinct was to run! But where?

Amanda had jumped to her feet and was at her side. ''Mom…it's all right. Mom!''

The edge of alarm in her daughter's voice forced Alyssa to fight for control. The object of this morning's visit hadn't been to make the situation worse for Amanda. It had been to help her, to make things better. And now…

Alyssa patted the arm wrapped around her shoulders, even though her fingers still trembled lightly. ''I'm all right. I just… For a moment, I…''

Amanda was not mollified. ''Let me get Jeff.''

Alyssa shook her head. ''No! I'm fine. As you said…it's going to be hard. But if everyone else can face it, so can I. I'd feel like a traitor if I left Dad alone. He can't hide from it, and neither should I.''

''What if *he* asked you to leave?''

''I wouldn't do it.''

''Mom, there'll be photographs. They're not pretty.''

Alyssa fought down another moment of panic. "I'll still be there," she said bravely.

Amanda squeezed her mother's hand, but her eyes remained worried.

A tap on the door caused both women to jump, then giggle, releasing of some of their tension. Jeff poked his head inside before the rest of his large body followed. "What's going on?" he demanded. "It sounded like an argument, but now you're laughing!"

Amanda recovered first. "Who wouldn't laugh? Have you looked at yourself in a mirror yet today?"

He rubbed his rumpled hair and straightened his lopsided bathrobe. "I just woke up! Leave me alone."

Alyssa seized the moment to gain a little time on her own. "How would you like the same treat I gave Amanda?" she asked. "Breakfast in bed."

Jeff grinned. He wasn't too sleepy to turn on the charm. "You're offering?" he asked.

"I'm offering."

As she left the room, she paused long enough to kiss her son's bristly cheek. But once she was outside the door, the smile she wore disappeared. If Amanda only knew how much she truly did want to turn her back on the future! On all the days when she would have to walk proudly into court and listen to things being said about her father and her mother...and not show any emotion. All the days when she would be forced to remember a past she had done her best to forget.

The dream. The phantasm again pushed itself into her consciousness, making her cover her ears to drown out an echoing sound. She had to stop thinking about it! It was like a curse, afflicting her. A piece of film to be run over and over, so real and yet so fantastic.

With haunted eyes, Alyssa pushed away from the wall and hurried downstairs to the kitchen.

JEFF AND AMANDA LOOKED at each other after their mother left. Each knew what the other was thinking.

"Will she be all right?" Amanda asked, requesting an off-the-cuff medical/psychological opinion.

"God, I hope so," Jeff replied, running his fingers through his hair. "What was that about?" he asked, referring to the assignation he had interrupted.

"I advised her to leave town when the trial starts, but she refused."

"Is that a good idea?" Jeff asked, frowning.

"Probably a better one than staying here. It's really going to be rough, Jeff. Even rougher than we thought. And with a television camera in court... I saw some pictures yesterday. Photographs of the remains." Her voice wavered, prompting Jeff to take her hand. She looked at him. "I didn't think it would affect me, but it did. Those bones were *Margaret.* When we used to go to the lodge, when Mom and Dad didn't know we were there... We *played* around that willow tree, Jeff! We played on her grave. She was our grandmother!"

The Baron siblings, once they reached a certain age, had followed the example of their elders. No one talked about the lodge. No one talked about Margaret. No one talked about Margaret's disappearance. Not even when the skeletal remains were found had they done more than worry about their grandfather and their mother. The past seemed vaguely off-limits, and Margaret a long-lost entity. Until now.

Jeff lightly stroked her fingers. "I know what you mean. I've thought of that, too." He drew a long breath. "In my occupation, I should be used to death. And to bones. We even had a human skeleton at med school we called Harry. But somehow, this…this is different."

"I'm worried about how Mother will react. She has memories of Margaret, memories of the real, live, breathing person. She loved her."

"What about Granddad?"

"Granddad is stronger. It will be awful, but he'll get through it."

"But Mom may not?" Jeff speculated.

Amanda agreed. "We'll have to watch her closely. There's something about the way she looks sometimes.…"

"I've arranged for time off during the trial. George owes me for the time he took when he eloped with Marge. Which reminds me—Cece and I have arranged something. The Saturday before the trial starts, we're getting married. Just family, in church. Then we're going to the Dells for the rest of the weekend, but we'll be back in time for the start of the trial. I'll be in court every day that Mom is. I'll watch out for her, so you won't have to worry. You'll have enough to think about without that."

Amanda gave her brother an impulsive hug. "Oh, Jeff, that will mean so much."

"I'll be rootin' for ya, kid," he said in his best boxing-movie imitation. Then he held her away from him to study her face. "I heard a rumor yesterday," he said. "Something I didn't believe.… Is there something going on between you and Ethan Trask?"

Amanda blinked. She felt warmth rush to her

cheeks, so she spun away to hop back in bed, tucking the tail of the overlarge T-shirt she slept in under her legs as she drew her knees up toward her chin. "Who said that?" she asked.

"It's making the rounds at the hospital. It's also spreading around Worthington House. Cece heard it."

"Since when have you two listened to gossip?"

"Since it concerns you," he replied. He looked at her suspiciously. "You haven't denied it."

"I don't think I should have to! Ethan Trask is the last person I'd pick to get involved with. He's way out of my league."

Jeff's eyes narrowed. Amanda tried to hold his gaze, but ended up looking down at the bed cover and brushing away a few crumbs. She sensed rather than saw her brother frown. "I should certainly hope so," he said. "Hard, unyielding men don't make good husbands. I wouldn't want you getting mixed up with someone like that."

"Should I warn Cece off?" Amanda asked innocently.

At first Jeff didn't get the connection, but he soon grinned. "She already knows all my worst faults, and she still wants to marry me."

"More fool her," Amanda teased. Then she had to protect herself from Jeff's sudden attack with her spare pillow.

Laughing, he collapsed on the bed at her side, making the mattress bounce under his weight. "I wish I could give her a better honeymoon," he complained. "Hawaii or Tahiti or someplace like that."

"I doubt the place will matter," Amanda said, turning over to prop her head on her elbow.

"Not when she has me." Jeff grinned again, then

glanced at her bedside clock. "Oops. Gotta go. Duty calls in less than an hour." But before he moved away, he paused. "I meant what I said about Ethan Trask. The man gave me the willies."

"You acted like you wanted to punch him."

"I wouldn't have minded," Jeff admitted.

"He didn't ask for this case, remember."

"But he didn't turn it down, either."

"Why would he?"

"You tell me."

"You're being unreasonable, Jeff."

"And you're getting angry. Why?"

Amanda was stymied. Jeff gave her a quick smile and left the room.

TESSIE GREETED Amanda at the office with a fistful of telephone slips. She went through them quickly, separating the most urgent from those that could wait. One that piqued her interest was from Conrad Frayen, the longtime head of accounting at Ingalls F and M. He'd left a message saying it was extremely urgent that she call him.

Conrad Frayen was not the sort of man to overreact. Deliberate in both manner and disposition, he had held his position for a good fifty years. In fact, they'd celebrated his fiftieth year with the company only about a year and a half ago. If Conrad said something was extremely urgent, it was.

Amanda tucked her purse into the usual desk drawer and reached for the phone. The voice that answered her call was dry with age, almost reedlike.

"I'm not sure if this is something I should be doing or not," Conrad said. "I've thought about it for two days, but after last night...I couldn't sleep a wink. I kept thinking about what I'd said and what he said, and I just knew I had to call you. I'm worried about something that might look bad for your grandfather, Amanda. Ethan Trask and his assistant came to see me the day before yesterday. Actually, his assistant talked to me the day before that, got a little of the story and left. Then he came back with reinforcements." Conrad paused for breath, giving a slight wheeze. "It's about some trouble the F and M had about the time your grandmother disappeared."

"What kind of trouble?" Amanda asked.

"Money trouble. Maybe even a little worse than we're in today. Place was going to close if we didn't get some quick cash."

Amanda frowned. She hadn't known the company had been in a similar condition before.

"Judson and Margaret owned some bonds," Conrad continued. "Judson wanted her to sign her part over to the company, along with his, of course. He'd only added her name to them out of sheer stupidity. I told him not to, but he wouldn't listen. Well, she refused. She wouldn't do it. And Judson was really upset."

"What happened?" Amanda breathed, afraid that she already knew.

"Judson got her to sign them before she left. That's what he told me. He cashed them in at the bank, and we were able to save the F and M." Conrad paused. "Ethan Trask seemed mighty interested. I'm afraid he's taking the wrong spin on what happened. I know Judson. I've worked for him ever since he took over the company after his father passed on. He's not the sort of person to cheat...or to kill. But Ethan Trask's going to put me on the stand. He's going to make me say things that will *look* terrible for your grandfather. I don't want to do it, but I don't see how I can refuse. He took my statement. It's all on record, even if I suddenly die. Kept me up all last night thinking about it.''

Amanda's gaze alighted on the brown envelope Carlos Varadero had pulled from his pocket. In her upset state, she'd forgotten about it. She'd looked through everything else and had seen no mention of Conrad Frayen. His testimony must be in the envelope. ''You did what you had to do, Mr. Frayen,'' she said reassuringly.

''But I feel like I've betrayed Judson. I started to tell him earlier, but I just couldn't make the words come out. He's been good to me, fair. I wouldn't want to say anything that would—''

Amanda cut in. ''He'd want you to tell the truth, Mr. Frayen. So do I. Thank you for calling, though. You've done nothing wrong. I probably would have contacted you later in the day myself.''

''How would you have known?'' the accountant asked.

''Ethan Trask has been ordered to give me any information he collects pertaining to the trial.''

''Well, then…'' Conrad Frayen sounded noticeably happier. ''I don't feel half so bad.''

Amanda smiled tightly and disconnected. He might not feel ''half so bad,'' but she certainly did. She felt worse. The noose around her grandfather's neck was tightening bit by bit. His motive for murdering Margaret had now been strengthened.

She walked over to the envelope and opened it. As she expected, it contained a copy of Conrad Frayen's statement and also one by Fred Dryer, her grandfa-

ther's bank manager. With a sick feeling, Amanda
added them to the contents of the box.

THE NEXT ELEVEN DAYS were hectic. Amanda worked
from sunup to well past midnight, poring over endless
pages of notes and absorbing as many details about
the case as she was able. She interviewed prosecution
witnesses, going over their accounts, looking for discrepancies. She even talked to a couple of potential
witnesses in Chicago that Leo, her investigator, had
found. She spoke with experts, making arrangements
with those she might call to testify. She found people
who would act as character witnesses for Judson. She
had several sessions with Peter, both to refine her own
strategy and to speculate on the prosecution's. She
worked again with her grandfather, trying to pull from
his mind all the information she could, while also
starting to prepare him for an appearance on the stand.
She hadn't formally talked to him about that yet,
though.

The only bright spot in the entire period was near
the end, when Jeff and Cece were married. As they
had requested, the wedding was quiet, but it was also
quite beautiful. Cece wore a pale blue dress, befitting
her widowhood, and a fingertip veil, with her dark
hair shining loosely around her radiant face. Jeff, in
a dark suit, looked extremely handsome and in love,
certain that this time he wasn't making a mistake.
When Cece tossed her bouquet, it was playfully
aimed at Amanda. Everyone clapped and teased her,
and Amanda took it in good spirits. After the small
reception at the Ingalls's mansion, Cece kissed her
mother and a visiting aunt goodbye, while Jeff made

the rounds of his family. Then they were off to start their life together.

The little group they left behind broke up shortly afterward, but the feelings of goodwill lingered. Amanda placed the bouquet in a small vase of water on her bedside table, and as she lay in bed that night, trying to fall asleep, she periodically reached out to touch a cream-colored rose petal.

THE NIGHT BEFORE the start of the trial was stormy. The wind blew rain against the windows in sheets. Amanda couldn't sleep. Her stomach was tied in countless knots, her nervous system set on high. The next day, Tuesday, was going to be the start of one of the most difficult periods in her life. She had been working so hard, trying to cover every angle, that she couldn't switch her mind off. She hadn't seen Ethan Trask more than three times in the past eleven days. Undoubtedly, he had been working just as furiously as she had. Tomorrow she would see him. Tomorrow…in the courtroom.

Her stomach lurched. Peter had warned her she might react this way. It wasn't unusual, he said, for a lawyer to have pretrial jitters. The best thing, he advised, was exercise. Go out for a run, ride a bicycle. But she couldn't do either, not in the middle of the night in the rain. Instead, she paced from one side of her room to the other.

Finally, unable to stand confinement any longer, she went downstairs, being careful to make as little noise as possible. She was just about to enter the kitchen when she came upon an unexpected scene: her grandfather pouring a cup of tea for both himself and her mother. He was wearing the robe Amanda had bought him for Christmas—a garnet-red velvet with black piping around the collar and sleeves. Her mother looked fragile in a pale yellow wrapper that emphasized the golden strands of her hair. Alyssa wore no makeup; her grandfather hadn't shaved.

Judson poured the tea and slid a cup toward Alyssa. Then he sat down across from her and took her hand. No words passed between them, but words were unnecessary. Life had not been easy for either, but through it all they had remained close. Now they were to be tested again.

Amanda turned silently away, unwilling to interrupt, even though she knew she would be welcome.

CHAPTER TWELVE

THE MORNING the trial began broke clear and bright, with few aftereffects of the storm the night before. The media were out in force, blocking the entrance to the courthouse and clogging the halls inside. Ethan pushed his way through the crowd, murmuring answers to questions when he chose to and ignoring others. He was wearing a dark, charcoal-colored suit cut of lightweight wool, a white shirt and a tie with splotches of black, gray and red. There was not a crease out of place or a speck of unwanted dust. He'd had his hair cut three days before so it wouldn't look "fresh"; his shoes were shined, his nails buffed. He could have been a knight suited up in his best armor, ready to joust.

He brushed through the doors into the courtroom assigned for the trial. Like all the other courtrooms he had seen in this building, it was huge. Decorative plaster molding graced the high ceiling, while rich walnut paneling covered most of the walls and was repeated in the judge's bench, the jury box, the attorneys' tables and the carved wooden railing that separated the well from the straight-backed pews of the spectators' gallery.

As was the custom, the prosecutor's table was closest to the jury. Ethan placed his briefcase on the flat surface and flicked open the catches. As he started to remove some of its contents, a commotion erupted in the hallway outside. He didn't need to turn around to know that Judson Ingalls had arrived.

He heard the swell of noise as the doors opened and closed. A voice caused a pang to shoot through his system—a woman's voice, Amanda!—assuring someone that everything would be all right.

He steeled himself to face her. He felt more than heard the small group come through the railing's low-slung gate and collect at the defense table. Then he looked over, straight into her eyes.

She stood a little apart from the others. Today she wore a neat black suit with a pale pink blouse. Her hair was brushed away from her face, her makeup applied with care, her nails lightly enameled. She, too, had come dressed for battle. But beneath her polished exterior, her blue eyes looked bruised from fatigue, and if he could be one to judge, she was several pounds lighter.

Their gazes held, sparked and quickly broke apart.

He examined the others who were with her. Judson Ingalls he recognized immediately—a tall, straight, refined man dressed in his Sunday best, with a thatch of white hair above a strong and determined face. Their eyes met. Judson Ingalls nodded in acknowledgment of their differing roles. Ethan nodded shortly in return.

At Judson Ingalls's side was a tall, slender woman who had confronted middle age with amazing ease. Blond, fine-featured, she held herself proudly, but there was a strong tension just beneath the surface of her movements. She said something to Amanda and gave her a quick hug before drawing the others back toward the gate. Alyssa Baron, Ethan decided.

Jeff Baron was there, his concern still masking itself as anger. A pretty, dark-haired woman was at his side, holding on to his arm. Jeff looked at him and glared. Ethan showed no emotion.

Just as the small group found seats to the rear of the defense table, another cluster of people arrived. A second tall, blond woman—this one greyhound lean and a number of years younger than the first—rushed up to Judson Ingalls to give him a quick hug. A quiet, handsome man pulled her away, leading her back to the others, who had contented themselves with leaning across the railing. A plump man and woman murmured platitudes, and an older man with white hair patted Judson on the back.

The Ingalls family…presenting a united front.

Ethan arranged several yellow legal pads and a handful of sharpened pencils in front of him and sat down.

THE JURY was agreed upon with amazing swiftness. It took only three hours to cull the crowd of candidates to fourteen people—eight men and six women, two of whom were retained as alternates. Heeding Peter's admonition, Amanda had used her period of questioning to subtly start bringing the prospective jurors around to her point of view, as well as connecting with them on a human level. In the end, she was fairly happy with the mix achieved—different races, different ages, different levels of education. Anyone with obvious prejudice had been excused; so, too, had anyone unduly influenced by the media coverage. The only remaining point to bother Amanda was that Ethan seemed pleased as well.

They broke for lunch, then afterward came back to

begin the trial itself. A jolt of electricity might have been set loose in the courtroom. Everyone felt it. It was the sort of tension that kept people on the edge of their seats, afraid to blink because they might miss something.

Judson, most highly affected by the spectacle, stumbled slightly as he came to take his chair. Amanda quickly reached out to assist him, aware of the gasps from the assembled onlookers. He was pale, much paler than she had ever seen him. She whispered words of assurance in his ear. What he was feeling was natural, she said.

Her own stomach fought with the cup of coffee and piece of dry toast she'd eaten for lunch. Now she wished she'd had nothing. She glanced at Ethan. He looked calm and cool and very confident.

"Please rise. Court is now in session," a court officer called, and Judge Eustace D. Griffen ascended to the bench. While everyone remained standing, the judge instructed that the jury be brought in. Soon the fourteen people, looking self-conscious and sober, filed into the room and took their respective seats in the jury box.

The jury was sworn in and the judge addressed them, giving an overview of the trial process: first would come the opening statements, then the prosecutor would present his witnesses, with cross-examination by the defense counsel, followed by the defense counsel presenting her witnesses, with cross-examination by the prosecution. Next there would be time for rebuttal by both sides—an interval when no new evidence could be introduced, only witnesses brought to refute charges made during testimony. Finally, the closing arguments would be presented, and the judge would then give the jury instructions as to the law.

"I want to reiterate," Judge Griffen said, tilting down his chin so that the jury got the full effect of his basset hound expression, "that in this case, as in all cases, the defendant is presumed innocent. The state has to prove that he is guilty beyond a reasonable doubt. You are to consider only the evidence presented in this court. I also want to remind you that opening statements are not evidence. They are merely a prediction, a forecast—a road map, if you will— that tells you in a clear and concise manner what the evidence will be. The lawyers are not allowed to draw inferences at this time, nor will they." He looked at Ethan. "Are you ready, Mr. Trask?"

Both Ethan and Amanda knew they had been served notice not to stray from the appointed path.

Ethan stood up. "Your Honor, I request that all witnesses be excluded from the courtroom."

"Any argument?" the judge asked Amanda.

She got lightly to her feet and shook her head. "No, Your Honor."

The judge ruled, "Motion carried," and any witnesses present had to leave. That included Liza, whose protesting whispers forced Amanda to turn around and quietly add her directive to the judge's. Once the courtroom settled down again, the judge looked at Ethan and prompted, "This time, Mr. Trask?"

"May it please the court," Ethan said as he stood up, the traditional beginning. He walked to the podium facing the jury. "My name is Ethan Trask. I am the prosecutor assigned to this case by the state of Wisconsin. First, I want to thank you for answering the call. Service on a jury, particularly one that is sequestered, is difficult. You will be away from your homes, separated from your families, but what you are about to undertake is one of the highest duties of citizenship in a free society.

"As prosecutor, it is my obligation to present evidence for you to weigh in your deliberations as to the guilt of the defendant. You must decide if the defendant, that man—" he pointed at Judson casually, but with the deadly aim of a seasoned gunfighter "—killed his wife, Margaret Ingalls.

"Evidence will be presented to show that theirs was a troubled marriage. They they had many arguments, which became particularly intense in the last months of Margaret's life. That they argued about her lovers and about money. Evidence will show that he was infuriated by her life-style and by her neglect of their daughter. It will also show that he was in dire need of money because the business that had been in his family for several generations was about to fail. That he tried to make his wife sign a series of bonds they owned together so that he might cash them, and she refused.

"You will hear how they fought again one last time the night she disappeared. You will hear about the blood on the carpet of the floor of her room, and how he hid that carpet away. You will hear about the bullet that was found in a baseboard of the room, how the gun that fired that bullet was one of a matched set belonging to him.

"You will hear from experts who will tell you the blood on the carpet was Margaret Ingalls's. You will hear how science today can match blood found on an object to that of its previous host, even if that host is now nothing more than a collection of bones. You will hear from an expert how the body of Margaret Ingalls was identified through her dental records; how the poor, sad remains had to be pieced together, sometimes like a jigsaw puzzle, in order for the cause of her death to be determined. You'll hear how the body was discovered buried on the defendant's lakefront estate.

"You will hear how forty-two years ago he pretended that his wife had run away. And how, in all those passing years, he never made the slightest attempt to find her. You will hear all of this and much, much more." Ethan paused, looking closely at each juror in turn. "As the judge said," he continued, "at the end of the trial he will give you instructions as to the application of law in this case. It will be your obligation to examine all the evidence you have seen and heard presented here. And in so doing you will find that the defendant, Judson Ingalls, is guilty of first-degree intentional homicide, as charged."

Everyone's attention was riveted on Ethan. His voice had rung with complete conviction. His body was poised, waiting. Then he walked back to his place at the prosecution table and sat down.

"Ms. Baron?" the judge requested.

Amanda squeezed her grandfather's hand and stood up. She was aware that every eye had now turned to her, not only those present in the courtroom, but those in many homes as well. The red eye of the single television camera seemed to bore a hole into her back. She consulted her notes, drew a deep breath, then took Ethan's place at the podium.

"Ladies and gentlemen, I, too, would like to thank you for heeding the call to duty. Service on a jury is more important to the spirit of American justice than any war waged to gain the right to serve. Rights are easily lost, and are regained only at great cost. That you are willing to answer such a high call speaks of your quality as a citizen.'' She took a nervous swallow of water from a glass waiting on the edge of the bailiff's desk. Her voice had sounded thin at first, unsure. But as she continued to speak, it had grown stronger, surer. She did her best to quell the nervousness.

She looked at the jurors, one by one. They were everyday, ordinary people, not monsters waiting to attack her grandfather. What she had to do was *talk* to them, and thinking that, she felt her nervousness lessen.

''The state must prove its case,'' she began. ''That is what the judge said. And it must be proved beyond a reasonable doubt. Circumstantial evidence is not proof. Gossip and innuendo are not proof. The state must *prove* its case.

''You will hear how Judson Ingalls loved his wife, how it is inconceivable that *he* could have murdered her. Margaret had a fatal flaw—she thought only of herself. You will hear about the life she led. How it was wild and reprehensible to the sensibilities of mainstream society. You will be told about a party the night she disappeared, that there were a number of guests. People who were supposed to be her friends.

''Margaret Ingalls died. That is the only provable fact the prosecution can claim. The rest is pure speculation. And because it is speculation, you will have no other choice than to find Judson Ingalls not guilty of the charge made against him.''

She glanced at Ethan as she walked back to her seat. He was busy writing something on a notepad and gave no notice that he had even heard her.

She met her grandfather's eyes. There was pain deep inside them because of the way she'd been forced to refer to her grandmother, but there was also something else: pride.

She gave him a quick smile and sat down, reviewing in her mind if she'd remembered to say everything she'd planned to. She thought she had.

THE PROSECUTION'S first witness was the workman who had found Margaret's body. Bob Sheehan sat uneasily in the witness chair. It was painfully obvious that he was unaccustomed to wearing a suit. He kept tilting his head and stretching his neck as if the tight collar of his shirt were strangling him.

Ethan moved toward the stand. He smiled at the man, displaying an easy charm. "Would you state your name, please, and where you live."

"Bob, er, Robert J. Sheehan. I live in Casner, Wisconsin."

"And what is your occupation, Mr. Sheehan?"

"I'm a heavy-equipment operator."

"What, exactly, does that mean?"

"I run 'dozers and graders and excavators, things like that."

"Backhoes?" Ethan questioned.

"Yes, sir, backhoes."

"Would you tell the court, please, what you were doing on August sixth of last year?"

Bob Sheehan shifted in the chair. "I was working a job for Joe Santori. He's a buddy of mine. He asked me to come out to Timberlake Lodge. We were going to check a water line that runs from the lodge to the lake.''

"What happened when you started to check that line?"

Bob shifted again. "Well, everything started out fine…as usual, you know. I'd dug a ways up from the lake, then I came to this old willow tree. It wasn't exactly in line with the pipes, but it was going to be hard for the backhoe to get past. Joe looked at it. It was a scraggly thing, mostly dead. Only a few branches had leaves. And Joe said to take it down—a willow tree shouldn't be so close to the water pipes anyway. He said he'd square it with Mr. Ingalls.'' Bob glanced at Judson, then looked quickly away again. He was growing more uncomfortable by the second.

Ethan made an attempt to settle him. He moved closer to the witness stand and draped an elbow on the railing. "How long have you been a heavy-equipment operator, Mr. Sheehan?"

"Ten years.''

"Do you like the work?''

"Mostly.''

Ethan went back to the scene at the lodge. "Did you take the willow tree down?''

"Yes. I got behind it and pushed it with the front blade. Then I dragged it off a piece.''

"What happened next?''

"Well, I started to dig again. Then…''

"Yes?''

Bob Sheehan swallowed. "Then I saw what I'd uncovered.''

"What was it?''

"Bones. Human bones. I yelled for Joe and Pete.

They were back down toward the lake. They came running...they could tell I was upset.''

Ethan went to the prosecutor's table and dug into a file. From it he extracted a series of photographs. ''I'd like to show you these pictures, Mr. Sheehan. They're marked state's exhibit numbers 1 through 13. Would you look at them and tell me if this is the area in which you were working and if this is the site where the body was found?''

Bob looked dutifully at each picture. He visibly flinched at the last few. ''Yes,'' he said. ''That's it.''

Ethan retrieved the photographs. ''Your Honor, I request that these photographs be entered into evidence.''

The judge looked at Amanda, who gave the photographs a quick survey.

''No, objection, Your Honor,'' she said, bobbing up and then down again.

''May I show these exhibits to the jury, Your Honor?'' Ethan asked.

The judge gave gruff approval, and the courtroom waited as the jury looked through the glossy prints.

When they were through and the evidence given over to the court's clerk, Ethan returned to his line of questioning. ''What happened after you found the remains, Mr. Sheehan?''

''Joe ran to get someone at the lodge. This guy came down, Cliff Forrester. Then a woman. He sent her to call the police.''

''Did you stay around to talk to the police?'' Ethan asked.

''Well, I was still kind of shaken. We all were. I hung around, but not for any longer than I had to.''

Ethan nodded, indicating that he considered the

man's feelings perfectly understandable. Then he lightly tapped the railing before the witness and said, "Thank you, Mr. Sheehan, that's all."

Amanda rose to her feet. She nodded to the witness. "Only one question, Mr. Sheehan. What was the condition of the remains when they were uncovered?"

"Well, the bones weren't all in one piece. They'd been messed up in tree roots, and the backhoe didn't do them much good, either."

"So they were disturbed, broken up?"

"Yes," he confirmed.

Amanda, too, thanked him and sat down.

Ethan rejected the chance for reexamination and the witness was excused.

Amanda glanced at her grandfather. He still appeared pale, but he was holding up. She'd told him before they came into court that day to be sure to look at the witnesses as they testified, to listen to what they said. She'd even given him a legal pad to write down any discrepancies or comments he might have. It would make him feel more in control.

She glanced over her shoulder into the spectators' gallery as Ethan Trask stood up again. Her mother also looked pale, her face drawn into a tight mask. Jeff was holding her hand. Cece gave her a wobbly smile. Amanda swung back around, her eyes catching on Ethan as he moved into the center of the room.

"Your Honor," he said, "the state calls Paul Schmidt."

As the courtroom waited for ex-Chief Schmidt to be escorted into the room and sworn in, Amanda's gaze stayed on Ethan. He was constructing his case with care, laying the groundwork so that the jury could easily follow the sequence of events. She watched as he consulted his notes, his long, nicely put-together body taut like a cat waiting to spring. She remembered that body as it once had been, taut against hers, straining to get even closer. She dragged her gaze away, angry with herself for letting her thoughts stray. To help anchor herself, she murmured encouragement to her grandfather and received in return a nod and a tight smile.

Chief Schmidt took the stand.

There was a subtle change in Ethan's demeanor; he didn't show the same friendliness as he had to the last witness. "State your name, please," he clipped.

"Paul Jonathan Schmidt."

"Your occupation?"

"I'm retired from active duty with the Tyler Police Department, where I served first as a deputy for eighteen years, and then as chief for the next seventeen years."

"When did you retire, Chief Schmidt?"

"Last December."

"Ten months ago?"

"Correct."

Chief Schmidt looked more accustomed to wearing a suit than Bob Sheehan had, but even though he should have been used to appearing as a witness on various police matters from all his years of service, he didn't look comfortable now. He shifted his weight and reached for the glass of water a court officer provided.

"Chief Schmidt," Ethan said, drawing his attention again. "You and your assistant were the first officers on the scene at Timberlake Lodge."

Amanda jumped to her feet. "Objection, Your

Honor—leading the witness.'' She had to show Ethan that she wasn't going to be a pushover in court. She had the sense that he was testing her.

''Sustained,'' the judge said.

Ethan rephrased his question. ''Chief Schmidt, were you and your assistant the first officers on the scene at Timberlake Lodge?''

''Yes.''

''Who called you?''

''A call came in to our dispatcher and the dispatcher sent word on to me. The caller identified herself as Liza Baron.''

''Who is Liza Baron?''

''Judson Ingalls's granddaughter. She'd been living at the lodge for a few weeks. She and the caretaker, Cliff Forrester, were the only persons living there. It was kind of run-down.''

''Just answer my questions, please. Who was the officer you brought with you?''

Chief Schmidt's lips had tightened. ''Lieutenant Brick Bauer.''

''Was Lieutenant Bauer your next in command?''

''At the time, yes.''

''Who else did you call, Chief Schmidt?''

Chief Schmidt frowned. ''Who else?'' he repeated.

''Yes. You made another call, didn't you? Whom did you call?''

''Oh...I called Judson Ingalls.''

''Why?''

''It was his property.''

''Do you consider yourself a friend of Judson Ingalls?''

Chief Schmidt bristled. ''Yes! Is there something wrong with that?''

Ethan ignored the question. "What did you tell him, Chief Schmidt?" he asked.

"That there was an emergency at the lodge… which there was!"

"What did he say?"

"Objection, hearsay!" Amanda inserted.

The judge hesitated, then said, "Overruled."

"What did he say?" Ethan repeated.

"He asked me if it had to do with Liza. If Cliff had gone crazy and—"

"Objection, Your Honor!" Amanda shot to her feet again. "What the witness is about to say is totally irrelevant to this case!"

"Sustained. Please direct your comments to this case and this case alone, Chief Schmidt," the judge directed.

Ethan glanced at Amanda. His dark eyes gave nothing away. He turned back to his witness. "Did you tell him that a body had been found?"

"I believe I said something about that. I told him it was probably old Indian bones."

"Did he come to the lodge anyway?"

"Yes. He arrived there the same time we did."

"Did he go with you to the burial site?"

"No."

"Where did he go instead?"

"I have no idea. I saw Liza run out to meet him. He probably went off somewhere with her."

"Did you ever talk with him again about the body?"

"Well, yes. A couple of times."

"What did you talk about?"

"I let him know that the body we found was an adult female's, and that she had been fairly tall."

"How soon did you know that?"

"The coroner's office in Sugar Creek came back with that right away."

"Did you make that information public?"

"Not immediately."

"Why not?"

"We were in the process of investigating the case!"

"Yet you told Judson Ingalls."

"I thought he should know."

"Because he was your friend?"

"Because the body was found on his property!" Chief Schmidt snapped.

Ethan changed his tack again. He knew just how far to press a witness, and how to leave subtle messages in the minds of the jurors without actually saying the words. He pretended to consult his notes, but Amanda had the idea that he knew exactly where he was going next and didn't need any prompting.

"Would you tell us who was present at the burial site that day?"

Chief Schmidt swallowed some of his indignation. "There was Joe Santori and two of his men—Bob Sheehan and..."

When Chief Schmidt's mind seemed to go blank, Ethan went to the prosecution table and withdrew a police report from his file. "Your honor, state's exhibit number 14." He passed it to Amanda before handing it to the witness. "Is this the initial incident report you filed on August sixth of last year, Chief Schmidt?"

Chief Schmidt examined it. "It is."

"Would you read the names, please?"

"Joe Santori, Bob Sheehan, Pete Riley and Cliff Forrester."

"Cliff Forrester was the caretaker of the lodge?"

"Then he was, yes."

"Who was the caretaker before him?"

"Philip Wocheck."

"Where is Mr. Wocheck now?"

"He's retired, just like me," he said. Then he went for a stale joke: "We're both old war-horses put out to pasture."

Some people in the gallery chuckled, and members of the jury started to laugh as well before quickly changing their minds, unsure if laughter was allowed. Chief Schmidt seemed encouraged by the reception of his attempt at humor. His shoulders became a little less fixed, his mouth more relaxed.

Ethan used the break to pass the evidence to the court clerk.

"When you arrived at the site," he said, turning back, "what condition was it in?"

"Joe and his men had been digging a ditch. They'd been at it a while. A dead tree had been hauled off to one side."

"Where were the remains?"

"Mostly in one section of the partially dug ditch."

"Was the skeleton in one piece?"

"No."

Ethan showed him the previous state's evidence. "Look at these photographs," he said. "Is this what you saw?"

"It is."

"What did you do from that point?"

Chief Schmidt shifted in his chair again. "I called in the crime-scene boys from Sugar Creek. They roped the area off and started taking pictures. After that, I basically got out of the way. They know what they're doing.''

''What was your last act at the scene?''

''I posted a guard overnight, then I supervised the removal of the body. It was taken to the lab in Sugar Creek.''

''Why did you post a guard?''

''Because I wasn't sure if the crime-scene people were through yet.''

Ethan nodded. Then he said, ''Your witness.''

Amanda pushed away from the table. She started to speak, but was stopped by the judge.

''It's been a long day, Counselor. If this is going to take more than fifteen minutes, I want to call a halt now.''

''I just have a few questions, Your Honor.''

The judge smiled. ''I noticed the last time you said you only had one question, you had two.''

Amanda grinned. ''I promise, Your Honor.''

He leaned back in his chair and swung around to face the witness.

Amanda approached the stand. ''Chief Schmidt...you testified that the area was disturbed. Will you tell us again what disturbed it?''

It was easy to tell that Chief Schmidt felt on firmer ground with Amanda. His whole expression was more relaxed. ''A backhoe,'' he said. ''One of those machines that has a digging arm the operator can extend from the rear. He lowers it and uses it like a scoop.''

''And a tree had been removed?''

''It was off to one side, but I could easily see the hole it had been taken from.''

Amanda retrieved the first series of photographs

herself and handed them to Chief Schmidt. "And the body was found at that point...across from the spot where the tree was located." She had Chief Schmidt mark the proper point on a photo, asked him to sign it, then requested permission to pass it to the jury after showing it to Ethan. "So the remains were disturbed by this backhoe as it did its work. Just how badly were the remains 'disturbed'? And be specific, if you can."

"Objection," Ethan interrupted, rising to his feet. "The witness is not an expert."

"I'm just asking him to tell us what he saw," Amanda explained.

The judge said, "Overruled."

Chief Schmidt answered promptly. "A number of the bones were apart. Some were broken, the skull in particular."

"Thank you," Amanda said and sat down.

Ethan again declined the opportunity for reexamination.

The judge dismissed the witness, then dismissed court for the day, telling everyone to be back for nine o'clock the next morning. He admonished the jury not to discuss the case among themselves or with anyone else. "Don't listen to anything, don't read anything," he said. Then he told them not to hesitate to tell their tender if they had a special need. "I'm sure we could even come up with a late-night pizza if any of you wanted it."

The jury went off happily, leaving the crowded courtroom on its feet. The judge, too, then stood down, and the television camera was switched off.

Amanda felt her shoulders slump. She was exhausted. The day already seemed forty-eight hours long, and she would probably be up well past midnight preparing for the next day's ordeal. Still, she pulled herself back together and turned to greet her family, who had come around the railing to offer encouragement to Judson and herself. She suffered the hugs and the pats and the kisses...and the words uttered with false conviction.

Over Cece's shoulder she saw Ethan Trask. He was all alone, quietly gathering his materials. As he was about to walk away, he looked up and caught her glance. He held up four fingers.

Amanda murmured an excuse and broke away. She stopped a short distance from him. Nettled, she asked, "What is it? What does *this* mean?" She held up four fingers of her own.

His features might have been carved from some kind of warm stone. They were hard and unyielding, but they also had been formed by the hands of a master sculptor. "I counted four questions. Possibly five," he said. Then he gave her a light smile and walked away.

Amanda could only stare after him. If it had been his plan to disconcert her, he had succeeded.

CHAPTER THIRTEEN

THE INGALLS CLAN gathered at the house and, along with well-wishers from the community, continued in their attempt to put a positive face on the day's proceedings. Herbert Ingalls, Judson's younger brother, was there from Milwaukee, along with his daughter, Irene, and her husband, Everett Bryant. Anna and Johnny Kelsey stopped by, as did Britt Hansen, Annabelle Scanlon, Elise Fairmont and Tisha Olsen. There were so many people, in fact, that Clara pressed Archie into service in order to keep a fresh supply of food and drink available.

Amanda was anxious to get to her office. Now that she had a more complete blueprint of Ethan's strategy for the trial—from his own lips in his opening statement—she wanted to rethink her strategy, shore up the defense's strengths, lessen their liabilities. But everyone seemed to need her there. As she moved from one small group to another, she was forced to repeat the same assurances: yes, the day had, indeed, gone well; and yes, they were off to a good start.

Herbert, standing next to Judson, looked the yin to his brother's yang. Where Judson was still vigorous for his age and cared about his appearance, Herbert, who had never been particularly active, dressed like a man who had other things on his mind. From his unkempt patch of snow-white hair to his woefully-in-need-of-a-good-polish shoes, he was a man who could easily be underestimated. Until you looked in his eyes. In them was the same sharp intelligence and stubborn sense of correctness that ran rampant in the character of most Ingalls men.

Herbert finished off a delicate sandwich in two bites, then pronounced, "Looks like a good jury to me. That truck driver seems fair. So does the accountant. I'm not so sure about that frizzy-haired housewife, though. She seems a little…strident. Why'd you accept her, Amanda?"

"The defense can excuse only a certain number of jurors without explanation, Uncle Herbert. There were others I'd rather not have had to deal with, so I excused them and not her."

Everett Bryant, Alyssa's cousin by marriage, broke into the conversation. He was a big man in every way: big frame, big girth and a big heart that was sometimes hidden by an overblown manner. "How many do we have to get on our side, Little Mandy?" he asked, using his pet name for her. He enjoyed giving people pet names, whether they approved of his choice or not.

Amanda smiled. She had always liked Everett. "Actually, Mr. Trask has to get them on *his* side," she corrected.

Everett laughed heartily at the point she'd made, uncaring if the two men beside him laughed or not. His good humor brought a tiny smile to Judson's lips.

"But to answer your question," she continued, "the decision has to be unanimous."

"What happens if it's not?" Herbert asked.

"Then the judge would declare a hung jury and the whole thing would have to be retried again…with new jurors. But I doubt that will happen. Judge Griffen has a reputation for holding a jury's feet to the fire to make them come up with a decision. He doesn't like to waste taxpayers' money.''

''Now that judge,'' Everett declared. ''He's a corker, isn't he? He looks as if he got a taste of something sour when he was a child, and the face he made stuck! Old Sour Face, that's what I think we should call him!''

Amanda edged away as Everett continued to expound on his idea.

The women present were broken into two groups, one occupying the couch and chairs by the bay window, the other gathered nearer the fireplace. Alyssa was in the latter, and Amanda veered toward her when she saw the barely concealed distress on her mother's face.

No one else seemed to notice, but Amanda had become supersensitive to her mother's moods as the trial drew near. Something was wrong, something worse than the terrible fact that her father was on trial for the murder of her mother. Only Alyssa wouldn't admit it. What could be worse? Amanda wondered. Then she trembled inside at the possible answers.

Alyssa seemed to shake herself from a dream when Amanda stopped beside her. She smiled her beautiful smile and reached out to lightly encircle her daughter's waist.

Irene Bryant, Herbert's daughter, hugged Amanda, too, enveloping her in a cloud of expensive perfume. Irene was a woman who was resisting middle age even as she lost the battle of the bulge. She encased her overly endowed form in the latest styles bought from one of the more exclusive stores in Milwaukee, and she insisted on covering any gray hairs with a brassy shade of red dye. Irene was a silly woman, but she was kind. "Amanda, dear, you were wonderful today!" she gushed. "Frankly, when you first said you were going to become a lawyer, I didn't think you'd do it. But you did, and I'm *so* impressed!"

Amanda smothered a too-wide smile. "Thank you, Irene. I'm flattered." She glanced around the group. With some relief her gaze settled on Elise Fairmont.

Elise was the town's chief librarian. Just that summer she had taken Tyler by surprise and married the architect who had come to salvage construction of their new library.

"I saw Bea going into Gates Department Store the other day," Amanda said, naming Elise's sister. "She was putt-putting along in her wheelchair, going up one of the entrance ramps. It must be quite an amazing difference for her, finally agreeing to a motorized version."

Elise smiled brightly, looking much younger than her fifty-three years. Marriage seemed to agree with her. "She's beginning to complain that it's not fast enough. Robert's told her her next step will be learning to drive a car, but she's still resisting that. I think she's afraid I won't drop by as often if she learns to drive. But that's silly. It would open her world up even more."

Annabelle Scanlon chortled. She and Bea were good friends, since both liked to gossip. Amanda knew that Annabelle was one of the forces actively working against her grandfather this past year, as she spread rumors around town, spread lies. But Annabelle was also Cece's mother, and as such, she was now a part of their extended family. Maybe that would stop some of the gossip about them....

"At least she's come around to tolerating Robert," Annabelle said. "I remember a time when she hated the man, absolutely hated him!"

A shadow of pain passed over Elise's face at the reminder.

Amanda jumped in. "How is Robert?" she asked. "I haven't seen him around town lately...but then, I've been so busy."

Elise responded gratefully. "He's working with the construction people and, of course, he still has his classes at the university. He can't wait to get the new library finished so we can move into the house and get started renovating it." The house in question was the old library building, which Robert had discovered to be of particular architectural interest.

"When might that be?" Annabelle asked. She was always looking for new grist for the gossip mill.

"Next spring? We hope to open the new building in May."

Alyssa murmured her pleasure.

Amanda squeezed her mother's hand and moved on to the other group. This assemblage was younger: Liza, Britt, Cece. Tisha Olsen was at home with them, even though she was older by a good twenty years.

Tisha owned and managed the Hair Affair, Tyler's most popular hair salon. She was a tall, well-built woman with a generous mouth, you-don't-fool-me eyes and a mass of bright red hair piled into an elaborate knot on the top of her head. The unlikely object of Judson's affection, she had loyally stationed herself in the courtroom each moment that her busy schedule allowed.

Tisha was first to speak. "Ethan Trask is quite a looker, Amanda. We have a bet going in the salon, and maybe you know the answer. Is the Terror from Madison married, or is he fancy-free? I say he's married, but his wife kicked him out because he was such a bastard to live with. But then, I'm not the best person to ask, not with what he's doing to Judson." Tisha was not shy about stating her thoughts. "Personally, I'd like to wring his neck."

Liza giggled. "My feelings exactly."

Amanda was glad for the delay before she was expected to answer. She took advantage of those precious moments to collect herself. "Actually, I don't know. I don't believe he is. He doesn't *seem* married…I mean—"

"You know, there's a rumor going around about you two," Tisha said directly.

Amanda's cheeks grew warm when everyone looked at her.

Liza frowned. "What rumor? I haven't heard any rumor. If it's about Amanda and… Tell me! Amanda?" Liza's expression grew more suspicious as her sister's color deepened.

"It's nothing. It's silly," Amanda denied.

"Juanita caught them necking in the hallway at Worthington House," Tisha supplied.

Was Tisha taking revenge because Amanda had refused to let her sit beside Judson in court? Amanda wondered. "That's not true!" she denied again, this time with more force. "We weren't necking. We were…"

Cece came to her rescue. "Rumors flash through Worthington House like wildfire. I sometimes wonder how. It's just as bad in the convalescent wing as it is anywhere else in that place. I mean…does someone hobble from room to room with a walker, spreading the latest news? Or do the patients have some kind of code they tap out to send messages?''

Britt Hansen grinned. ''Jimmy's great-aunt always knows things before I do!'' Inger Hansen, her deceased husband's aging relative, lived at Worthington House. ''And Grandmother Martha…she never says anything, but I'm sure she does, too. She wasn't surprised when I told her I was going to marry Jake.''

''No one was surprised that you're marrying Jake,'' Cece teased.

''Or you Jeff,'' Britt retorted with a smile. Britt had suffered through a difficult period after her husband's death, trying to keep the farm that had been in her family for generations, as well as support four active, growing children. She had come upon an idea for a specialty yogurt, had gained national attention and now was reaping the rewards. The lines of worry that had once been so prominent on her girl-next-door face had disappeared completely, and her naturally pink cheeks again complemented an array of freckles and her strawberry-blond hair. ''Where is Jeff, anyway?'' she asked.

''He had to go to the hospital,'' Cece said, sighing. ''He was supposed to have these next couple of weeks off, but George called. They were swamped. He asked if Jeff could come in…just for a couple of hours, he said. I probably won't see him again until after midnight.''

Liza continued to watch Amanda. Amanda knew her sister's curiosity had not been answered, and that she wasn't going to be happy until it had been.

"Where's Margaret Alyssa?" she asked, trying to stave off further questioning.

"Cliff's gone to get her," Liza said flatly. "Susannah volunteered to baby-sit whenever we have need of her during the trial."

"I've heard Susannah's just about through putting the finishing touches to the bed and breakfast she wants to open," Britt contributed, "and that she's going to call it Granny Rose's! Isn't that a great idea?"

The others agreed, but it was easy for them to see that Liza had business with her sister.

Britt was first to move away. She stood up, murmuring, "I think I'd like another of those sandwiches Clara's serving. I wonder if she'd give me the recipe for the filling?"

Cece followed suit, then Tisha...both agreeing with Britt that they had suddenly grown acutely hungry.

Amanda sighed once she and Liza were alone. "Well, you certainly chased them away."

"There's only one thing I want to know from you—have you gone over to the enemy camp?"

"Liza!"

Liza swept thick blond hair back over one shoulder. "I don't think the family should be the last to know."

Amanda sat forward. "Know? Know what?"

"Whatever it is that's going on between you and Ethan Trask."

"*Nothing,*" she began heatedly, then quickly lowered her voice, "is going on between me and Ethan Trask."

"Now that I think of it," Liza mused, "I did see you looking at him funny during the few minutes I was allowed in the courtroom today."

"He's an amazingly good lawyer!"

"And he looked back!" Liza declared.

"It was coincidence...."

"Sure. Right. I believe that!"

Amanda felt a sharp flash of anger. Liza had for-
saken the family for several years to go off and do
her own thing in Chicago. She hadn't seemed to care
about the turmoil she'd left behind. She was upset, so
she'd left. Well, they'd all been upset. They all
missed Ronald Baron. They'd all been devastated by
his decision to end his own life. Now...now Liza
dared to lecture her, Amanda, about family loyalty?

Amanda opened her mouth to say something pithy,
then just as suddenly closed it. What the family did
not need right now was feuding members. She rubbed
a weary hand over her eyes. She was tired...
exhausted. Her nerves were raw and on edge.

She said levelly, "My only passion at the moment
is to get Granddad absolved of this charge. I don't
have time to get involved with anyone right now. And
especially not the man I'm having to fight against in
court. That would be pure insanity."

"Insane things happen."

"Maybe they do to you, but not to me."

Liza tilted her head. She thought about what
Amanda'd said, then she contended, "You could be
wrong about that, you know. We are sisters. Everyone
told me to leave Cliff alone. They said he was crazy,
that he might hurt me. But did I do what they said?
No-o-o."

"I can't fall in love right now, Liza."

Liza sat back. "Fall in love? I was thinking 'fall
in lust.' This is more serious than I expected."

Amanda's hands tightened into fists. "I didn't
mean that."

"It's what you said."

"I'm tired. My mind—"

Alyssa interrupted them. She placed her hands on Amanda's shoulders and told her she had a telephone call. "Someone named Peter?" she asked uncertainly.

Amanda bolted from the room as if the call were extremely urgent and she had been waiting for it for hours. *Why* had she said that to Liza? she wondered as she fell back against the study wall. She hadn't meant it. She didn't love Ethan Trask. She couldn't! She barely knew the man. In all the times they'd been together since she'd first seen him a few weeks ago, they'd spent approximately thirty minutes alone. *But what a thirty minutes!* a voice in the back of her mind insisted.

PETER WAS FULL of compliments for the first day in court. He'd slipped into the rear of the gallery shortly after jury selection and had stayed for most of the afternoon.

"Why didn't you come by the house?" Amanda complained. "I'd have liked to have everyone meet you."

Peter grunted. "I'll meet them later. Let me get through with this book first. The darned thing's giving me fits."

"Is there anything I can do?" she asked. "Do you need someone to act as a sounding board?"

"I'd say you have enough on your hands right now, wouldn't you? No, I just can't make a couple of scenes do what I want." He sighed. "I don't know…maybe I'm not as good a writer as I hoped. Maybe I should just chuck it all and supplement my income by fishing."

"Do you usually catch a lot of fish?" Amanda asked.

He chuckled. "No. That's why I thought I should write."

Amanda shook her head, chuckling as well. "I'd say you should just stay at it awhile longer. Those scenes will come around."

"Your confidence is appreciated."

"So is yours," she said.

He paused. "Seriously, Amanda, you did fine today. I watched the jury, and they responded to you. They listened to everything you had to say."

"What about Ethan?" she asked.

She sensed Peter's shrug. "He knows his way around a courtroom, but you were aware of that. Just keep doing what you did today."

"Will you be in court tomorrow?"

"I'll try."

Amanda said goodbye and rang off. She was partway up the oak stairway, on her way to the second floor to change into something more comfortable to wear back to the office, when the front doorbell rang. She looked around. No one else was about, so she went back down to answer it. Before undoing the latch, though, she checked to see who was there. They'd been having trouble with the press making calls at all hours of the day and night. This morning an enterprising reporter from a Chicago newspaper had even climbed a tree, trying to discover which bedroom was Judson's. Brick had been called to put an end to that, and afterward the onslaught had lessened...at least temporarily.

The identity of the person on the front porch surprised Amanda. It was Edward Wocheck. She opened the door and greeted him uncertainly. "Mr. Wocheck?"

He was wearing a well-tailored dark suit that set off his handsome, strong-featured face. There was something slightly foreign about him, even discounting the vaguely British touch in his pronunciation.

"I wonder if it would be possible for me to speak with your mother," he asked.

Amanda pulled the door farther open even as she wondered at this turn of events. To her knowledge, a Wocheck had not crossed the threshold of the Ingalls home since the day Edward Wocheck, *this* Edward Wocheck, had stormed out the front door after discovering that he was not considered "good enough" marriage material for the daughter of the house.

"Certainly," she said. "We're having a few people in, but you're welcome to join them. It's just relatives and friends from town," she explained when she felt him hold back.

"I wonder," he said, "if you'd tell her that I'd like to speak with her for a moment? I'd rather not..."

Amanda understood. "Of course," she said and motioned toward a brocade-covered chair. "Make yourself comfortable and I'll be back in a moment."

Amanda made her way to her mother's side. "Turnabout, Mom," she said. "Now someone wants to speak with you."

Alyssa laughed and excused herself. She was smiling at Amanda as they moved into the front hall. Then the smile dissolved in surprise. "But I thought you said..." Astonished blue eyes turned to her daughter.

Immediately Amanda realized her mistake. Her mother had thought the caller to be on the phone. "Oh! No. Mr. Wocheck just stopped by."

Her mother was more flustered than Amanda ever remembered seeing her. She became even more so when Edward Wocheck took her hand. As quickly as she could Alyssa pulled her hand away.

"I wanted to see how you were, Lyssa," he said, his voice gruff with restrained emotion.

Amanda turned away and went quietly up the stairs. She didn't think either one of them noticed.

ETHAN PICKED at his baked fish with the tip of his fork. Food didn't interest him.

Carlos, sitting across the table, motioned to the elegance of their surroundings. "You are wasting the moment, my friend. Such beautiful luxury, such wonderful fare. My steak almost melts in my mouth. And the mushrooms..." He kissed his fingers and offered thanks to heaven.

"I must not be in the right mood," Ethan murmured.

Carlos lifted an expressive eyebrow. "You have not been in the 'right mood' for many days."

Ethan sighed, abandoning any show of eating.

"It is this case," Carlos decreed. "You do not like trying it."

"It's not that," Ethan denied.

"You admit...you do not enjoy bringing the grandfather of Amanda Baron to justice."

"I never said—"

"Few men would," Carlos continued. "She is very hard to resist. She is smart, she is beautiful, she is innocent of the baser realities of the world. She has not seen life as we have seen it. In her domain there are few rough edges or deprivations."

"Your poetic nature is showing again," Ethan murmured dryly.

"At least I *have* a poetic nature. Many bad things have happened to me also, amigo. When my family was forced to leave our home, we brought nothing except what we could carry. One of my uncles died, as did several of my cousins. The boat we crossed the water on would have been condemned for other uses. And when we arrived at our destination, people did not want us. We spoke only broken English, our skin was much too dark. My father had been the doctor of our village, but here, for many years, he swept floors. I could be angry, too, my friend. But I choose not to be. Life is too short not to be enjoyed. That is an old saying, but it is so very true."

"What I feel has nothing to do with Amanda Baron," Ethan maintained stubbornly.

Carlos cut another piece of steak. "Maybe so, my friend. And if you continue to tell yourself that, maybe you will come to believe it."

CHAPTER FOURTEEN

THE NEXT DAY started with three of the prosecution's expert witnesses.

First, the crime-scene expert testified about what had been done at the site of the body's discovery. Ethan took the man through the technicalities of proper police procedure as it pertained to the situation. The jury was told how in this instance every piece of possible evidence had been gathered, marked and sent either to the crime lab or to the coroner's office in Sugar Creek.

With a mental apology to the officers who had once made up the now-defunct Tyler Police Department and to those still serving under the new regime, the Sugar Creek Sheriff's Department, Amanda challenged the credibility of the police work. Her aim was to create doubt, to spotlight any sloppiness. If she could show that the police were inept in one way, it would be easy for the jury to believe that they might also be inept in others. They were not infallible. She succeeded in getting the investigator to admit that the procedure had been rushed because of the approach of darkness and the arrival of a thunderstorm. She also got him to admit that the investigators from Sugar Creek placed little weight on the discovery of a ''bunch of bones''—his words—because they fully expected them to belong either to an ancient Indian who had once called the rolling hills home, or to a pioneer settler. Such discoveries happened occasionally in the area, he said.

The second witness was the Sugar Creek coroner. He explained the process used to identify a body so long buried. He testified about the discovery of Margaret Ingalls's dental records and how he had made a match to the teeth of the remains. He then testified that the skeleton had been sent on to the State Forensics Laboratory in Madison to determine the cause of death, because the laboratory in Sugar Creek, on a county level, was not set up for such a determination.

Amanda jumped on the fact that the coroner had been forced to forward the remains to a laboratory in Madison. She brought up the disruption of the bones by years of entanglement with the willow tree's roots and by their rough handling by the backhoe—how the skull had sustained the worst damage. Then she came back to the admitted inadequacies of the county coroner's office. By the time she was through, the coroner was steaming. He glared angrily at her as he stalked away from the stand.

The judge then called a short recess, but soon they were back at it. Ethan called the forensic anthropologist from the state laboratory who had made the determination of cause of death. He took the woman through the entire process, paying attention to each small detail, and continuing to add to the trial's growing list of exhibits. Her testimony was long and complicated, from skeletal reconstruction to the eventual finding of the probable cause of death—massive blunt trauma to the head from a single, severe blow.

As Amanda stood to start her cross-examination, the judge lifted a hand. ''You look as if you're wind-

ing up for a long one, too, Counselor. Let's take a
break for lunch, then we can all come back rarin' to
go. Members of the jury, my instructions still stand.
No talking among yourselves about the case, no talking to other people and no reading anything that you
shouldn't. We'll meet back here at two o'clock.'' He
banged the gavel and stood. As the jury walked out,
so did he.

Through lunch Amanda did her best to keep her
family's spirits lifted, but that was hard to do when
her own felt so weighed down. So far she'd been able
to make small inroads into the prosecution's case, but
she wasn't sure how much good she had done.

Judson was the calmest of them all. "I didn't kill
Margaret. I *couldn't* kill Margaret. The truth will win
out in the end," he insisted.

After lunch, Amanda did her best to plant seeds of
doubt in the minds of the jurors. "Could a fall have
caused the injury?" she asked the forensic expert.
"How badly had the remains deteriorated?" "What
about damage made upon discovery?" "Was that the
reason it took *ten full months* to determine the cause
of death?" "Oh—the laboratory was swamped with
too much work. They were rushed with other cases.
Could that possibly have influenced the finding in this
case? Could it have been rushed as well, sacrificing
accuracy?"

The forensic anthropologist came off pretty well,
but Amanda seemed to score a hit with the jury about
the rushed conditions of the laboratory. She saw a few
displeased frowns directed at the witness.

She'd planned one last question. "Tell me," she
requested, "were there any other signs of violence on

the remains? I'm speaking, of course, about violence in the past. Say…a bullet mark?''

The anthropologist shook her head. ''No, none. I'm positive.''

''You're positive?'' Amanda repeated.

''I'd stake my reputation on it.''

Amanda smiled slightly. ''Thank you.''

Ethan got slowly to his feet. He knew exactly what she'd done—twisted and maneuvered until she had the expert exactly where she wanted her. She had made the woman look bad and then had given her an opportunity to redeem herself…which she'd done in no uncertain terms. The tables had been nicely turned, and the prosecution's witness had just helped the defense.

Amanda let her smile gain strength as he continued to look at her. She doodled a small star on her legal pad. *One for our side,* she thought, then turned the pad to a clean page.

This time Ethan, too, had only one question. ''If some of the bones were broken and some bits were missing, is it possible, Miss Harris, that in your search for bullet markings, you might have missed something?''

The forensic expert realized that she'd been caught. She started to stammer.

Ethan didn't force her to answer. ''Thank you, no further questions,'' he said.

Amanda's smile dimmed. He had completely destroyed the point she'd established, by using her own line of reasoning against her.

The next witness was Joe Santori.

Ethan took him through all the formalities, then received confirmation of his link to the case. Joe told of Liza's plan to renovate the run-down lodge, and her request that he give her an estimate of what the job would cost.

"I wanted to check the water line out to the lake," Joe explained. "It's an old place, been there a number of years. The system they used had a well for drinking water but took water from the lake for everything else. I was told the pipes to the lake had been there for fifty years or more. Before I came up with an estimate, I wanted to check their condition."

"So you arranged for the services of a backhoe?"

"Yes, I did."

"And the backhoe operator found the body?"

"Yes, he did."

"What did you do?"

"I ran to get Cliff Forrester at the lodge. He was caretaker of the place."

"And did Cliff Forrester arrange for the police to come?"

Joe nodded. "Yes." Joe sent a look toward Amanda and Judson, showing his regret at what might come.

"Did you get the contract to repair the lodge?" Ethan asked.

"Yes."

"Give us an idea, please, of what that work entailed."

Joe drew a deep breath. "Well…some work had already been started in the entryway. Liza wanted to enlarge it. We had to patch the roof in spots, go through the place and look for rot, reinforce a section of the veranda, take down old wallpaper, refinish the floors…general things like that. The basic structure was pretty sound. What we did was mostly cosmetic."

"Did the work you did include pulling up baseboards?"

Joe's voice tightened. "Yes."

"In the room that was once Margaret Ingalls's?"

"In that room, too."

Ethan closed in. "And did you find something in a baseboard in Margaret Ingalls's room?"

Joe shifted his large, muscular body. "Yes."

"What was it?"

"A bullet."

"How did you find this bullet?"

"When I was pulling the baseboard away from the wall, it fell out of its hole. I had a little time to kill one day, so I started messing around in a room we hadn't started to work on yet."

"Margaret Ingalls's old room?"

"Yes."

Ethan searched through a series of poster boards for one on which a diagram of the room was drawn. "Is this a diagram of that room?" he asked.

"Yes," Joe confirmed.

"Would you please mark the place where the bullet hole was located?"

Joe took a red marker, hesitated a moment, then placed an *X* on the diagram. He also signed it, as Ethan directed.

"Let the record show that the witness has indicated a position on the south wall," Ethan said. "Your Honor, I would like to enter this as state's exhibit number 101." He positioned the diagram on a stand so that the jury could see it, then returned to his questioning. "What did you do with the bullet after you found it, Mr. Santori?"

"I gave it to Liza Forrester," Joe said.

"Forrester?" Ethan asked.

"Her maiden name was Baron. She'd just married Cliff Forrester," Joe explained.

Ethan produced another piece of evidence. It was in a plastic zip bag and had both police and trial exhibit tags attached. He handed it to Joe Santori. "Is this the bullet, Mr. Santori?" he asked.

Joe examined the slug of metal. "Yes."

Ethan formally placed the bullet into evidence as state's exhibit number 102. He then thanked the witness and sat down.

Amanda tapped her pencil on her legal pad, where she'd made a few notes. When she looked up, she smiled at Joe and moved away from the defense table.

"Mr. Santori," she said, "I wonder if you'd mind looking at state's exhibit number 101 again, please." She didn't take the diagram to Joe; instead, she invited him to come off the stand. Joe looked ill at ease as he complied.

"Mr. Santori," she said, "would you please repeat what you said a moment ago about the baseboard? You said it was here...in this spot?" She indicated the *X*. "Is that where the bullet was positioned?"

Joe frowned. "I think so. It was in the baseboard on that wall. When I pulled it away, I heard a 'clunk.' If I'd fit the board back onto the wall, the hole should have been right about there."

"Is that the spot you marked?" she asked.

Joe answered, "Yes."

She indicated to Joe that he could be reseated.

"Where is that piece of baseboard now, Mr. Santori?"

Joe shrugged. "I have no idea. I put it on the junk pile at the site, and someone hauled it off, I suppose."

"The police didn't ask you for it?" she asked.

"No."

"Did they even talk to you about it?"

"No."

"You mean," she asked incredulously, "something they consider so important now, they didn't even bother to talk to you about then?"

"No one talked to me," Joe said honestly.

"What about the bullet?" Amanda asked. "Did the police talk to you about the bullet?"

"Not that I recall."

Amanda went to the evidence table. She picked up the small zip bag.

"When you found the bullet, Mr. Santori, did you mark it in any way, so that if you saw it again later you'd recognize it?"

Joe frowned. "No."

She waved the plastic bag. "So the bullet in this bag might be any bullet, mightn't it?"

"Objection, Your Honor!" Ethan thundered. "Calls for a conclusion!"

"I'm merely following a logical train of thought, Your Honor," Amanda defended. "Surely the prosecution can't object to that."

"I do object," Ethan repeated. "Defense counsel—"

The judge motioned them to his bench. Amanda knew she was playing a risky game.

Ethan frowned darkly as he stood at her side.

Amanda tried not to glance at him for more than a second.

"Now look, you two," the judge grumbled, his hand over the microphone. "This case has been going very smoothly. I don't want that to change. Mr. Trask, I'm going to sustain your objection. Ms. Baron, rephrase your question."

Some of the fierceness had disappeared from Ethan's brow as he settled again at his table.

Amanda drew a breath. "Mr. Santori," she said, "you testified that you did not mark the bullet in any way. Tell me, can you be positive that this is the same bullet you found in the baseboard in Margaret Ingalls's room?"

Joe hesitated. "Well, when you put it like that...no."

"Thank you. No more questions."

Ethan stood up. "Mr. Santori, when did you find the bullet in Margaret Ingalls's room?"

"When?" Joe asked. By now he was getting tired of being on the stand.

"Yes. What date?"

Joe took a moment to think. "It was mid-December. The Ingalls family was going to have a party at the lodge over Christmas, and they wanted as many rooms finished as possible."

"And when did you give the bullet to Liza Forrester?"

"A week after I found it."

"A week," Ethan repeated. "A week is a long time, Mr. Santori. Why did you wait that long?"

Joe shrugged his thick shoulders. "I wasn't sure what to do with it."

"Why not?"

"I wasn't sure if it was important."

"So the police didn't know about the baseboard or the bullet in a timely manner, did they?"

Joe shrugged again. "I suppose not."

Amanda stood up as Ethan sat down. "Mr. Santori, why didn't you give the bullet to the police?"

Joe shook his head. "Old Chief Schmidt was retiring and a new captain was coming in from Sugar Creek, a woman. Karen Keppler. The whole department was in an uproar."

"So they could easily have made a mistake in procedure?"

Ethan jumped to his feet. "Objection!"

Amanda patted the railing between herself and Joe. "I withdraw the question, Your Honor." She tried not to smile as she made her way back to her table.

A rumble came from the spectators' gallery, causing the judge to rap his gavel. Once the courtroom had quieted, Judge Griffen looked at the two attorneys. "Is the witness excused?" he asked.

Both Ethan and Amanda nodded. The judge saved a special look for Amanda. It silently warned her to behave.

Ethan called his next witness. It was Brick Bauer.

Amanda watched as Brick walked to the stand and was duly sworn in. In his dark Sheriff's Department uniform, with his short black hair, his compact muscular body, his squared features and his no-nonsense attitude, he seemed the ideal spokesman for law enforcement. Brick settled into the witness seat.

Ethan moved toward the center of the room. "State your name and rank, please, Officer, and which department you're affiliated with," he requested.

"Donald Martin Bauer. I'm a lieutenant with the

Sugar Creek Sheriff's Department. Currently I'm posted at the Tyler substation.''

"How long have you been with the Sheriff's Department, Lieutenant Bauer?"

"Since last December, when the Tyler Police Department was taken over by the county."

"And before that?"

"I was an officer in the Tyler Police Department for ten years. I became a lieutenant after five years of service there."

The judge interrupted. "Mr. Trask...if I may. We're already late taking our break, and I promised the jury I'd be consistent. Court is adjourned for thirty minutes."

As the courtroom emptied, Amanda turned to her grandfather. "Are you all right?" she asked softly. It had been a rough day of testimony.

"I'm fine...fine," he assured her.

Family and friends surrounded them. They were the only people left in the courtroom except for a guard and a couple of clerks. Ethan, she could see, had gathered his briefcase and disappeared. She thought of their unpleasant clash and experienced a slight remorse—the kind of sorrow one gladiator might feel when forced by circumstance to drive a sword into the vital organs of another. The gladiator would do it, but he—or she—would feel badly after.

Again there was a sense of false optimism surrounding the well-wishers, as if everyone had determined that by not giving in to despair and worry, they could keep away an unwanted verdict.

The crowd broke up, anxious to make good use of the break. Some went to the snack bar Amanda had pointed out to them yesterday, others to the cafeteria a little farther away. She went into the nearest bathroom to dampen a paper towel and pat it over her face. One day soon she would have to apologize to Joe for putting him through that, but she had points she'd needed to establish, and his testimony had helped establish them.

A stall door opened and Liza appeared, blinking in surprise. "Oh! I didn't know that was you. I heard someone out here, but I thought..." She looked closely at her older sister. "You look like hell. Do you need to sit down?"

Amanda forced a smile. "No, I'm fine. A trial is just...draining."

"How did it go today? I'm here to meet Cliff— we're going on to Madison for a meeting he has with some wildlife people. The rat won't tell me anything at all about the trial. He says it wouldn't be right, since the witnesses were banned. I told him it might not be right for a witness to sleep with him, either. He didn't particularly care for that!"

"Pretty well," Amanda prevaricated, answering Liza's question.

"Well, let's hope it goes just as well tomorrow. I've been served notice that I'm to testify."

"Oh dear," Amanda sympathized.

"'Oh dear' is right. Amanda, isn't there some way I can get out of this?"

Amanda looked up into her sister's worried face. She shook her head. "Short of going to jail for contempt, no."

Liza sighed deeply. "Damn."

She held the door open as they walked back into the hall. Then they separated, Liza to find Cliff, Amanda to make her way into the quiet courtroom.

One clerk was still at her desk, industriously writing something; the court reporter had also returned, marking his tapes of the morning's proceedings and preparing strips of clean tape. Soon everyone would be back. Amanda sat down at the defense table and started to read over her notes, but movement at the table next to her drew her attention.

Ethan had returned early as well. He glanced up and caught her gaze. Amanda looked quickly away. After the morning they'd spent...

He came to stand next to her. Amanda's nerve endings started to vibrate. She tried to make them stop. She hadn't let herself think about what she'd said to Liza at home yesterday, her stupid slip of the tongue. But being with her sister just now had brought it all back. She couldn't be so idiotic as to think that she might be falling in love with him. She *couldn't!*

He spoke quietly, so that the other people in the room wouldn't hear what he said. "I'd have fought harder to get you off this case if I'd known how good you are."

She looked up, surprised, but covered her reaction quickly. "A compliment, Mr. Trask? From you?"

He gave the ghost of a smile. "Maybe I'm just warning you that the gloves are off from this point onward."

"The better to feel me with, Mr. Trask?"

A light kindled in the back of his dark eyes. Amanda mentally backtracked. Maybe she shouldn't have reminded him of their indiscretion. Even if *she* was thinking of it.

"The better to *beat* you with, Ms. Baron. I intend to win this case."

"So do I, Mr. Trask," she retorted, and he moved away.

Amanda's heart was thundering as people started to file into the gallery. What had just happened between her and Ethan? She wasn't sure. Had he complimented her? Threatened her? Or had he done both? And why, oh why, had she challenged him as she had? Did she enjoy seeing the spark of memory in his eyes? Did she like to demonstrate the power she had over him—a power that no one else seemed to possess?

Love? No. Lust? Yes. That had to be what it was, just as Liza had said. And Liza would know. Her sister had had more experience in such matters by the time she was eighteen than Amanda had ever had.

Amanda's gaze flickered across to the man sitting at the next table. In his dark suit, he looked both handsome and intense. *Love?* her mind insisted. Maybe, she conceded, and quickly forced her thoughts away from the personal and back into the trial.

THE JURY RETURNED to its box, Brick Bauer returned to the witness stand and the judge called the proceedings to order.

Ethan took up where he had left off, as if there had been no interruption. "Lieutenant Bauer," he said, then, in an aside, he asked, "do people call you Brick?"

Brick nodded, then said, "Yes," when he remembered that he needed to speak for the record. "It's a nickname."

Ethan continued. "Through the testimony of Chief Paul Schmidt, we have learned that, along with Chief

Schmidt, you were one of the first officers called to the scene when Margaret Ingalls's body was discovered. Is that correct?''

Brick cleared his throat. "It is."

"We have also learned that you are the officer responsible for finding Margaret Ingalls's dental records in Chicago. Is that also correct?"

"It is."

Ethan lifted another plastic bag. Amanda recognized its contents instantly. She glanced at her grandfather, who sat very still. His gaze was riveted on the gun.

Ethan removed the weapon. Both bag and gun were marked with evidence tags. "Have you seen this gun before, Lieutenant?" Ethan asked.

"Yes, sir, I have."

Ethan pivoted. "Your Honor, I want to place this article into evidence as state's exhibit number 103." He handed the gun to Amanda for her inspection.

Amanda's hands trembled as she touched the cold metal. With its ebony grips and her grandfather's initials inlaid in silver, it was an exact match to the gun in the wooden case. She nodded stiffly. "No objection," she said, then she coughed to cover the trembly note that had been in her voice. She didn't want the jury to know that the feel of the gun had disturbed her. She glanced quickly at her grandfather. To her relief, he sat stone-faced, his attention fully focused on Ethan Trask.

Ethan continued, "Would you tell us where you've seen this gun before, please, Lieutenant?"

"I found it at Kelsey Boardinghouse in the room of Philip Wocheck."

"Would you tell us, please, what you were doing in this room?"

"My aunt is Anna Kelsey. She and my uncle own Kelsey Boardinghouse. Philip Wocheck is one of their boarders, only he broke his hip a number of months ago and has been undergoing rehabilitation in Worthington House, a retirement center and nursing home in Tyler. With Mr. Wocheck's permission, my aunt has been taking care of his room. She asked if I would move some boxes in his closet. When I did, the bottom of one of the boxes broke and the gun fell out."

"Would you please tell us where Mr. Wocheck is employed?"

"He's retired. He used to work as caretaker and gardener for Mr. Judson Ingalls at Timberlake Lodge."

Ethan paused, letting the information sink in. The fact had been established before, but he wanted it repeated at this point. A moment later he continued, "What is it about the gun you found that makes it special, Lieutenant?"

"Objection," Amanda broke in. "Calls for a conclusion."

"Sustained."

Ethan lifted the gun again. "Look at the gun, Lieutenant. Would you please tell us what you see on the handle?"

Brick complied. "The initials J.T.I."

"And what do those initials stand for?"

"Judson Thaddeus Ingalls. The gun is one of a pair registered in his name."

"A pair?" Ethan asked.

"A matched pair, a presentation set."

"When were the guns registered, Lieutenant?"

"In October of 1948."

"What type of gun is this?"

"It's a thirty-two caliber double-action revolver."

"Explain that to the jury, please."

Brick looked at the interested faces of the jurors. "*Caliber* is the measurement of the diameter of a gun's bore. The size of the hole in the barrel," he went on to explain more simply. "It's measured in hundredths of inches, or millimeters. In this case, this gun's bore is thirty-two one hundredths of an inch across. *Double-action* means that the gun can be fired simply by pulling the trigger."

Ethan nodded thoughtfully. "So if a bullet were fired from this gun, it would have to fit inside its bore—the barrel?"

"Yes," Brick confirmed.

"By that you mean the bullet would have to be a thirty-two caliber? Is that correct?"

Again Brick confirmed the fact.

Ethan moved closer to the jury. He looked into each face. "Tell me, Lieutenant," he asked slowly, meaningfully, "what was the size of the bullet found in the baseboard of Margaret Ingalls's room?"

"Thirty-two caliber."

"Were tests run to match the bullet with this gun?"

"Yes, sir, they were."

"And what did the tests show, Lieutenant?"

"That this gun, registered to Judson Thaddeus Ingalls, fired the bullet that was found in the baseboard of Margaret Ingalls's room at Timberlake Lodge."

"Thank you, Lieutenant," Ethan said swiftly, having successfully pulled from the police officer exactly what he wanted.

Members of the jury were visibly affected. Some,

with eyes wide, shifted uncomfortably in their seats, while others sat stiffly, troubled by what they'd heard.

Amanda recognized the hit the defense had taken. She knew she had to do something, and do it quickly. But as she got to her feet, a clerk came to whisper something in the judge's ear. The judge glanced at his watch and frowned. He said, ''I'm going to end this session for today. We'll take up again tomorrow morning at nine.'' Then he gave his same warning to the jurors and banged the gavel. A court officer proclaimed, ''All rise!'' as the jury was shown out of the room and the judge disappeared into his chambers at the rear of the courtroom.

Amanda closed her eyes in frustration. Now the jury would be left with the image of Judson firing a bullet in Margaret's room. It wouldn't matter that it was Judson's *gun* that fired the bullet and that Judson might have been nowhere near it at the time. The jury had been imprinted with a certain idea. The interruption had worked beautifully in the prosecution's favor.

Amanda drew another star on a clean sheet of yellow ruled paper and slipped it surreptitiously onto the table near Ethan's elbow.

She had the satisfaction of knowing that her unexpected action startled him. His eyes followed her all the way out of the courtroom.

CHAPTER FIFTEEN

AMANDA SAT at the table in the breakfast nook off the kitchen. In front of her rested an empty bowl that had once contained a double portion of Royal Fudgenut Ripple ice cream—packed with sugar, packed with cholesterol, packed with sodium and packed with fat. And she didn't care. It had tasted delicious and had been exactly what she needed. Most days if she wanted a sweet, she'd virtuously choose Britt's low-cal yogurt. Today she'd needed something much more decadent. Only, after consuming the Fudgenut Ripple, her feeling of apprehension returned much too soon. The calorie-packed ice cream had proved a temporary fix at best. As she pushed the bowl away, her mother came into the room. Amanda tried to find the reassuring smile she usually wore, but the effort was only partially successful.

"I thought I heard someone up," Alyssa said quietly. "I wondered if it was you."

"Yep…just me." Amanda indicated the sticky bowl, and her mother shook her head with mock dismay.

"I thought I broke you of that habit years ago," she said.

"I revert to childhood after two a.m.," Amanda teased.

Alyssa wrapped her silk robe more closely around

her slender body and sat down across from her daughter. Without her makeup, it was easy to see the lines of worry around her mouth and the tiny marks on her forehead caused by frequent frowning.

"Want some?" Amanda asked.

Alyssa started to agree, then shook her head. "No, my stomach wouldn't like it. It hasn't liked most things I've put into it lately."

"What little that is," Amanda murmured.

Alyssa ignored the tiny prod. "I've heard from Janice and David," she said. "They're back from their trip and are coming to Tyler tomorrow to be at the trial. It will be so nice to see them again. It seems so long since..." Alyssa's words trailed off as her mind became occupied with other thoughts.

A nervous tic pulled near the point where Amanda's jaw hinged, and she rubbed the spot to make it stop. It came from holding her teeth together too tightly for too long a period of time. She started to get up, to rinse her bowl with water so that Clara wouldn't be annoyed with her the next day, but she was stopped by her mother grabbing hold of her wrist. Alyssa's fingers were surprisingly strong.

"We didn't do very well today, did we? That gun..." Alyssa's voice wobbled on the word. "That gun," she repeated, then she shook her head, her eyes haunted. "I have to tell you something, Amanda. Something I probably should have told you long ago, but just couldn't. I wasn't sure if it would help or if it would... I—I keep having these *dreams!* I'm a little girl again. I remember things, I remember people. But nothing makes sense! It's all jumbled up! It—it's about the night my mother died."

Amanda covered her mother's hand, making no attempt to release her fingers even though her wrist hurt. She'd known all along that something else besides the trial was bothering her. "What do you remember?" she asked. "Do you remember your mother being killed?"

Alyssa shook her head. "No! I..." She drew in a trembling breath. "It's like I'm looking at myself from outside. I can *see* me. And that's not right, because in dreams people don't seem themselves—at least, not like that."

"What happens?" Amanda questioned softly.

"In the dream tonight, as usual, I—I was in my mother's room. Dad says I really wasn't there, that I was upstairs in bed asleep, but that's where I *see* myself. People were arguing...a man, a woman—" Her voice broke. "Then I remember a gunshot, and that my hand hurt. It was a tingly kind of fire, as if the shot had reached out to touch everything in the room. It burned me...made my ears hurt! I was so afraid! I was crying. Then another man came. He picked me up and brought me to my room. Phil, I think. He called me *malushka*."

The name struck a familiar chord in Amanda's memory. Phil had called her that, too! He'd done it when Ethan had interviewed him. What had Phil said? That she reminded him of her mother...then he'd used that word. "Do you know what it means?" Amanda asked. "Have you heard it before?"

"It was a pet name Phil used to call me. It's Polish. I think it means 'little girl.'" She drew another uneven breath. "Phil was always so sweet to me. His wife died shortly after Edward was born. He told me he'd always wanted a daughter, too. So I guess, in a way, I was his 'little girl.'"

"Who was the man? Do you remember?"

Alyssa became agitated again. "No. No."

"Was the man Granddad?"

Alyssa couldn't remain seated. She jerked to her feet and held on to the back of the chair. "I don't know."

"Was it someone else?"

Alyssa searched for an escape route. Her frantic gaze moved from the door to the window. "I don't know," she repeated. "I don't...I can't... It's all a dream! It wasn't real!"

Amanda moved quickly to her mother's side, wrapping her in a reassuring embrace. Even though Alyssa was both taller and years older than she was, Amanda was the stronger of the two at that moment. When Amanda pulled back, she saw that her mother was unconsciously rubbing her right palm, as if trying to erase a memory.

Gently, Amanda intervened. She took the offending hand and held it between her own. She smiled softly.

Tears formed in Alyssa's eyes. "I wanted to tell you," she whispered, "but...I was afraid. I didn't want to say anything that might hurt Dad...or Phil. Not when it's probably just some kind of crazy—"

"Dreams aren't real, Mom. You probably heard someone say something the next day. You might even have heard the shot. Phil did. He's going to testify soon that he heard it from outside the building as he was walking by. If he heard it, you might have, too. That's not unreasonable."

"But what about my hand?" Alyssa whispered thinly.

Amanda knew she had to do something to calm her mother. After the trial, if she was still upset, they might have to take her to a specialist to see if they could get to the bottom of what was bothering her. "Haven't you always told me you have an overactive imagination?" Amanda teased.

Alyssa smiled weakly. "Yes," she said, wiping at her cheeks.

"Then don't worry about it. There's nothing you've told me tonight that changes anything in the trial. Dreams can't be admitted as evidence. Not by either side." Amanda paused to see if her words had had the desired effect. Her mother looked less agitated. Amanda took her bowl to the sink, rinsed it, then said, "Come on. Let's get to bed. Tomorrow is going to be another long day."

Her mother's smile, stronger now, was her reward.

AMANDA HAD two main questions for Brick Bauer the next morning. She asked if, in his experience, the fact that a person owned a gun meant that it was he or she who always fired it. She received no as his answer. Then she asked if, when Liza gave him the bullet, he had tried to question Joe Santori. The answer again was no. Ethan, of course, attempted to mend the inroads she'd carved into the jurors' minds, but she could sense that yesterday's damage had been somewhat muted.

A ballistics expert was called to take the stand. He went through a long process explaining how markings are made on a bullet as it passes through the barrel of a gun, and how those markings are unique to each weapon. He then produced some photographs of slides showing tests he had performed on the gun. The tests confirmed his opinion that the bullet found in the baseboard of Margaret's room was a match to bullets fired from Judson's gun. The markings were the same.

On cross-examination, Amanda asked, "Is there a way to tell *when* a bullet was fired from a gun? I'm speaking of years, not hours." "Can you tell one year from the next?" "Then this bullet you're speaking of could have been fired anytime from October 1948 to—let's say a five-year span—1953?" Upon receiving confirmation of that fact, she sat down.

Ethan didn't bother to stand up. He just fired the question from his seat: "But, Mr. Matthews, is it not also correct that the bullet could have been discharged on a warm summer evening in late July of 1950, on the day Margaret Ingalls was killed?"

"Of course," the expert readily agreed.

"Thank you," Ethan said.

Amanda had no comeback.

Next, Ethan called a forensic pathologist. The list of letters after the man's name was almost as long as the name itself. His years of service to the state of Wisconsin were also impressive. He even *looked* intelligent, with his high forehead and studious expression.

Ethan's line of questioning centered around one concept: "Is it possible for a bullet to pass through a body without hitting any bone and still inflict a grievous wound?" The answer was yes. Ethan poked and prodded to keep the man on the stand a little longer, but the original question was the one he had been going for.

Amanda decided to get a little more specific during her cross-examination. "Tell me, Dr. Petrasonovich," she said, "in your opinion, would a soft tissue wound like the one you've described cause a great loss of blood?''

''That's hard to say exactly,'' he replied. ''There are so many variables. It would depend upon where the person was hit. In the arm, in the stomach, in the leg, in between the ribs…''

''The victim would have to die quickly—does that help you to be more specific?''

''Yes. Then the person would have to be hit in a major vessel, an artery. And yes, there would be a great loss of blood.''

''Thank you, Dr. Petrasonovich. No further questions.''

She had been planning to ask about the most likely place a bullet might hit an artery without leaving a trace on bone. The expert she'd consulted before the trial opened had suggested the side of the neck, the carotid artery, which would play beautifully on her plan to raise doubts about the trajectory of the bullet in the baseboard. The murderer would have to have been amazingly tall, or else would have to have stood on the bed or held the gun high over his or her head.

But Amanda decided against asking the question. *Where* the bullet might have struck didn't matter so much as the picture the jury now saw of a person bleeding to death, of a large amount of blood. Ethan would still have to introduce the carpet to connect the blood and the bullet to the corpse. And the amount of blood on the carpet was not in keeping with the great amount of blood the witness had just testified to. She had caught Ethan in another bind. She would just leave it at this point, and see if he could wiggle his way out.

Ethan took her place before the witness. ''If the

heart was pierced, would there be a great loss of blood?''

''No, because the heart would stop beating.''

Ethan sat down.

Amanda stood. She didn't move away from the table. ''But what is the probability of a bullet doing such a thing? It would have to enter the body, hit the heart, then exit the body without striking a bone, and still be traveling at enough speed to embed itself in a baseboard.''

''That probability is extremely small,'' Dr. Petrasonovich granted.

Amanda resumed her seat. Ethan bounced up.

''But possible?'' he asked.

Dr. Petrasonovich smiled slightly. ''Yes, possible,'' he said.

''Thank you.'' Ethan resumed his seat.

Amanda glanced at the jury, wondering if the lawyers had lost them during this little byplay. They hadn't. Each face was intent, interested. She heaved a mental sigh, relieved because she felt she'd gained a point.

After the midmorning recess, the next witness Ethan called was Liza. She came into the room proudly defiant, lifted her hand to take the oath, then sat in the witness box, her blue gaze fixed on Ethan.

He made no effort to ease into her testimony. ''State your name, please,'' he requested briskly.

''Mary Elizabeth Baron Forrester. Most people call me Liza.''

''What is your relationship with the defendant in this case?''

Liza lifted her chin. ''He's my grandfather.''

''Do you love your grandfather, Liza?''

Anger sparked in Liza's eyes. "When I said most people call me Liza, I meant my *friends*. Not you! Definitely…not you!"

Ethan didn't react. "Just answer the question. Do you love your grandfather?"

Liza bristled again. "I don't see where that's any of your business. My feelings for my grandfather are personal. They have no part—"

Ethan wheeled to face the judge. "Your Honor, I'd like to have this person declared a hostile witness. As you can see, she definitely feels personal animosity. And in order for me to question her adequately—"

"Objection!" Amanda called.

The judge stopped everyone by raising his hand. "Objection overruled. Your request is granted, Mr. Trask. Proceed."

Liza glanced at Amanda. Amanda had tried to get her sister to see reason. She'd been afraid that this would happen. But Liza wouldn't listen. Now Ethan Trask was no longer bound by the rules that prevent a lawyer from cross-examining his own witness. He could use leading questions, put words into her mouth, and Amanda could do nothing about it.

"Let's start again, Mrs. Forrester," Ethan said. "Is it not true that you love your grandfather?"

Liza sputtered.

"Answer the question. It's very simple. You do love him, don't you? Or is there a reason that you don't?"

"Of course I love him!" Liza snapped.

"Is it not also true that you came into possession of the bullet that Joe Santori found at Timberlake Lodge? He told you where he found it, and still, knowing that the police were investigating the murder of your grandmother and knowing that your grandfather was a prime suspect, you did nothing?''

"I gave it to the police. I gave it to Brick!''

"But not until a period of time had elapsed.''

"It was just a few days, a week at most.''

"Why? Why did you hesitate? Were you afraid that it might look bad for your grandfather? That the police might take the bullet and match it to a gun your grandfather owned?''

"Objection, Your Honor, he's not letting the witness answer!'' Amanda interrupted.

"Overruled. But, Mr. Trask, give her a chance.''

Ethan nodded shortly, his dark gaze riveted on Liza. "Were you afraid it might look bad for your grandfather?'' he repeated coolly.

Liza set her jaw. "I was busy. We were working on the lodge, trying to get it ready for Christmas. My family was planning a party.''

"And you just forgot.''

Liza didn't like the skepticism she heard in his voice. "Have you ever planned a party, Mr. Trask?'' she retorted. "Or renovated a building? There's an amazing amount of work to do.''

"Your Honor—'' Ethan complained, turning to the judge.

"Answer the question, Mrs. Forrester.''

"I thought I had, Judge.''

Ethan persisted. "And I thought you said you loved your grandfather. Does that mean you'd do anything for him…including conceal evidence?''

"I didn't conceal—''

"You also found a rug in the attic at Timberlake Lodge, didn't you, Liza?''

Liza sulked. "Yes.''

"A rug that had once been on the floor of your grandmother's room there."

"Yes."

"You found it hidden away in the attic among many other things that once belonged to your grandmother, didn't you?"

"I wouldn't say they were 'hidden away'! They were just…there."

"In the attic?"

"Yes."

"What articles did the room that used to be hers contain?"

"I don't understand."

"At the time you found the rug in the attic, was her room empty? Did it have any furnishings? Did it have any reminders of the person who used to live there, except for a portrait and a mirror that Margaret must once have gazed into?"

"It was empty, but…"

"Do you remember the room *ever* having furnishings?"

"I wasn't allowed to go to the lodge."

"But you went anyway, didn't you?"

Again, Liza lifted her chin. "A few times," she admitted, "when I was a child."

"Did the room have furnishings at those times?"

"No."

Ethan turned away. "No further questions."

Amanda approached the stand where her sister sat. She held a small plastic bag she had picked up from the evidence table. As directed by the judge before the trial started, Amanda gave no indication that she and Liza shared a familial relationship. She even went out of her way to pretend that they didn't.

"Mrs. Forrester," she said formally, "it has been established that Joe Santori gave you a bullet that he said he found in the baseboard of Margaret Ingalls's bedroom at Timberlake Lodge. Before you turned it over to the police, did you mark it in any way so that you might know it at a later date?"

"Mark it?" Liza asked, frowning.

"Scratch the base? Examine the bullet for any peculiarities that would make it unique?"

Liza shrugged. "I just put it in a drawer. I didn't look at it."

"I would like to show you state's exhibit number 102. Can you swear that this is the bullet Joe Santori handed you?"

"Your Honor!" Ethan interrupted.

"I have no idea," Liza answered without hesitation, before the judge could speak.

"Your Honor!" Ethan protested more strongly.

"Sit down, Mr. Trask," Judge Griffen ordered. Then he gave Liza a firm look. "I'd appreciate the chance to make a ruling before you answer the question. Remember that in future, please. Proceed, Counselor."

"So this bullet might be any bullet. You have no way of knowing?"

"That's correct," Liza agreed.

"Thank you," Amanda said and walked sedately back to the defense table.

Ethan sat very still. Amanda knew that he was weighing his options. In the end he decided to pass. "No questions, Your Honor," he said.

"The witness is excused," Judge Griffen intoned, and Liza stepped away from the stand. As she moved past Judson, her back to the jurors, she gave him a bright, confident smile. The smile included Amanda, and when Amanda glanced around at Ethan, she knew that he had seen it. She could sense that he was annoyed. He still thought they were ganging up on him.

The next two witnesses after lunch were rather dull in comparison to the fireworks with Liza. But then, that was the way it had always been with Liza. People who followed her, no matter who they were or what they were doing, always paled by comparison.

The first was Joe Campbell, the dry cleaner from Tyler, who had found traces of blood on the Oriental rug that had been sent in for cleaning. He testified about how some punch had been spilled on the beautiful old piece during a Christmas party at the lodge, and how Alyssa Baron, Judson's daughter, had sent it to his shop to be cleaned. He also told how Karen Keppler, Tyler's new police captain and the person who'd spilled the punch, had called to tell him to charge the bill to her.

"At this point, had you cleaned the rug?" Ethan asked.

"No, sir. You see, I could get the punch out, no problem. But the blood...that blood looked pretty old. That's what I told Captain Keppler. I told her the rug would have to be sent to Sugar Creek for special treatment, and the price would go up accordingly."

"What did Captain Keppler do then?" Ethan asked.

"She confiscated the rug as possible evidence. Had one of her men come to the shop and take it away. I think she didn't want it cleaned by mistake. As if I would."

Interest picked up for a moment when Ethan introduced the rug into evidence, but the courtroom settled back down again as the next witness took the stand.

The man was the blood expert who had matched the DNA of the blood on the rug to the DNA of the skeleton, thus typing the blood as Margaret's. The man had graphs and charts and photographs. He was avidly involved in his craft and probably extremely good at it, but he was almost too good. It was hard for him to connect with the jury. He insisted upon giving each little detail, which made Ethan's task difficult.

During her cross-examination of the two men, Amanda's questioning concerned the amount of blood on the rug. She had each point out the marked area of bloodstain on the exhibit—an area approximately six inches in diameter—and from the blood expert, she received an estimate as to the amount of blood required to make such a stain. The man hesitated to be specific, but she finally narrowed him down to four or five ounces. Her next question gained his confirmation that when a person donates blood they give one pint, or sixteen ounces. So the amount of the blood on the rug was approximately one quarter the amount taken from a person during a blood drive, nowhere near the amount lost when a person bled to death.

Ethan couldn't let her latest inroad into his case stand. He rattled off a series of questions on redirect of the last witness, mostly smoke and mirrors to get the jurors' minds off what Amanda had accomplished. This time he *used* the blood expert's tendency to give confusing details, and by the time he was through, everyone was ready for the day to end. Even the judge seemed relieved to bang his gavel and abandon the courtroom.

Amanda felt worn, her nerves jangled. The intensity of battle had increased as each day passed. She gathered her things as her grandfather was surrounded by family and friends. As quickly as she could, she broke away from them to find a quiet spot where no one would see her or talk to her. She desperately needed a moment of peace.

In an out-of-the-way alcove, she fell back against the wall and closed her eyes. Her breath came as fast as if she'd been running a race, and her heart thundered. If this pace kept up, she would fall apart! She had no idea where the defense stood at this moment. They might be winning or they might be losing. She was glad her grandfather never asked.

One thing he'd said, though, had floored her: he admired Ethan's ability. He also admired what he saw of the man—integrity, confidence, determination. Her grandfather had always been definite in his likes and his dislikes. He made up his mind quickly, and afterward it was hard to shake him from his decision. She wondered what the rest of the family would think if they knew.

She calmed her agitation by taking long, deep breaths, made the muscles in her neck and shoulders relax, then forced her expression to look less harried. She even managed to avoid reacting unduly when she emerged from her bolt hole to head for the stairs and discovered that her timing had placed her in the hall at the same moment as Ethan. He was walking with Carlos, talking to him. At first neither man saw her. Then Ethan, as if sensing her presence, looked across the short space that separated them.

His words must have stopped in midsentence, because Carlos looked at him questioningly before seeking out the cause of his abstraction. When the investigator discovered Amanda, his confusion lifted.

No one moved. Then Amanda, who'd had more time to recover, nodded at the two men and started for the stairs again. Ethan and Carlos followed two steps behind her. No one spoke until they were at the base of the curving stairway.

"Quite an interesting day, Counselor," Ethan said, his voice drawing her around. "Just as tomorrow will be."

"I'm sure," Amanda replied. "Considering all that you have in your bag of tricks."

"Not tricks," Ethan corrected. "Facts."

She tilted her head, looking up into his dark eyes. "Have you ever doubted yourself, Mr. Trask? Have you ever asked yourself if you just might be wrong?"

The dark eyes narrowed. "The state doesn't pay me to be wrong, Ms. Baron," he said levelly.

"No, it pays you to prosecute innocent people."

"It pays me to prosecute people who *say* they're innocent. Otherwise they wouldn't come to trial."

"You're a hard man, Mr. Trask."

"As hard as I have to be, Ms. Baron."

Their attention was drawn to Carlos, who stood shaking his head sadly.

"What's wrong with you?" Ethan snapped, giving the first sign that he might be feeling just as on edge as Amanda from the wear and tear of the trial.

"I find it sad," Carlos said, "that two people who are so obviously right for each other must continue to be apart."

"Two peop—" Ethan repeated, shocked that Carlos would come out with such a statement.

Amanda blinked, equally shocked.

Carlos smiled slightly, enjoying the effect his words had had. "Two people," he repeated. "You, Ethan. And you, Amanda…if I might call you that."

Ethan's hands had curled into fists. Amanda didn't know if he wanted to hit his companion or not, but if she had to bet on the outcome of a fight, she'd put her money on Carlos losing.

"I never saw you as Cupid, Carlos," Ethan said tightly.

The man's smile broadened. "A person plays the role in life that he is given," he said.

"A person should value his teeth!" Ethan returned.

"A person must speak the truth. You have said that many times, my friend."

Eyes wide, Amanda witnessed the byplay between the two men. At first, her face had flamed. Now she was fascinated. She didn't notice the people moving about the great lobby or hear the noises associated with their business in the courthouse. Her gaze moved from Ethan to Carlos and back to Ethan. He had argued against Carlos saying what he had, but he hadn't argued against the content. Did that mean Ethan thought them right for each other, too?

Ethan glanced at her, saw her interest and quickly decided to make a strategic retreat. Grabbing hold of his friend's arm, he murmured brusquely, "See you in court tomorrow, Counselor," before he walked away, dragging Carlos with him.

But he couldn't prevent the reassuring wink Carlos gave her, or the answering smile of comprehension that Amanda returned.

Ethan *did* think them right for each other!

CHAPTER SIXTEEN

THE NEXT DAY was extremely difficult for the defense. Ethan called a procession of witnesses who had known Judson and Margaret during the span of their marriage—people from the community and others who had been Margaret's friends in the Chicago area. He even produced a woman who had once worked as a maid at Timberlake Lodge.

The testimony from the people who knew Judson and Margaret underscored the marital difficulties experienced by the pair. As Peter had warned, Ethan painted a picture of a man unable to control his wife's actions, a man insanely jealous of his wife's lovers, a wealthy man whose wife spent money like water, a man who resented his wife's inattentiveness to their child. All Amanda could do was try to deflect the damage. She got each witness in turn to say that Judson loved his wife and affirm how he had tried to hold the marriage together.

The former maid identified a note she'd kept all these years, the note Margaret had written the last day of her life to tell Judson that she was leaving him, a note that Ethan introduced into evidence. The maid testified about the arguments she'd overheard between Judson and Margaret, and about the disrupted state of Margaret's room the morning after their final argument. She also told how that next morning Judson, distraught, had ordered all the guests immediately ousted from their rooms and from the lodge, and had ordered Margaret's room cleared of all its furniture and the room locked. She described how servants had rolled up the rug and put it in the attic, and how they'd moved everything else upstairs as well.

Amanda could only try to show that the maid had mixed fact with gossip. She was an older woman now; her mind was fuzzy on some of the finer points in the past. But Amanda couldn't push her too hard. Abigail Simpson looked like everyone's version of a sweet old grandmother. She didn't want the jury to think that she was behaving like a bully.

Late that afternoon, after the recess, Ethan called Conrad Frayen to the stand. Ingalls Farm and Machinery's longtime accountant was so thin he seemed in danger of breaking as he wheezed his way to the witness box. Once there, though, he met Ethan's gaze with proud resistance.

"Judson Ingalls is my friend," Conrad repeated more than once during his testimony, even though his words were struck from the record.

Still, Ethan was able to pull the information from him that he wanted. Conrad admitted to financial troubles at the F and M forty-two years ago, and how those troubles had suddenly cleared up after Margaret's disappearance. How Judson had told him he'd managed to get Margaret's signature on the bonds they jointly owned just before she left Tyler.

Amanda could do little with Conrad's testimony. What he'd said had hurt them by adding to Judson's growing list of reasons for wanting Margaret dead. The idea Ethan managed to get across was that Judson had forced his wife to sign the documents. Amanda couldn't fight that unless she put her grandfather on the stand. And it seemed, with each passing day, that she had no other choice.

The last witness for that day was Judson's bank manager. Fred Dryer took the stand dressed in his nattiest suit, his thinning hair combed neatly to one side, and he told everyone that, yes indeed, Judson had come to his bank to cash in the bonds he and Margaret owned. Ethan asked if he had verified Margaret's signature.

"I did," Fred Dryer confirmed, "but I didn't really need to. I'd seen it enough over the years on her numerous bank drafts!"

Amanda didn't bother to cross-examine him. There was nothing for her to refute.

EVEN THE FAMILY realized how badly the day had gone. There were no false smiles or bracing words of assurance when court was adjourned. As they filed into the old Victorian later, they might have been going to a wake.

"What can we do?" Liza demanded. Since being dismissed as a witness, she had stationed herself firmly in the spectators' gallery.

Unaware of the pressure they were applying, they all turned their eyes on Amanda. Once again they were in need of her reassurance. And once again, she tried to oblige. "We do what we've been doing all along," she said. "From what Peter tells me, you can't take one or two days out of a trial and decide you're either winning or losing. And no one can ever tell with a jury. What we consider a terrible blow, the jury might barely notice. So when we go into court tomorrow, we don't act as if today was the end of the world."

She turned to her grandfather. "Granddad, you once said you wanted to tell your side of the story. Do you still want to do it?"

Judson looked at her. "Yes."

"In all likelihood Ethan will rest his case tomorrow, the day after at the latest. We'll put on a few witnesses ourselves, but shortly after our side opens, you'll be put on the stand. Is that what you want?"

"It is," Judson said firmly.

Amanda reached out to hug his neck. "Then that's what we'll do," she said.

The family settled a bit, but Amanda could sense that they were worried.

AMANDA ARRIVED at the courthouse quite early the next morning. She wanted time to collect herself. Thinking of what lay ahead, she hadn't spent an easy night. She knew Ethan had yet to call Phil Wocheck, his most important witness, and she expected him to do it today. She wanted to be ready.

She stopped by the snack bar for a cup of coffee and found Carlos already there, nursing a cup himself. The Cuban smiled at her, the sweet charm of his expression warming her as it always did. Against her instincts, Amanda stopped. She didn't want to talk with him about Ethan. She wanted to think only of the case. But she seemed unable to help herself.

"Good morning," she murmured.

"Good morning," he replied. "You are here early. So is Ethan...but he is already in the courtroom, so you do not have to worry."

"I wasn't worried," she protested, even though she had looked furtively around.

Carlos shook his head. "I thought we were all through with that, but I suppose everything will just have to wait until after the trial, since that is the way the two of you are determined to play it."

"We're not playing—" Amanda began.

"Yes, you are," Carlos interrupted. "And if you are not careful, you may play yourselves right off the field. That is why I said what I did. The two of you are much more alike than you think. So much pride. So much fealty to the past." He took a sip of coffee. When she said nothing, he continued, "I told you once before that Ethan trusts no one. I did not tell you why. He did not grow up as you did, surrounded by people who loved you, people who looked after you, people who protected you from harm. Ethan grew up in a place much different, where people did little to watch out for one another, where people did not care. His mother worked very hard to support the two of them, but I am sure there were many nights as a child when he went to bed hungry. He did not tell me this, but I know it.

"Many of his friends from that time are in jail now...or are dead. It was that kind of world. But it could not destroy Ethan. He was smart. He went to college, he went to law school...but before he could do any of the things he had planned to do for his mother, she died.

"Now he has no one to soften the edges. He has worked for so many years with people who are the worst we humans have to offer that he has hardened his heart. Or at least, he has tried to do so. It is because his heart is so tender that he must work to harden it. Does that make sense to you, Amanda Baron?"

It made perfect sense to Amanda. She knew exactly what Carlos was saying. One of the reasons she had never wanted to go into criminal law was that she would have such a difficult time living with the outcome of each case. Was the person innocent or was he guilty? Had she just assisted a criminal to get back on the streets or had she put an innocent man in jail? Ethan solved the problem by not giving an inch. But that did something to a person after a time, especially when there was no one to make life easier.

She could also identify with his frustration concerning his mother. She felt a similar distress about her father's death. Why hadn't he come to her? Told her what was happening? She would happily have come home from school and tried to help. But he hadn't told her; instead, he had taken his own life.

"I understand," Amanda said softly.

Carlos smiled. "Good," he said, and seconds later, Amanda walked away.

ETHAN SAT at the prosecutor's table, going over his notes. After today's first witness, he would call Phil Wocheck, and he wanted to be sure that he had thought of everything he wanted to ask him.

He sensed movement at his side and looked up to see Amanda settling at the adjacent table. For a moment, all thoughts of the trial were wiped from his mind. His memory whipped back to the day before yesterday, when Carlos had waxed poetical about love and life and what he thought ought to take place between them. At times Ethan wished he had his friend's easy way of looking at things. It was so simple in Carlos's eyes: if Ethan cared for Amanda, he should tell her. But it wasn't so simple. Nothing was *ever* that simple.

She looked up. His gaze didn't waver. Wordless communication passed between them; flushing, Amanda jerked her eyes away.

Ethan shifted in his chair. *Holy God!* he thought. *If I'm not careful, I* am *going to leap on her across the table!* He hadn't forgotten the accusation she'd once made—an accusation that he had dismissed, but obviously should not have.

He forced his gaze back to his notes and tried to concentrate. But he was highly aware of her, and highly aware of his own awareness. Finally, unable to conquer the situation, he pushed away from the table and walked out of the room.

When he came back a half hour later, onlookers had started to filter into the gallery, the press had staked out the halls and Amanda was nowhere to be seen. He went back to his notes and was again interrupted by Amanda's arrival. This time, though, she was in the company of her grandfather. While friends and family settled into their seats, Ethan was aware of the resentment and anger directed toward him. Yet as he met Judson Ingalls's eyes, he saw neither emotion. Lacking, too, was any evidence of arrogance or cockiness. Instead, pride mixed with pain in the gaze of the man who stood accused. And for the first time in Ethan's memory of similar situations between himself and a defendant, he was the first to look away.

The judge and jury arrived, and the courtroom was called to order. The day's first witness was Zachary Phelps. Ethan knew he had two problems with this witness: he, too, was Judson's friend; as well, the ex-police chief's mental faculties were such that his testimony could be easily challenged. But Ethan was betting on Amanda's reluctance to tear the man apart.

With some hesitation, Zachary told of the day following Margaret's disappearance. How Judson had told him, "Margaret's gone and it's all my fault." How distressed Judson had been while showing him the note Margaret left. He also admitted that Judson had never mounted a search for her.

Ethan sat down, satisfied with the testimony. He watched as Amanda straightened. Today she wore a dark red suit that complemented her hair and her coloring. She looked efficient and competent…and wholly desirable. Ethan savagely disciplined his thoughts.

"Chief Phelps," she said, moving closer to the stand, "you know Judson Ingalls well, do you not? Would you consider yourself his friend?" Upon receiving confirmation, she asked, "Did Judson Ingalls ever tell you why he didn't try to find his wife?"

Zachary Phelps nodded. "He did. He said that this time if Margaret wanted to leave, he'd let her. He wasn't going to try any longer to make her stay where she didn't want to be."

"And you believed him?"

"I believed him."

Amanda spared Ethan a glance as she sat down. He returned to his feet.

"Yet you *are* aware that Margaret Ingalls's body was found at Timberlake Lodge?" The question was a strong reminder of the fact.

"Yes," Zachary Phelps agreed.

"Thank you." Ethan settled back at the table, signaling his dismissal of the witness.

The next witness was Philip Wocheck. The old man hobbled into the courtroom, leaning heavily on a walker. He needed some assistance getting into the witness chair.

Ethan waited as a court officer sprang forward to help, then he drew a breath and began. He took the old man through all the preliminaries—his name, his connection to the case. Phil answered slowly, his accent lending weight to his solemn attitude.

"Would you tell us, please, what you were doing the evening of July seventeenth of that year?" The question was brisk yet polite.

"I was digging a hole to plant a tree."

"What kind of tree?"

"A willow tree."

"Did anything happen while you were digging the hole?"

"It was hot that day—that was why I waited until late afternoon to dig. Still, I became thirsty. At dusk I went to get a drink of water. When I did, I heard two people arguing. Then I heard a shot."

"A gunshot?"

"Yes."

"Where were you when you heard all of this?" Ethan asked.

"Outside of Margaret Ingalls's bedroom."

"What did you see next?"

"A man...a man running away from the room."

"Did you recognize that man, Mr. Wocheck?"

Phil shrugged. "It was almost dark...."

Ethan came closer to the stand, his veneer of politeness eroding. "What did you do next?"

"I went into the bedroom through the French doors."

"What did you find there?"

"Clothes…on the bed, a suitcase half full of lacy things, feathers. She was going away."

"What else did you see?"

Phil hesitated. "I saw her."

"Margaret Ingalls?"

"Yes."

The courtroom rumbled with comment. The public had not known before that Phil Wocheck had seen Margaret Ingalls dead. The judge banged his gavel for silence, then he nodded at Ethan to continue.

"Where was she?" Ethan asked.

"Lying on the floor by the bed."

"Was she dead?"

"Yes. There was blood…much blood. On her face, on her hair. On her shoulder. I checked her pulse. There was none."

"What did you do next?"

"I saw the note on the mantelpiece. It was her paper, the color of lilacs and smelling of her scent. The note said she was leaving."

"What did you do then?"

Phil answered simply, "I helped her to go."

By now the silence in the courtroom was deafening. No one spoke, no one moved, no one even seemed to breathe.

"Explain, please," Ethan urged softly.

"I wrapped her in a shawl I found on the bed and carried her out to the tree hole. I dug a little deeper. I put her in. I put in dirt. I put in the tree. And I put in more dirt, until it was done."

"My God," a person in the gallery breathed. Other people began to murmur as well. The judge banged his gavel again to silence them.

"Then what did you do?" Ethan asked, his body taut.

"I went back to her room."

"And what did you do there?"

"I finished packing her clothes, then I hid the suitcase in the potting shed where I worked."

"Did you find a gun?"

"Yes."

"What did you do with it?"

"I took it to my room. I do not like guns. I did not want anyone else to be hurt."

Ethan stepped back, his gaze intent. "Did you recognize the gun? Had you ever seen it before?"

"A gun is a gun. I do not like guns."

"Answer my question, Mr. Wocheck. Had you seen it before?"

"Yes, I think so."

"Who did it belong to?"

"Margaret Ingalls."

"Don't you mean Judson Ingalls?" Ethan demanded.

Phil shrugged. "One...the other...both. I do not know."

Ethan moved forward again, aware that everyone's attention was riveted on him. He used his next question like a rapier thrust. "Why did you do it, Mr. Wocheck? Why did you go to all the trouble of burying Margaret Ingalls's body and then hiding her suitcase and the gun that killed her?"

"Objection!" Amanda protested. "No basis in fact. The prosecution has not yet established that the gun did, indeed, kill Margaret Ingalls."

"Sustained," the judge said.

Ethan repeated the question, this time leaving out

the disputed fact about the gun. "Why did you do it?" he demanded.

"Because she was a bad woman. She hurt people. She wanted to go, so I helped her go!"

"Don't you mean...you helped your employer? You *knew* that Judson Ingalls had killed his wife, so you went to great pains to cover up the fact."

"Objection!" Amanda cried even more strenuously.

Ethan continued his questioning as if there had been no intervention. "Did Judson Ingalls *direct* you to do all those things, Mr. Wocheck? Did he *order* you to do them?"

Amanda jerked to her feet. "Your Honor! Mr. Trask is—"

"Mr. Trask is skating a very fine line," the judge interrupted. "Mr. Trask, be extremely careful."

Ethan nodded. He kept his gaze on the witness, who continued to stare past him. Philip Wocheck was a stubborn old man. Ethan *knew* he was continuing to hide something. "Did he, Mr. Wocheck?" he insisted.

"No." The answer was gruff.

Ethan rested a hand on the low railing that fronted the jury box. "Margaret Ingalls had many lovers, didn't she, Mr. Wocheck?" he said softly, yet there was danger in that softness. "You know the color of her notepaper. You even know the scent she used.... Were *you* one of her lovers?"

Ethan had wanted to shake the man, shake out of him the testimony he resisted giving. He was only partially successful.

Phil's arthritic hands curled into fists as his body stiffened. An angry fire burned in his eyes. "I am an

old man, Mr. Trask. I forget many things. But I would
never forget *that!* No! I was never Margaret Ingalls's
lover! She was not the kind of woman I *could* love.
She hurt her husband, she hurt her child—'' His de-
nial stopped, instantly cut off, and Ethan had an inkling that he had hit on something. Instead of trying
to protect Judson Ingalls, was Phil Wocheck somehow, in some way, trying to protect the *child?*
Alyssa?

Ethan swiveled his head, his eyes searching for the
woman in the crowd. He couldn't find her. His mind
raced, but he could make no further connections. He
pressed Phil with a few more questions that the man
obstinately refused to answer, saying he couldn't remember. Then Ethan sat down. Suddenly the case felt
askew, as if it had shifted slightly off center. He
watched as Amanda approached the witness.

AMANDA'S HEART thumped wildly. She sensed that
something had happened, but she didn't know what,
or how to capitalize on it. She glanced at Ethan and
then at Phil. Something Phil had said… She straightened her shoulders. She didn't have time right then
to figure it out. She had to ask questions, dispel the
notion Ethan had built that Phil was covering for her
grandfather.

''When you found the body, you said there was a
lot of blood. How much do you mean? Was there a
huge puddle on the floor…on the rug? Did you have
to step over it?''

Phil looked at her. Amanda wondered if he thought
it inappropriate that she, Margaret's granddaughter,
should ask such a question. He answered slowly. ''It

was on her head, her neck, her shoulder. Some was on the rug.''

"Some. Is that all you saw? Was there blood somewhere else in the room? On another spot on the floor? On the bed?''

"Your Honor,'' Ethan complained, "defense counsel should ask one question at a time.''

"I apologize, Your Honor,'' Amanda said. Still, she looked at Phil.

"Only there,'' he murmured, "where I said.''

"What about other wounds?'' Amanda asked.

"I don't remember,'' Phil replied.

Amanda moved closer to the stand. "Was something else happening at the lodge the night you found Margaret?'' she asked.

Phil huffed in disdain. "A party. She was always having parties.''

"With many guests?'' Amanda asked. "How many? Ten...twenty?''

"I do not know. They made a lot of noise. More than ten.''

"Both men and women?''

Phil huffed again. "She always made sure to have many men around.''

Amanda stopped walking. "Is it possible that the man you saw running from Margaret's room was one of the men from the party?''

She waited for an objection from Ethan, but it didn't come.

"I do not know,'' Phil said, sticking to his story.

Amanda felt her own sense of frustration with Phil. If only he could be a bit more specific...he was specific enough when he wanted to be!

''Thank you,'' she murmured and returned to her seat.

Phil was excused, and when Ethan rose to say that the state rested, Amanda touched her grandfather's hand. One plateau in the trial had been reached; they would now start the climb toward another.

ALYSSA LEANED BACK against the rest room door, her body trembling uncontrollably. What Phil had said… He had heard two people arguing…. Just like her dream! Then a gunshot… *Just like her dream!* A low keening sound echoed hollowly throughout the marble-tiled room. The sound came from her, but she wasn't aware of making it. She simply knew it was a product of her body, just as she knew that Phil hadn't told the whole truth just now. There was no question, there was no reason—she just *knew!* He said he'd come into the room and seen…Margaret! But he hadn't! He'd come into the room and seen…her! Alyssa! A little girl. She had been standing there, looking at Margaret, looking after the shadowy man, then she had slowly transferred her disbelieving gaze to Phil….

What was dream? What was reality?
She had to talk to Phil.

Edward! Edward! her mind cried. But Edward was in London. He'd gone there on business shortly after the trial started, and he wouldn't be back for several days.

When this was over, she had to find out the truth! It was either that or go insane—just as everyone undoubtedly thought she'd already done. She hadn't been able to sit through the rest of Phil's testimony. When he had started to talk about the blood, she'd clambered blindly over everyone's feet. She'd had to get away!

Jeff had followed her. At this moment he was waiting in the hallway outside.

She knew she needed to pull herself together.

For Jeff's sake. For Amanda's sake. For Liza's sake. For her father's sake. For her *own* sake!

The hardest part came in finding the courage to do it.

CHAPTER SEVENTEEN

AMANDA WATCHED as her grandfather approached the witness stand, his back straight, his head held high. He raised his hand, and in a resolute baritone, swore to tell the truth.

For the past several hours, Amanda had used the defense's opening witnesses to cultivate a more positive image of her grandfather during his marriage to Margaret. The jury had been told how Judson freely gave Margaret money, gave her affection. Again they were told about Margaret's way of life—her lovers, her ability to drive even her friends to the point of irritated distraction. Amanda even produced an expert witness who cast more doubt on the prosecution's story about the bullet that had magically inflicted a mortal wound in Margaret's body without touching bone and still had enough forward impetus left to embed itself in a baseboard.

Finally, as Monday afternoon wore on, the time had come to put her grandfather on the stand. Amanda gave him a moment to settle in, then she started to question him, taking him easily through the preliminaries. She included his military service in Europe during the war, having him tell how he had helped in the rescue of a village official's family and won a medal from both France and his own government as a result.

She then guided him into talking about his marriage to Margaret. In his own words, he told of the difficulties they'd experienced, made worse by his absence during the war. How he had tried to keep their marriage together despite everyone's, including his own mother's, negative opinion of his wife. How he had even moved to Chicago to try to make Margaret happy. Then, after his father's death and his subsequent inheritance of Ingalls F and M, how they had moved back to Tyler, and Margaret had started to throw lavish parties at Timberlake Lodge, scandalizing the local population with her wild behavior and her fancy friends. How he had turned a blind eye because he loved her.

"Did she take lovers over this period?" Amanda asked.

Her grandfather's chin dropped. "Yes," he replied softly.

"What happened the last time you saw her?"

"We had an argument. I needed her to sign the bonds in order to keep the F and M on its feet. If I didn't find some money, the place was going to go under, and half the people around Tyler would lose their jobs. But she wouldn't do it. She said it served the local yokels right. I couldn't make her see…" His words trailed away.

"What happened in the end? Did she sign the bonds?"

"Yes. That was the last thing I saw her do. I'd kept on at her all afternoon, trying to get her to change her mind, trying to get her to see that she wasn't hurting only me. Finally, she signed them. She said she'd do it just to shut me up. Then she told me to leave, she didn't want to see me again…and I did."

"Did you see the gun?"

Judson shook his head. "No."

"How did the gun come to be in Margaret's room?"

"I gave it to her. Some months before she'd become worried about ruffians in the area—the lodge was rather isolated. She was so worried that I gave her the gun for self-protection. I never expected her to have to use it. It was more…reassurance."

"Where did you go after you left Margaret?"

"I walked around the lake."

"Did you see anyone?"

"No."

"How long were you gone?"

"A couple of hours? I never really looked at a clock."

"Was it light when you returned?"

Judson shook his head. "No, it was dark. It had been dark for some time…maybe a half hour?"

"Where did you go when you returned to the lodge?"

"To Margaret's room. I—I wanted to try to patch things up again. But she was gone. I found her note on the mantelpiece. It said she was leaving me."

Amanda handed him the note in evidence. "This note?" she asked.

Judson held the note as if it burned him. "Yes," he choked.

Amanda allowed him a moment to collect himself. She returned the note to the evidence table, then asked, "What happened then?"

"I—I picked up one of her scent bottles and threw it at her dressing table. I was upset. I loved her! I didn't want her to leave!"

"Even though you knew she had other lovers?"

"Yes!"

"Even though you had just recently argued about her other lovers?"

"Yes!"

"Even though she ignored your child?"

"Yes! Yes!"

Amanda hesitated, then she asked softly, "Did you murder your wife, Mr. Ingalls? Did you direct that she be buried on the grounds of Timberlake Lodge? Did you pretend that she had run away, when all the time you knew exactly where she was? Did you never try to find her for that same reason?"

Ethan was on his feet, ready to object to her barrage of questions, but Amanda quickly repeated only one. "Did you murder your wife?"

Her grandfather looked at her with bleeding eyes. "No," he whispered thickly. "I couldn't kill her. I loved her! I still love her!"

Amanda dropped her head. She felt drained, just as she knew her grandfather did. "No further questions," she murmured and made her way back to her chair. The eyes of some members of the jury followed her, while others continued to watch Judson. She thought she saw tears in one or two pairs.

Ethan took his time about standing up. He didn't seem to want to jump in too quickly. His voice, when he spoke, was low, modulated. "Did Margaret ever make you angry, Mr. Ingalls? Did she ever make you *very* angry?"

For the remainder of the afternoon and all the next morning, Ethan tried to break Judson's credibility. He questioned everything Judson had said, except for his war record. That he left alone. In the end he could not break him, but he had inflicted enough damage that Amanda wasn't sure anymore if her grandfather's story was believed. She tried to make quick repairs, getting her grandfather to repeat certain aspects, but in the end she had to stop. She could see that he was wilting badly. He couldn't take much more.

She looked at Ethan, wondering if he would continue to press, but even though he must have scented blood in the grayness of her grandfather's face and in the increasing dullness of his answers, he held back. When his opportunity for recross came, he declined. He didn't go for the jugular when he could have. He didn't take the easy way, forcing mistakes from an exhausted old man.

Amanda rested her case. No rebuttal witnesses were called. Both sides closed. Then, after lunch, closing arguments were heard. Both lawyers summed up their cases, Ethan reviewing the evidence he had presented, Amanda watering her seeds of doubt.

In the end, after the judge had given the jury their instructions as to the law, all any of them—lawyers, defendant, and observers alike—could do was wait as the twelve selected men and women retired to the jury room to deliberate.

THE HOURS THAT FOLLOWED were torture. Judson spent the evening sitting in his study, reading one of his favorite books, and walking in the backyard. Alyssa disappeared into her room, taking her meals there as well as her rest. Jeff, Cece, Liza and Cliff tried to resume as much of their normal life as they could, but all found it difficult. Even baby Maggie was fretful. Amanda tried to work at her office, but ended up coming home.

Crazily, she took out her frustration on the front door. The darned thing had squeaked for years every time someone came or went, and she wasn't going to put up with it any longer. Liza had once told her it was a reassuring sound because it stayed the same. To Amanda it was a symbol of the not-so-happy past. In jeans and an old shirt, she attacked the hinges with a vengeance. When Clara asked her what on earth she was doing, she replied, "It's time for things to change for the better, Clara, and I'm going to make a start right here!" Then she aimed a can of graphite spray and pressed the nozzle. It worked! No more squeak.

The following afternoon, Peter came to the house, and Amanda introduced him to everyone. He explained that he had just finished the revisions to his manuscript and sent it off to his publisher. He also commended Amanda on the masterful job she had done in her grandfather's defense. He had been in court yesterday, he said, and he couldn't have done a better job himself.

Amanda thanked him but remained unconvinced. Right now she didn't feel like hearing congratulations. Only one thing could persuade her that she had helped her grandfather.

Word came at 5:17 p.m. Amanda had just looked at her watch for what had to be the hundredth time in ten minutes when the ringing telephone broke the silence. Everyone looked at her, including Clara and Archie, who had joined the family group. Amanda walked across the room to pick it up. "Thank you," she said, then she announced calmly, "The judge wants us back in the courtroom at six-thirty. The jury has reached a verdict."

Relief warred with trepidation. Someone was sent to find both Judson and Alyssa.

At six-thirty, everyone was back in the courtroom. If it had seemed as though an electric wire had been attached to each seat at the beginning of the trial, that was nothing to the voltage that flowed through the courtroom now. Every nerve was exposed. Agitation was barely suppressed.

Amanda and Judson sat stiffly at the defense table. Ethan waited on the prosecution's side. The judge swept into the court, called for the jury to be brought into the room, then before the verdict was read, issued a warning.

"There will be no demonstrations in this court-room. No one will be allowed into the well, and no one may approach the jurors. If the jurors wish to speak with the press, they may do so outside this courthouse. Have I made myself understood?" Judge Griffen gave everyone a hard look from his sad and solemn basset hound eyes. He reserved his longest look for the media reporters crowded into the back of the courtroom. Then he turned to the jurors.

"Members of the jury, we've been informed that you have arrived at a decision. Mrs. Delahousey, are you the foreman?" Upon confirmation, the judge continued, "Please give the paper to Mr. Williams so that I may see it."

The court officer brought the paper to the judge, who read it and then handed it back. "The verdict is in order," the judge decreed. "The court may publish the verdict. Will the defendant please stand?"

Amanda pushed away from the table at the same time her grandfather did. Her heart thumped rapidly; her knees felt weak, wobbly. Uncaring at this point what anyone thought, she threaded her fingers through those of her grandfather. His hand was icy cold. She looked into his eyes and tried to smile. She was aware of her mother behind her, of her brother and sister and the rest of their family and friends. She was aware of the jury, of the grave faces of the people she had been talking to, trying to convince these past days.... She was aware of Ethan, waiting just as tensely as she was.

The court officer started to read, "The state of Wisconsin versus Judson Thaddeus Ingalls, case number..." The words blurred, became fuzzy. Amanda fought for clarity. "...finds as follows," the officer continued, "not guilty on the charge..."

Amanda felt as if a fist had hit her hard in the stomach. Her grandfather stiffened, then he swayed, catching himself by balancing his fingertips on the table. The crowd in the gallery started to make excited noises, and some members of the press made a dive for the door, causing the judge to bang his gavel. "Order!" he intoned. "We will have order. Continue, sir."

The officer proceeded with the formalities, after which the judge formally released Judson from the legal process. Then he banged the gavel a final time and left the bench.

From that moment, the horde in the gallery nearest them couldn't be stopped. They rushed the rail, a few people coming around to hug Judson and Amanda and to pump their hands in congratulations. Excited noises filled the room as the pandemonium continued. Amanda's emotions were carried along with the crowd's. She had time only to glance at Ethan as he quietly repacked his briefcase and shook the one or two hands that offered consolation. There were no laurels for the loser.

Outside the courtroom the media surrounded them. Smiling hugely, Amanda spoke freely for the first time. So did her grandfather. With some of his accustomed dignity cast aside, he told everyone how joyous he was at the outcome. He had Tisha on one side, Alyssa on the other and Amanda next to her mother. Judson managed to hug them all. That was the photograph spread across the front page of the local newspaper.

THE PARTY CONTINUED late into the night. Champagne had been uncorked; Clara had several cakes prepared. She'd been sure of a positive outcome all along, she claimed.

Amanda went from group to group, happy and yet with a strange sadness lingering in her soul. She tried to keep an eye out for her grandfather, to be sure that he wouldn't exhaust himself. Jeff was doing the same thing. In fact, Jeff had told her that when one o'clock came around, he was going to call a halt to the celebration so that Judson—and their mother—could rest.

Shortly before the appointed time, Amanda noticed that her grandfather was missing. She searched the groups in the two main rooms, and when she didn't find him, she checked the study. Then she looked on the back porch, one of his favorite spots, especially at night. He loved the feel of the quiet air, he said. It was there she found him, sitting in one of the twin high-backed rocking chairs that had been considered old when he was born. His gaze broke away from the moonlit yard when he heard her approach.

"It's you, girlie?" he asked softly. Voices sounded far off in the house, filled with laughter and happiness and good cheer.

"It's me, Granddad," she said. "Are you all right? Do you want everyone to leave? Jeff was planning to roust them shortly, but he can speed things along, if you like."

"I'm fine…fine," Judson murmured, his gaze returning to the yard.

Amanda claimed the chair at his side. Sitting in one of the old rockers gave her a feeling of continuity, of a blood tie solid and unbroken, a tie that held people together from one generation to the next.

Judson sighed, a deep heartfelt sound. "You did a good thing, girlie," he said quietly. "For me, for your mother…for our family. I didn't want to shame them by being sent to jail."

"As you said before, Granddad, the truth won out."

"Did it?" Judson asked. "Did it really? I'm not so sure. Right now people are happy. But what about tomorrow? I know I'm innocent. I know I didn't kill Margaret. But what about them? Won't some of the people in this town still wonder? The jury said 'not guilty,' it didn't say 'innocent.' There's a difference."

"People won't think that!" she denied.

"What about your Mr. Trask? He believes I did it."

"He doesn't know you! All he has to go on is what he was told."

"Which means I still *look* guilty. The evidence was pretty persuasive. I might have voted to convict myself, if I'd have been on the jury."

"Granddad…"

Judson turned to her and smiled. "Shh. It's all right. I'm not ungrateful. What you did for me was wonderful, Amanda. I'll never forget it. Now...if you'll forgive me, I'm tired. I'm so tired I can barely think anymore, and I'm just rambling on." He patted her hand. "Go back to the party. Enjoy yourself. You deserve it. Just let me sit out here and enjoy things in my own way. I'm fine...fine." He withdrew his hand and turned away. He wanted to be alone.

Amanda moved to the door, but before going inside, she paused to look back at him. Possibly he had arrived at the reason for the sadness she felt deep inside. In the midst of their celebration, she, too, had sensed that their victory was bittersweet...because Margaret was just as dead. *Someone* had killed her. And if not her grandfather, who?

THE DAY AFTER the end of trial, Ethan packed his few personal possessions in a box, then started work on clearing away the materials left in his temporary office. The secretary on loan from the district attorney's office would be gone in another two days. She was needed elsewhere. So as far as he was concerned, the office might as well be shut down, too. In a way, it would be good to get back to Madison, to his real office, to his real secretary, to his apartment.

Carlos tapped on the door, but didn't wait to enter. He carried a newspaper, and without a word, placed it under Ethan's nose.

On the front page was a photo taken just after the trial. A jubilant Judson Ingalls had his arms around three women, one of whom was Amanda.

"Would you like me to cut it out?" Carlos asked. "So you might have something to remember her by?

Since you will not swallow your pride and go talk to her.''

''Shut up, Carlos,'' Ethan said reflexively, pushing the paper aside.

Carlos shook his head. ''I never thought you were a bad sport. Should you not at least congratulate her on her win?''

''You really like to rub it in, don't you?''

''I have never been as sure as you that Judson Ingalls was a murderer.'' Ethan looked at him and Carlos shrugged. ''It was only a feeling.''

''Then you must be happy that I lost.''

''You did not lose, my friend. Justice won. Remember? Anyway, I came to tell you that I have been reassigned. I must leave this afternoon.''

Ethan paused. He looked at the Cuban and realized that he would miss him. It came as something of a shock that he should feel that way. He and Carlos had worked on cases before; they had also parted before. But this was the first time he'd felt regret. The Ingalls case had been odd from the beginning. It was even more odd at the end. ''Let's hope it won't be too long before we work together again,'' he said.

White teeth flashed. ''Invite me to the wedding. That is all I ask.''

''Shut up, Carlos,'' Ethan said quietly, this time in camaraderie.

The men shook hands, and Carlos turned away.

Ethan's attention went back to the box. He didn't know that Carlos had stopped to speak with someone until he heard a feminine voice say the investigator's name. A familiar feminine voice. Amanda Baron!

Ethan's head jerked up, his gaze immediately locking on the two figures in the doorway. The notebook he held slipped out of his hands and crashed to the floor.

Carlos grinned. "A salute for the bride-to-be," he teased. Then he formally lifted Amanda's hand, bowed over it and touched the soft skin with his lips. "May you be forever happy, Amanda Baron. And may you help my friend to be happy, too."

She murmured something that Ethan didn't hear.

When Carlos finally took his leave, Amanda remained in the doorway, seeming uncertain of her next move. Then she followed through with a decision to enter. She examined the room. "So this is your lair," she remarked.

She looked perfect today—bright chestnut hair curling freely to her shoulders, creamy skin, beautiful dark blue eyes, soft kissable mouth. She wore white slacks and a nubby cotton sweater in a delicate shade of pink.

"This is it," he agreed, reaching to retrieve the fallen notebook.

Her gaze was focused on him when he looked at her again.

"I often wondered what your office was like," she said. She moved to the window that overlooked the public green, leaned closer to glance outside, then turned back to face him. "I was here the first day you came to Sugar Creek—in the courthouse, I mean. I saw you when you came to set up this office."

Ethan frowned.

"But you didn't see me," she continued. "You walked right past me in the lobby."

Fascinated, he watched as she started toward him. She stopped just out of reach. "I thought you were extremely handsome," she confessed. "I'd seen your photograph in the newspaper.'' She glanced at the newspaper on his desk and saw the page it was turned to. Smiling slightly, she murmured, ''At least you haven't taken to throwing darts at me yet.''

Ethan didn't know what she was talking about. ''Carlos brought that,'' he said.

''Carlos is amazing.''

''Carlos talks too much.''

''Does he say things you don't want him to?''

''Sometimes.''

She continued to look at him. Then she said, ''He told me about your mother. I'm very sorry.''

Ethan's lips tightened. ''He shouldn't have done that.''

''He thought I'd understand.''

''He still shouldn't have.''

''He says you're a very private man, that you hold things in. That you won't let yourself feel—'' she stepped even closer to lightly touch his chest ''—in here.''

A shudder raced through Ethan's body.

''He says,'' she continued, ''you need someone to—''

Ethan swept her hand away. It was either that or pounce on her. The trial was over. The constraints that had once separated them were now erased. His action was instinctive.

Her smile faltered. ''Are you angry that my grandfather won his freedom?''

''The jury made its decision.''

''But are you angry with the decision that it made?''

''I've lost before.''

''But not often.''

"No."

Her blue eyes pleaded with him to bend slightly. Enough so that she might be able to reach out to him again. Ethan stood stiffly, incapable of bending. He had held himself aloof for so long.... As a child, when his friends had started down the path to petty and then serious crime. In high school and in college, when others his own age had been having fun in one form or another, and he had had to work to bring in what little extra money he could. When his scholarship to law school had allowed him to dream of a better life for himself and for his mother, and she had died. When his reputation for unyielding prosecution had made him look more like a machine than a normal, living, breathing person.

Amanda's cheeks brightened. "I told myself I shouldn't come here today," she said tightly. "I said, 'Amanda, you'd be an idiot. There's something going on between the two of you, something that could be *amazingly* special, but if he doesn't want to acknowledge it...' Then I said, 'Amanda...if you don't go, you'll be a typical Ingalls. You'll be burying your head, hiding from reality. You'll be acting out what happened to your mother all over again.' She loved Edward Wocheck once. Edward Wocheck loved her. But Granddad objected. And Mother let it happen. She let Edward walk away! I know I'm a romantic...everyone in the family says I am. So I might as well act like one, even if I feel like a fool. I can't let you just walk out of my life, Ethan, and pretend that I—that you... Not when...not when—"

Her words broke off. Seconds passed, seconds in which the hands of time seemed barely to advance. It wasn't so much what she'd said as the depth of feeling with which she'd said it. Ethan's thought processes scattered.

Once again her blue eyes pleaded. She had come so far, exposed so much of her soul. But Ethan couldn't make himself speak, make himself move.

Her body jerked. As close together as they stood, he felt the violence of the movement. Then with a little cry, she tore herself away and disappeared out the door.

Still unable to break his paralysis, Ethan could only stare after her.

AMANDA HURRIED down the curving courthouse steps. She tried not to run; she didn't want to call attention to herself. What she'd done in there just now was bad enough! She'd known that he was hard even before Carlos had tried to convince her that he wasn't. She should have heeded her first impulse and stayed away from him! She should never have come here today, should never have thought to reach out to him. *Oh, please, don't go away, because I think there might be something between us!* No wonder he had looked at her in so...so stunned a manner. She'd sounded like something out of a forties movie! It was one thing for Carlos to seem so sure of Ethan's feelings. It was something else entirely for her to confront Ethan himself. How would she ever face him if they met again? Her body burned with embarrassment.

She advanced across the lobby and out the main doors. Her goal was to get into her car and leave the dust of Sugar Creek far behind her. As humiliated as she felt at that moment, she'd even be willing to leave the state!

The little red sports car waited in the parking lot.

She jumped in and turned the key. Nothing happened. She turned the key again. Again nothing happened.

Of all days! Of all times! She beat her fists against the steering wheel, then jumped back out. She'd walk if she had to! She would not stay in Sugar Creek! She started off down the busy street.

Above the noise of traffic she heard the sound of someone running. Whoever it was was close behind her and getting closer. She glanced over her shoulder. Ethan! In his well-made suit, in his carefully chosen tie...

Amanda didn't hesitate. She, too, started to run. She didn't want his pity or his patronizing words. But she'd left it too late. Strong fingers wrapped about her upper arm, stopping her, turning her around.

"Let go of me!" she demanded, fighting him, trying to pry loose from his hold.

His dark eyes burned down at her. "What you said just now...did you mean it? You don't want me to leave?"

"No, I lied!" she retorted angrily. "I always lie. Isn't that what you've thought about me from the first moment we met? You think my grandfather cold-bloodedly killed my grandmother, you think he and I together tried to put one over on the court, you think the whole town lined up against you...at my behest! That's what you think, isn't it? Isn't it? Why don't you just add jury tampering to your list of charges? Then we'd cover the whole spectrum!"

Amanda's chest heaved. Tears of anger and frustration were awash in her eyes, threatening to turn into a torrent. She was still so exhausted from the trial—mentally, physically, emotionally. She had convinced everyone else in the family to rest today, but she'd had to come to Sugar Creek. She should have stayed in bed!

She tried again to wrench herself free, and in the process bounced against Ethan's lean, hard-muscled body. He huffed, as if she'd knocked his breath away. Then she found that she couldn't draw back. His arms had wrapped around her, holding her tight. She wiggled until she realized that she was creating the wrong kind of friction. Only then did she become still.

"Did you mean it?" he repeated close to her ear, his warm breath tickling her skin.

Amanda sagged. What was the use? "Yes!" she admitted, vexed. "What are you going to do about it? Sue me?"

"You are the most maddening woman on the face of the earth...but I do care for you, Amanda Baron. I don't want to, but I do. If you tell me there's something special going on between us, I'll believe you. If you tell me it can become even more special, I'll believe that, too. I'll even believe your grandfather didn't murder his wife. To tell the truth, I was relieved when I heard the jury's verdict. You made an excellent case for reasonable doubt."

The compliment, coming from him, made Amanda feel proud. She tossed her head. "You didn't answer my question. What *are* you going to do about it?"

Ethan's smile was more relaxed, more genuine than she had ever seen it. Carlos had said he needed a softening agent, someone to help ease the blows that life had dealt him. Her? The thought struck her as extremely pleasing. She shifted in his arms, enjoying the novel experience of being so close to him, of not having to break away.

"I thought...this," Ethan said softly, adjusting her

chin. Then he lowered his mouth until it met hers in a kiss of such pent-up passion that Amanda was afraid she would swoon.

A car horn blared. Another joined in. Soon, most of the cars on the street were honking, causing Amanda and Ethan to break apart. At first they were disconcerted by all the commotion, then they grinned and waved at the jolly crowd of drivers.

"I wonder what my family will think," Amanda mused as they started back for the courthouse, arms wrapped around each other's waists.

"Will what they think make a difference?" Ethan asked.

"No. But they'll be surprised. It may take a little time for some of them to come around to the idea of us seeing each other." She hesitated. "I think you'll like them when you get to know them."

"Will they like me?"

"Yes…eventually."

He guided her toward his car, tucked her inside, then climbed behind the wheel.

"Where are we going?" she asked.

"To get to know each other better."

"Oh, you mean to talk."

Ethan's smile was slow. "Well, that too, I suppose. Let's just say, Carlos would approve."

As they drove out of the parking lot, Amanda saw her little red MG. She'd been angry with it at first for not starting right away. Now, she realized, things couldn't have worked out better if she'd planned them.

ALYSSA CURLED onto one end of the couch and forced herself to open the package of old photographs Liza had found in the attic at Timberlake Lodge. They'd been passed around to each of the children, but so far she'd refused to look at them.

She had to have courage, the same courage she'd found to make it through to the end of her father's trial. A great weight had lifted when she'd heard the verdict, but in a way, another weight had taken its place. Because *someone* had killed Margaret. If it wasn't her father, and it wasn't Phil…

The package started to shake in her hand. *Courage. Have courage!* she told herself. But her resolve failed.

She jumped up from the couch and stuffed the photographs back inside the drawer where she'd found them. Later, she would look at them. In a few days…after the old memories stirred up by the trial had faded.

She hurried across the room, longing for escape, but she paused in the doorway to look back. Someone had killed Margaret…and deep inside, Alyssa knew that somehow, some way, she was going to have to discover who.

READER SERVICE™

The best romantic fiction direct to your door

Our guarantee to you...

The Reader Service involves you in no obligation to purchase, and is truly a service to you!

There are many extra benefits including a free monthly Newsletter with author interviews, book previews and much more.

Your books are sent direct to your door on 14 days no obligation home approval.

We offer huge discounts on selected books exclusively for subscribers.

Plus, we have a dedicated Customer Care team on hand to answer all your queries on
(UK) 020 8288 2888
(Ireland) 01 278 2062.

Look out for the latest novel from

DIANA PALMER

PAPER *Rose*

Cecily is devoted to Tate, but their
passions remain unfulfilled. Shattered
by his rejection she leaves the man of
her dreams. But, when Tate becomes
caught in the middle of a shocking
political scandal, she knows they need
each other more than ever before...

MIRA®

Available from the Reader Service
February 2000 on sucbscription